BONES IN THE WILDERNESS

George Bellairs (1902–1982). He was, by day, a Manchester bank manager with close connections to the University of Manchester. He is often referred to as the English Simenon, as his detective stories combine wicked crimes and classic police procedurals, set in quaint villages.

He was born in Lancashire and married Gladys Mabel Roberts in 1930. He was a devoted Francophile and travelled there frequently, writing for English newspapers and magazines and weaving French towns into his fiction.

Bellairs' first mystery, *Littlejohn on Leave* (1941) introduced his series detective, Detective Inspector Thomas Littlejohn. Full of scandal and intrigue, the series peeks inside small towns in the mid twentieth century and Littlejohn is injected with humour, intelligence and compassion.

He died on the Isle of Man in April 1982 just before his eightieth birthday.

ALSO BY GEORGE BELLAIRS

The Case of the Famished Parson
The Case of the Demented Spiv
Corpses in Enderby
Death in High Provence
Death Sends for the Doctor
Murder Makes Mistakes
Bones in the Wilderness
Toll the Bell for Murder
Death in the Fearful Night
Death in the Wasteland
Death of a Shadow
Intruder in the Dark
Death in Desolation
The Night They Killed Joss Varran

BONES IN THE WILDERNESS

GEORGE BELLAIRS

ipso books

This edition published in 2016 by Ipso Books

First published in 1959 in Great Britain by John Gifford Ltd.

Ipso Books is a division of Peters Fraser + Dunlop Ltd

Drury House, 34-43 Russell Street, London WC2B 5HA

To
Dr. John F. Wilkinson
with happy memories of the lovely land of France

CONTENTS

Chapter I
What's Happened to Cheever?

When Samuel Cheever went on his holidays to France, nobody in Francaster bothered much about it. After all, shopgirls, office-boys, mill hands, even dustmen, were going abroad; why not Cheever?

But when Samuel didn't return, everyone began to sit up and take notice.

"What's happened to Cheever?"

When they asked his wife, who stayed at home ostensibly to look after the shop, she said she didn't know and she couldn't care less. Which was not quite true. They had been married for twenty-five years and had three married children. All that time, Samuel had been unfaithful to Annie, who knew every light of love he had slept with since the first time he'd betrayed her. When her husband didn't return from his holiday, Annie made sure that all Cheever's loves, past and present, were in town. She was satisfied that he hadn't eloped with any of them. Perhaps there was a new one…. That inference was very unlikely, because Cheever had left a substantial balance in the bank and an even larger wad of pound notes bricked-up in a cavity which had once contained an old wash-boiler in the cellar.

All Mrs. Cheever cared about was knowing that Samuel had gone for good. Or would he come back again, one day, like a bad penny? The uncertainty was disturbing.

Then the population of Francaster in general began to worry.

"What's happened to Cheever?"

They missed his fat, stocky figure, surmounted by a greasy bowler-hat pressed down to his ears. True, Cheever had left for his holidays clad in flannels and a blazer with a phoney coat-of-arms on the pocket, but that wasn't the man they knew. The day-to-day Samuel was seedy and shabby, like a lot of the second-hand articles in which he dealt. He described himself officially on his passport as a Furniture Dealer, but there were other things. Those who had articles for sale by night and behind closed doors missed Cheever most. They grew anxious and annoyed.

"What the 'ell's happened to Cheever?"

Finally, after Samuel had been absent a month and the mayor had commented on it to the chairman of the Watch Committee, Inspector Sadd, of the Francaster C.I.D., called on Mrs. Cheever. He was a tall, melancholy, well-mannered officer, with a heavy jowl across which he was constantly passing his hand as though wondering whether or not he'd shaved properly that morning.

"What's happened to Mr. Cheever?"

The shop stood in a narrow alley just off the town-hall square. A dark place with two windows badly in need of cleaning and full to overflowing with junk of every description. A bell on a spring over the door pealed as the policeman entered and a smell of old clothes, second-hand upholstery and dust met him.

Mrs. Cheever was sitting in an old rocking-chair trying to read the morning paper by the dim light from the windows.

NAKED PRINCESS FOUND DEAD IN BATH
FOREIGN ARISTOCRAT SUSPECTED

And a photograph of the victim with nothing on. Mrs. Cheever was lapping it up. Sadd had to ask her again.

"What's happened to Mr. Cheever?"

Annie Cheever was a little, muscular middle-aged woman with a mop of close-cut grey hair, a chubby face almost the colour of butter, and a huge bosom which, owing to her position in the chair, seemed to be supported by her knees. She had been rocking to and fro in ecstasy at the morning's news, and every time the chair tipped back, her short legs were raised a foot in the air. She wore a shabby skirt and a soiled grey jumper.

"How should I know? Your guess is as good as mine."

Sadd sighed. He'd expected this. The Cheevers were a secretive lot. They had much to hide and keep quiet about, and they were as close as a couple of oysters.

"Aren't you anxious, Mrs. Cheever?"

"No."

"Why?"

"He always turns up. He'll be back."

"He's been gone a month, hasn't he?"

"Yes. That's nothin'. He was once off for three months. But he came back, didn't he?"

If it was supposed to be a joke, Sadd's mournful face didn't register it. Cheever had once served three months in Strangeways Gaol for receiving stolen goods. The only time the police had ever caught him.

Sadd took out a small cigarette, lit it, and sat on a second-hand armchair near the door. There was a crack and the whole thing collapsed under him. He extricated himself from the parts, dusted himself down, and started to puff his cigarette again as though nothing comic had happened. But it had, at least, moved Mrs. Cheever. She sprang from the rocking-chair nimbly and reproached him.

"Now look what you've done! Who's goin' to make good the damage? If you *must* sit down, sit there ... ."

She indicated a wooden seat which Cheever had bought from the town council and which had once been one of many round the bandstand in the park.

"But I don't see why you need stay on. I've nothing to tell you. I don't know where my husband is any more than you do."

"What part of France did he go to?"

"All over the place."

"You were there last year, weren't you?"

"Yes. I left our Alice lookin' after the shop, and never again. The money her and her husband must 'ave helped themselves to is anybody's guess. When my 'usband started to talk about goin' to France again this year, I put me foot down. You'll go yourself, I sez to 'im. I'm not leavin' the shop. So he went on his own."

"Was he fond of France?"

"I'll say he was. He was there in the 1914-18 war and again at the start of the last war. Before 1939, he went quite a lot to stay with people he was billeted with in 1918. He was sweet on one of the daughters. I wasn't supposed to know, but I've me own ways of findin' out things."

"Did he speak French, then?"

"What he'd picked up there, though I must say he was never short of a word and always understood what

was said to 'im and could make himself understood, too.
I guess it was that woman saw to his eddication in that
respect."

"Has he gone to see his friends again this time?"

Mrs. Cheever sat down again and started to rock. The
arc described by the chair grew wider and wider and Sadd
grew anxious as to whether or not Mrs. Cheever would eventually take a toss right over the chair-back.

"He'd call, I know. He always did. It was this way.... My
'usband does a trade in antiques. Bein' in this business so
long, he's got to know what's what."

"I'll bet he has."

The rocking ceased. Mrs. Cheever's copious bosom
heaved.

"If that crack was supposed to be clever, I'm too busy to
bother with you any more. So, I'll bid you good mornin'."

"Don't be so touchy. I was simply agreeing."

"It was the way you said it. Now an' then, we get somethin' good comes in. Furniture, china, ecksetera.... My
'usband has good markets for gettin' rid of it. It mostly goes
abroad through men in the trade in London."

"Well? What has that to do with going to France?"

"I'll tell you, if you'll stop interruptin'. Last year, he
bought one or two good things on our 'olidays. We went on
a motor-coach trip. Nice was one of the places. There was
antique shops everywhere we called. Some was dear; others was very cheap. My 'usband picked up one or two odds
and ends and brought them home with 'im. You'd be surprised the prices he got for them. And you can get antiques
through the Customs without payin'. This year, he made up
his mind to go agen. Said he'd travel on the cheap and save
his foreign allowance to buy with."

"Did he take your allowance, as well?"

"What's it got to do with you? You can consider yourself lucky I've told you wot I have. I'm not forced to tell you anythin'. It's just out of the goodness of my 'eart, I've told you. And what do I get? Insults!"

Sadd smiled gently.

"I said, don't be so touchy. I was only joking. I appreciate what you've told me. But you must admit, I'm only asking you in your own interest. You want to know what's happened to him, don't you? Even if he's met with an accident and died—which I sincerely hope isn't the case—you'll have to find out sooner or later. You can't go on like this. Do you want us to help?"

Mrs. Cheever thought it out carefully, judging from her attitude, and then agreed she'd better know.

"After all, there's carryin' on the business, and money matters, isn't there? If he doesn't come back, I'll 'ave to prove somethin' to get the business, won't I? You'd better find out for me."

Spoken thus, it sounded easy. Sadd nodded as though it was.

"Very well. We'll make further enquiries. Did he book his tickets in advance?"

"I think so. He went to Hampole's Travel Agency, I know that. And to the bank.... They'll tell you. Let me know as soon as you can whether he'll be comin' back or not."

Sadd paused as if to ask another question. It all seemed so queer. He wondered if Mrs. Cheever knew a bit more about the disappearance of Samuel than she was making out. Perhaps she herself....

He shrugged his shoulders, bade her good morning, and the bell over the door tolled him out.

Hampole's Tea Shop was a few steps away in one corner of the town-hall square. They sold groceries and the windows were full of presents you could win by saving the coupons given away with quarter-pounds of tea. In addition they were travel agents. There was a lurid bill stuck on the glass panel of the door. COME TO FRANCE. It seemed like an invitation to Inspector Sadd.

Mr. Hampole was busy weighing out bags of soda. His daughter, Grace, looked after the travel and occupied a pen in one corner. Another poster stuck across the front of the desk. *Visitez le Côte d'Azur.* "It creates a h'atmosphere," Mr. Hampole had told his daughter when they put it up. "Vizity li Coaty dazzurr. It sounds good...."

The Hampoles received Sadd very kindly. They were a naturally cheerful couple and besides, Mrs. Sadd was a good customer.

"Good morning, Inspector."

Mark Hampole was a medium-built, solid, middle-aged grocer, and a widower with only his daughter, Grace, to look after him. They were a jolly pair who always seemed to have some secret joke between them and were in the habit of nodding, smiling or laughing at each other across the shop on even the busiest days. "Life wouldn't be worth livin' if it weren't for yewmour," was Hampole's favourite saying, and he lived by it.

Grace was a chubby girl in her mid-twenties. She had dark, striking features and a rosy complexion. She was being ardently courted by the French master of the town grammar school, who, it was locally rumoured, had a keen interest in the tourist section of the business. Hampoles were agents for Sweetman's Tours.

"What did I tell you? I said he'd be here sooner or later." Mr. Hampole giggled across at his daughter, who giggled back.

Sadd wasn't amused. He had little or no sense of humour and the twittering and chuckling of the Hampoles always put him out of countenance. It was like listening to a couple speaking a foreign language you didn't understand.

"What *did* you tell her?"

"That you'd be in sooner or later, asking about Mr. Cheever. Am I right?"

"Yes."

Hampole almost danced a jig in his glee.

"Travel department, forward," he called to Grace, and then his fun was interrupted by the arrival of grocery customers who kept him busy for quite a while.

Grace smiled at Inspector Sadd, who blushed. In secret, he thought her the bonniest girl in Francaster. Clever, too. Knew French very well and that was why her father had set her up in the travel line.

"Did you book the tickets for Mr. Cheever when he left for France, Miss Hampole?"

"Yes, Inspector. He didn't reserve any hotels, though. He wanted the cheapest form of travel and we gave it to him."

"Where did he go?"

"I'll look it up. Just a minute."

She giggled.

"What's so funny about a man vanishing, Miss Hampole?" said Sadd in a nettled, official voice.

"I can't help thinking of him when he called to pick up his tickets. He wore a blazer and flannels. A regular masher, he was...."

Mr. Hampole paused in his slicing of Danish bacon and the pair of them enjoyed a good laugh.

"I'm sorry...."

Grace Hampole apologised for her levity, and ran her forefinger down a column in a ledger.

"Here we are. Francaster, Newhaven-Dieppe, Paris, Nice."

"Is that all?"

"He asked if he could break his journey with the tickets. I said yes."

"Did he mention where he wanted to break it?"

"He talked of getting off at Cannes.... Oh, and Avignon and Arles. It all seemed a bit funny to me, I must say. Imagine Mr. Cheever in Avignon and Arles.... Or, for that matter, on the Riviera at all. In his blazer...."

Mr. Hampole paused in the middle of slapping butter.

"Imagine him.... In his blazer...."

He couldn't continue and was lost in gusts of mirth.

"Is that all?"

Sadd said it again, this time in an acid voice.

"Yes, I think so. Wait.... There was another place he wanted to call at, too. Let me see.... Ah, yes...Mâcon...."

Miss Hampole's mouth in saying it looked like that of a fish in an aquarium.

"Mâcon.... Spell it, please."

"M-a-c-o-n.... Circumflex over the A...."

"Eh?"

She leaned across and put a hook over the appropriate letter in Sadd's notebook.

"Where's that?"

"Not far from Lyons."

"Eh?"

"L-y-o-n-s.... Mâcon's a wine-producing place."

"Any size?"

"Twenty-one thousand inhabitants. Seat of the prefecture of Saône et Loire.... A county town.... I looked it up when Mr. Cheever asked about it."

"There should be some antique shops there, I suppose. Did Cheever specially enquire about it?"

"Only about breaking his journey there. He seemed to have looked it up beforehand. He knew where it was and all about it. He said so. He was that way. Liked showing-off."

"Well, thank you, Miss Hampole. That will be all for the present. You've been a big help."

Mr. Hampole signalled across to his daughter that he was proud of her by grinning and making a jaunty gesture with his head.

"Good day, Inspector. A pleasure, I'm sure."

Outside, the sun was shining and the people of Francaster were going peacefully about their daily business. A pleasant, large public square, with a big town-hall and gardens, and banks, shops and cinemas lining two sides of it. Sadd paused for a minute, getting his eyes accustomed to the daylight and his nose used to the fresh air after the dim, aromatic recesses of Hampole's shop. Then he crossed the square and entered the Home Counties Bank.

This was the largest bank in the town, formerly the Francaster Union Bank, and carried the marble pillars and sumptuous woodwork of days gone by. All four cashiers nodded at Sadd. The chief hailed him.

"Morning, Inspector. Not another lot of forged notes, I hope?"

"No. Nothing of that sort. Is Mr. Hobhouse in?"

The cashier disappeared and then returned to conduct Sadd to the manager's office, where Mr. Hobhouse himself was sitting, selecting victims for the next credit squeeze. The room was large and opulent and had once been the boardroom of the Francaster private bank.

"Hullo, Inspector. And what can we do for you?"

Mr. Hobhouse was a tall, grey-haired, fresh-faced, middle-aged man, who, on account of the size of his business was the acknowledged dean of the banking faculty in the town. His responsibilities rested lightly upon him and he was sociable and cheerful. He rang the bell on his desk and, when a junior appeared, he ordered a cup of coffee for Sadd.

"It's very kind of you, sir."

"You don't often call, Sadd."

They talked about Cheever over their coffee.

"Yes, he came here for his currency and travellers' cheques. He took the full hundred pounds' worth of cheques for himself and the equivalent of a hundred pounds in French notes for Mrs. Cheever. It was marked off on their joint passport."

"And his wife didn't go."

"So I gather. I shall have something to say about that to our friend when he returns."

"If he ever does."

Mr. Hobhouse raised alarmed eyebrows.

"Do you think something has happened to him?"

"I don't know, sir. But I've got a hunch we shan't see him again."

"Foul play?"

"Or else he's what is vulgarly called, done a bunk."

"But surely he'd have taken more money with him if he were running off. I'll tell you, in confidence, that he's quite a good balance here with us. I'd think he's rather comfortably off, you know. Over recent years he's done quite a lot of business in the antique trade and has drawn considerable sums from London dealers."

Sadd vigorously rubbed his heavy jowl.

"I don't know what he's done, sir. It may be foul play somewhere. Or else, perhaps he's got mixed up in something shady and gone to ground. We've had our eye on him for a long time. He was a bit of a twister, you know. He's served a term in gaol for receiving."

"So I heard. A bit of a man for the ladies, too. His wife hates him.'

"Has she said so?"

"Once or twice, when she's been a bit overwrought, she's expressed herself in no uncertain terms about him to one or the other of our tellers. She takes them into her confidence now and then."

"He hasn't drawn any money out since he left Francaster, sir?"

"No. Since word of his disappearance has got round town, we've kept a close eye on his accounts. They've been dormant since he left."

"Well, sir, I won't take up any more of your time. Thanks for the information and the very nice cup o' coffee. Would you mind letting us know at once if any cheques come through on Cheever's account?"

"Of course. Call again any time. Always glad to be of help."

Sadd wondered if he dared ask for a small overdraft, but thrust it from him.

"Good morning, sir."

"Good morning, Inspector."

Across at the police-station in the town-hall, Superintendent Ironside was waiting for Sadd.

"You've been a long time about it, Sadd."

It was always the same. Ironside was a very efficient officer and very quick-moving and thinking. He disapproved of what he called Sadd's pottering-about.

"I've done the best I can. It was quite a big job. It looks as if Cheever has come to some harm in France. He took two hundred pounds with him and that won't last long. Do we wait and see, or do we pursue it further? Interpol, and all that."

Ironside was still testy.

"Get your report typed out, and I'll see the Chief. I think we might make some quiet enquiries from the French police, through the proper channels, of course. But not a word of it has to get round town. We'd look soft if he turned up after all. I'll bet he's up to something shady somewhere.... Dope or smuggling or the like. He's a nose for crooked deals.... Well, get on with it; get your report in hand right away."

What's happened to Cheever?

This time the question was asked of the French police. They had quite a number of dead bodies on their hands, of course, some of them unidentified. Only one of those discovered over the past month tallied in any way with the description of Cheever, and that had been taken from the Etang de Vaccarès, a vast stretch of water in the Camargue, near the Rhône delta. Identification would be virtually impossible. The corpse had been in the water for perhaps three weeks or more, and the place was infested by birds of prey and rodents. Nothing but bones and a few shreds of clothing remained. Top and bottom sets of false teeth (enclosed) were taken from the upper and lower jaws.

The French police had tried to follow Cheever's pilgrimage across France with the assistance of their elaborate system of hotel forms and the like. He had arrived at Dieppe and had next cropped-up at Mâcon. He had stayed one night at the *Hôtel des Tilleuls* there. Then, the trail petered out.

"If he was doing it on the cheap, he might have travelled by train in the night and slept on the way. I've heard of people doing that. You can sleep under hedges in the day, too, if you travel by night. He was wanting to save his cash to buy antiques for profit."

Sadd seemed to think there was nothing strange in Cheever's antics.

"All the same, you'd better check on the teeth. That's one sure way of finding out if the body was what we're wanting."

Ironside waved a peremptory forefinger at his underling.

So, again the bell tolled for Sadd at Cheever's shop and there was Mrs. Cheever rocking again and reading about orgies and bottle-parties in the morning's news.

"You again. Any news?"

"Not yet, Mrs. Cheever."

"Well, what is it, then? Can't you see I'm busy."

"I won't keep you. Who was your husband's dentist, Mrs. Cheever?"

The rocking-chair ceased suddenly from its to-ing and fro-ing.

"Well! What a question. Why do you want to know?"

"Some teeth have been found in France and we just wondered...."

Mrs. Cheever could hardly speak for astonishment.

"Well! I've heard of some funny things in my time, but this caps the lot! My husband 'ud no more think of losin' his teeth than he'd think of leavin' his head behind. Why! he couldn't eat his food without them and you couldn't tell what he said when he spoke if he hadn't got them in. He hadn't a tooth of his own and wore top and bottom sets. He got new ones under the National 'ealth last year from Mr. Butterworth. But you're wastin' your time. He'd never 'ave parted with 'em. New ones would cost too much."

Sadd took all the abuse and left without saying much more. He didn't want to risk any uproar until they were sure of Cheever's fate.

T. J. BUTTERWORTH, L.D.S.

Sadd entered slowly. Butterworth was his own dentist and Sadd, too, had dentures top and bottom. He still remembered the horrors of forceps and gas. The receptionist approached.

"Good morning. Have you an appointment?"

"No, miss. Police."

"I know that, Inspector. Mr. Butterworth is engaged. He's operating...."

To confirm this, a man was helped out by the dentist and his nurse and placed in an easy chair to rest. He spat blood as he sat down.

"Ah've just 'ad th' lot out," he said feebly to Sadd by way of apology.

Mr. Butterworth, a tall man who resembled Mephistopheles in a white coat, turned his burning dark eyes on Sadd.

"Hello, Inspector. You got an appointment?"

"No, thank God! I just wanted a word with you, sir."

"Well, no need to be profane about it. What is it? Come in the surgery."

Sadd gingerly followed. The nurse was cleaning up and he averted his eyes. Then he produced the teeth from France.

"Did you make these, sir?"

Butterworth looked at the hideous objects as though he loathed them.

"They look like mine. Why? Where did you get them?"

"They were found in France. We wondered if they might belong to Samuel Cheever."

Butterworth grimaced.

"Cheever. I remember him. Very rough under gas. Went for me and blacked my eye. Had to get someone in to hold him down. Awful mouth of teeth. Pulled out the lot."

He smacked his lips, remembering his revenge.

"Could you check them in any way, sir?"

"Yes. I'll just take a look at the records."

Butterworth fumbled among some cards in a filing-cabinet.

"Here we are.... Yes, they're the ones I made for Cheever. Very short upper lip and narrow gums. You see...? I remember them."

"Could you swear to that, sir?"

Butterworth's dark, deep-set eyes bored into Sadd's from their pouched sockets.

"I'd have to make another check or two before swearing my life away. I'm almost sure, though."

Later, Butterworth confirmed they were Cheever's without a shadow of doubt. Materials, plate structure, teeth formations....

"What next?" asked Sadd of Ironside after the news which made it almost certain that the body from the Etang de Vaccarès was that of Cheever.

But that was already having attention.

The M.P. for Francaster, Mr. Fred Uncles, primed by his election agent, was already framing a question to be asked in the House.

What's happened to Cheever?

"I'll send Superintendent Littlejohn out to see about it," replied the Commissioner comfortably, when the Home Secretary rang up Scotland Yard.

Chapter II
The Miniature

It all started very badly. When Littlejohn and Cromwell got out of the train at Francaster, a thunderstorm was raging. Although it was a May afternoon, the station was almost in total darkness and people moved like wraiths in the gloom. Now and then, a flash of vivid lightning lit up the whole place, revealing surprised travellers carrying bags and tennis racquets, and coloured posters which mocked them. *Come to Blackpool in the Spring when the Weather's Good. Brighton is Ideal in May.*

Sadd dashed up to them. He wore a black plastic raincoat and looked as though he'd just been fished from the river.

"Superintendent Littlejohn? My name's Sadd. I've been investigating the case at this end...."

Sadd! Another good start! Littlejohn and Cromwell shook him by the hand. In the other, he held a dripping umbrella.

"No luggage, sir?"

"No. We hope to get back by the midnight train."

"Oh...."

Sadd didn't quite know what to say. If the pair from London thought they were going to solve the death of

Sammy Cheever in a few hours, they looked like being mistaken. They'd soon find out.

"Ever been to Francaster before? It's not always like this, you know. Up to an hour ago we'd hot sunshine. It'll be all the better for a storm. It'd got too sultry.... There's a car at the station exit."

It rained all the way to the police station and stopped as they pulled-up. A pleasant square with a garden in the centre. All the daffodils and tulips had been beaten to the earth by the storm. The shops and offices round the square had their lights on. Across at Hampole's shop, the owner put out his head to inspect the weather and nodded and grinned at Sadd like a Cheshire cat.

"A fellow called Sam Cheever, a broker and furniture dealer, went on his holidays nearly six weeks ago and never came back. They've just found his body in a pond in the South of France."

Littlejohn smiled. A pond! The Etang de Vaccarès was a huge lagoon which spread for miles.... But Sadd hadn't stopped to enquire.

"...A bit of a dark horse. There's no telling what will turn up before this case is finished, sir. Cheever was a one for the ladies. He'd even got one in France. This might turn out to be a crime of passion."

And with that, the Chief Constable and Superintendent Ironside entered and completely eclipsed the modest Sadd.

The purpose of Littlejohn's visit was simply a conference. Just that. All business entails conferences and journeys to and fro these days and the Chief Constable couldn't rest until they'd had one. So, Littlejohn agreed. It was a waste of time and money and the two Scotland Yard men left Francaster again that evening.

There were one or two other items in the Sammy Cheever file, however, mainly provided by Cromwell after a visit to Mrs. Cheever.

"Go alone," Littlejohn had told him, "and get to know all you can about Cheever and his French interests." It was a bit difficult getting rid of Sadd, but in the end, Cromwell found himself at the shop, the bell over the door jangled, and he was in.

Mrs. Cheever bore her widowhood lightly. After all, she had suffered none of the agonies and ceremonial of bereavement. Samuel had walked out of the door one day, dressed in his blazer, and nothing more had been heard of him until the report of his death had arrived, along with his dentures, from France. The French police had already buried his body, or what was left of it. They supplied Mrs. Cheever with the name of the cemetery at Arles, but she didn't show any inclination to go and mourn there. If the other six women of Francaster and the French trollop who had at various times in his life provided her husband with new experiences cared to go and weep for him at his tomb in Provence, that was their affair. Mrs. Cheever was too busy to bother. There were legal formalities in the offing whereby Mrs. Cheever would find herself financially independent, to say nothing of the *cache* of pound notes in the cavity behind the bricked-up boiler in the cellar.

"Good afternoon," said Cromwell.

At first, Mrs. Cheever thought a clergyman had called to offer comfort and condolences, but when Cromwell had announced himself and his business, she showed more interest and bade him take a seat on the form which had once faced the bandstand in the park.

"Smoke?" said Cromwell, who had already noticed that her chubby fingers were stained with tobacco.

"I don't mind if I do. I'm glad you've called and that London are sendin' somebody out to square things up in France. The lawyers say somebody'll 'ave to go out there and get proper proof and certificates. I don't know why, an' it's my opinion they're jest doin' it to line their own pockets at my eggspence. Now, with you goin', it'll save me quite a lot."

"I'm sure we'll be only too pleased to do all we can, Mrs. Cheever."

"That's nice of you. First kind word the p'leece have said to me since my late dear 'usband was took. The way they carried on, you'd think I'd been an' pushed 'im in the river myself."

So, now it was a river! Never mind.

"Perhaps you could give me some more information in case we need it on the other side."

"Ask me anythin'. I've 'eard those Frenchmen's a terrible lot to satisfy. What was it you wanted?"

"I believe your late husband had friends over there. Do you know their address?"

"Come into the back room."

The living quarters were almost as bad as the shop for hoarding dusty junk. Old pots and plates, second-hand books, brassware, and clothes on every available hook and receptacle. A silk hat on a marble-topped wash-stand and a large glass-fronted box of stuffed birds on the window-sill. The whole place chock-a-block with furniture of all kinds, and the only evidence of modest living there in a small island of linoleum-covered space containing a table full of dirty dishes, an armchair in which a huge black cat was fast asleep, and a dining-chair with the day's paper on the seat. Mrs. Cheever swept the cat and the news away and bade Cromwell make himself comfortable.

The address of Mr. Cheever's French friends was in a twopenny exercise-book which his widow drew, after a lot of rummaging, from a drawer in a bureau, on the top of which were piled a complete set of Calvin's *Institutes.*

Monsieur Henri Valdeblore,
    7, *bis*, Impasse Auguste-Friand,
    Mantes,
        S.-et-O. France.

Cromwell copied it out.

"I believe 'e works on the railway, or somethin'. My 'usband always went there every year till the last war broke out. They was friends in the 1914-18 war and kep' it up. I never went. Mr. Cheever used to say with not knowin' French, I'd be like a duck out of water."

Cromwell had heard about it all. The late Samuel had believed, no doubt, in keeping the women in his life apart from one another.

"Thanks. We'd better call there. Has your husband written to Mr. Valdeblore lately?"

"He wrote off jest before he left for the last time to say he'd be callin' to say how-do on his way south."

"And now, can you recollect anything particular in connection with your husband's last trip to France? Did he prepare long for it, or was he particularly interested in any kind of goods or antiques he intended buying there?"

Mrs. Cheever stood in deep thought for a minute.

"He'd got a good market for signed French minachures. You know the kind of thing. If you don't, I'll show you."

She started to rummage again in the bureau, puffing and blowing as she moved this object and that and talking over her shoulder in gasps.

"He brought some 'ome when we was there a year ago .... And, in confidence, I'll tell you, Mr. Cromwell, he made a good thing out of 'em. It seems some London dealer 'as demands for them in the U.S.A. of America. Mr. Cheever never paid more than five-pound for any one of 'em. And, believe it or not, 'e parted with four of them for over twenty pounds apiece. He said 'e was off for more .... 'ere we are ...."

She placed on the table, beside the dirty pots, a small portrait in a square black frame.

" 'e took that away with 'im. I suppose he wanted it with 'im as a sample or somethin'. His bag with 'is belongings came back from France yesterday and the police brought it here this mornin'. Cut me up 'avin' to sort out his things."

She squeezed a tear from her eyes and sniffed.

"I'm sure it must have done, Mrs. Cheever. A big ordeal, and no mistake."

"That's right."

Cromwell was fascinated by the little picture. It was set in a circular rim of brass not more than four inches in diameter and the whole mounted in the square frame of dark walnut. A piece of thin ivory pressed close to the convex glass and the lot sealed up at the back by a sheet of old, fly-blown notepaper.

The portrait itself was that of a woman. She was far from beautiful. A long anaemic face, set in a cap of exquisite white lace and tied with ribbons under the chin to form a complete frame of frills, which gave her an ageless look. She might have been twenty; or again, she might have been forty. Little curls of chestnut hair escaped from beneath the cap on her forehead and cheeks, but were no guides to her years. A yellow cravat, tied in a double bow, hid her throat, and a Paisley shawl or bodice her shoulders.

The expression was placid, almost bovine. A narrow forehead, a prominent arched nose, thin lips, and a long chin. The eyes were large and blue, and gazed from beneath well-pencilled eyebrows on a world which seemed to produce little reaction in them. In fact, the artist might have hypnotised the sitter to make her keep still.

Cromwell found it difficult to analyse why the thing attracted him so much. It might have been the subject, or the skill of the painter himself, who, of what might have been uninspiring material, had created a picture which made the rest of the contents of Cheever's seedy, sordid little home repulsive.

Cromwell turned it over in his fingers. The old faded paper which sealed the back was loose at one corner. He gently tugged it. It had been part of an old letter and perhaps a reminder to someone of what the picture was about. Just three lines of rusty ink on the yellow of the paper.

Clotilde de Montvallon.
Parti de Pont de Veyle,
Le 23 août, 1838.

That was all. She had left Pont de Veyle on the 23rd of August, 1838. Why?

Cromwell laid it back on the table and, as he did so, noticed the signature of the painter in the bottom left corner. J. Lepont, 1834.

"Not much to look at, was she?"

Mrs. Cheever's husky voice broke Cromwell's reverie. For a second he felt like telling her to shut up. Then, he was himself again.

"No, Mrs. Cheever. But it's so well done that you don't notice her defects, do you?"

"Funny, Mr. Cromwells, but I can't for the life of me think wot you can see about it. I told Mr. Cheever that. He sold all the other minnichewers, but kept that. Said it was the best of the lot. 'Why don't you sell it, then, if it's that valyuble?' I sez. But he jest says 'Ah,' and shuts up like a clam. Took it out of its frame, cleaned it up, he did, and he wrote off to Cannes, where we bought it, tryin' to find out more about it."

"You got it in Cannes, did you? Might I ask, where?"

"Oh, jest a shop in a side-street. Not far from the prom. My 'usband and the old woman as kep' the shop 'ad a lot of 'agglin' and arguin' before she'd part with it. I couldn't find me way there again, if you was to offer me a 'undred pounds. I do recollect she'd a monkey there, a real wicked one, that was climbin' over everythin' all the time. I remember playin' with it while Mr. Cheever an' the old girl made a bargain. It bit a piece out of the end of my finger, the ole devil."

Cromwell turned over the miniature again. He couldn't bring himself to leave it in the sordid surroundings of Cheever's back-room.

"Will you sell this, Mrs. Cheever?"

She automatically became the hard-bitten dealer again. Her face grew firm and her eyes greedy.

"Well, I do know me 'usband laid great store by it. It was the best of the lot he bought, you see, Mr. Cromwells. The dealer in London would give a lot for it, I do know. But seein' as it's you and you're doin' your best for me.... Ten pounds."

"Five," said Cromwell.

Mrs. Cheever gathered it from the table and put it back in the bureau drawer.

"I might as well put it away, Mr. Cromwells. After all, it's a souvenir of me late 'usband and very likely he wouldn't want me to part with it. I couldn't let it go at that. Mr. Cheever would turn in 'is grave."

Cromwell's eyes were now stony as well.

"You said he paid five pounds for it."

"Not this one, Mr. Cromwells. Not this one. I never knew how much 'e paid. It was all done in French, you see, and me sucking me injured finger on account of the monkey bitin' me. But I know he gave more than that."

Cromwell gathered up his bowler hat and put his big black shiny notebook back in his side pocket.

"Well, Mrs. Cheever, that's all for the time being. We'll do our best...."

"No offence about the minnychewer, I hope. But you do understand. He treasured it most of the lot. So much, that he didn't part with it when he sold the rest. He even took it abroad with him on his last trip."

"That's all right, Mrs. Cheever. No offence. It's too pricey for me, though. Well, good day to you, and thanks for the information. We'll let you know."

The bell jangled over his head as he opened the door, and above the noise of the bell, Mrs. Cheever's husky call.

"Hey! Mr. Cromwells!"

She had the miniature in her hand again and thrust it at him.

"Here, give me five. You're doin' me a favour lookin' into things for me. You can't say I'm not grateful. It's givin' it away at that price."

Cromwell didn't argue. He took the picture, thrust it in his pocket, and counted out five notes.

"Thank you."

Back at the police station, he found Littlejohn waiting for him. He continued to feel a strange exhilaration about the bargain he had made with Mrs. Cheever; not at the price he'd paid, but at the beauty of what he'd bought. It might be of importance to the case. After all, Cheever had been fascinated by it and, from what they had learned of Samuel, it hadn't been for the work of art or the beauty of the sitter. There had been something else ....

"I believe Cheever's possessions came back to-day and you sent them back to his widow?"

"That's right," replied Sadd. "There didn't seem to be anythin' of much importance there. We examined them. He travelled light. Just odds and ends of clothes and such and a little framed picture. Guess it was an antique he'd bought. We let his wife have 'em."

"Where were they found?"

Sadd nodded gravely.

"You may well ask. The French police are smart. I have to hand it to 'em. When they were told where his train tickets were for, they enquired all along the line. They found Cheever's bag in the railway left-luggage office at Mâcon. If he hadn't left them there, like as not, whoever killed him would have thrown them in the pond along with the body and we'd never have seen 'em again."

"Did you ever find out what he wanted at Mâcon?"

"Hadn't a clue. Nor had the French police. It's apparently a peaceful little market town, famous for wine. I looked it up in the library. It seems they make china there, too. An old place where there's bound to be antiques. That's what Cheever was after, you know. Antiques, to sell again after buyin' them on the cheap. He'd started a little racket in it, according to his missus."

"I see. In the course of your enquiries about him, and his movements, did you come across a place called Pont de Veyle?"

Cromwell didn't know why he asked it, but the name on the miniature and the place were still in his mind. Pont de Veyle.... The place Clotilde de Montvallon left in 1838.

"Beg pardon. What was the place?"

"Pont de Veyle."

"No. Never come across it. But I know who might know. Miss Hampole, who runs the travel agency here. I'll ring her up if it's important."

"I'd be grateful...."

Sadd looked at Cromwell with a puzzled expression. These Scotland Yard men!

"Hello Miss Hampole.... Yes, Sadd...."

They could hear her chuckling, heaven knows what about, at the other end of the line.

"Pont de Veyle.... That's it.... What? I can't hear you.... Oh, spell it. Of course...."

Cromwell wrote it down and Sadd passed it on piecemeal. And then they waited.

"She says she'll have to look it up in the French railway guide. Won't be long."

Miss Hampole was smart at the job. She was back in half a minute.

"She says.... Oh, you'd better speak to her. It's very complicated."

He passed over the instrument and Cromwell received the reply. It seemed perfectly clear to him.

Pont de Veyle was three kilometres outside Mâcon, the first stop on the railway between Mâcon and Bourg-en-Bresse. In fact, almost a suburb of Mâcon itself.

Cromwell fingered the miniature in his jacket pocket. What had Sammy Cheever been at?

He told Littlejohn all about it on the way back to London.

Chapter III
At the *Butte Verte*

It meant breaking the journey to the south, but as Sam
Cheever had obviously called on his old friend, Valdeblore,
at Mantes, a halt there might be worth the trouble. So,
Littlejohn and Cromwell had planned the same route as the
dead man. Newhaven-Dieppe, Paris, Riviera. Mantes was on
the line from Dieppe to Paris, midway between Rouen and
the capital.

It rained all the time and the sea trip was shocking.
Cromwell was violently sick and it took him an hour or so to
recover. Littlejohn had insisted on taking the sergeant with
him, although Cromwell's French was, like Cheever's, somewhat home-made, from the experiences of the last war. He
carried with him the usual luggage; an old gladstone-bag,
filled with all the equipment they might need on the case.
To the number of reference-books, Cromwell had added
a large French dictionary, a volume of French police procedure translated into English, and a phrase-book called
Comment-ça-va? and guaranteed to see any Englishman
through all his troubles in France.

Mantes-Gassicourt.

It was dark when they arrived. The name plaques slid
past the windows and officials on the platform shouted the

28

name of the station. The two detectives hauled out their baggage and looked around for the left-luggage office. They hoped to get a later train to Paris, stay there the night, and leave for Marseilles by 'plane next morning. The few passengers who had left the train had quickly disappeared into the darkness. Littlejohn asked a ticket collector. The man looked hard at him.

"Impasse Auguste-Friand, monsieur? It's near the cathedral.... 7 *bis*? That'll be Henri Valdeblore's place. The *Butte Verte*. It's a small café. You weren't thinking of staying there...? Because it's hardly the place where gentlemen like you...."

They found a stray taxi and were hurried through the town. A few broad avenues, full of newly-built offices and shops after the bad bombing of the war. Then, dark streets. Here and there, an electric light casting a bright pool on the wet pavement. A large hotel, and then two bars facing one another in a cul-de-sac. On the left, *Normandie Bar*, on the right, *La Butte Verte*. The taxi halted and they told him to wait. The man gave them a queer look, as though wondering what the business of such a pair might be.

The street was almost deserted. In the doorway of the shop next to the *Butte Verte*, a couple embracing in the shadows. On the edge of the pavement, a man in a peaked cap standing idly in the rain.

Littlejohn had not appealed to the police of Mantes. He'd felt an unofficial approach might be better and bring out more information. Now, he wondered.... He'd had no idea Henri Valdeblore kept a low bistro in an unsavoury quarter, a place in which, after all, Sammy Cheever might have been very much at home.

The *Butte Verte* was the size of a small shop, with a tall window across which was drawn a flyblown lace curtain to hide what was going on inside. There were transparent advertisements for beer and *apéritifs* on the glass panes of the door. Littlejohn lifted the latch and they entered. As they crossed the threshold, they were enveloped in a warm thick atmosphere dominated by the smells of alcohol and garlic sausage.

A resounding wooden floor, a long narrow counter with a zinc top, a shelf with bottles and glasses on it, and about half a dozen little tables. A bench, upholstered in worn brown leather, ran along one wall. A long, narrow room illuminated by two naked electric bulbs, and a door leading into the private quarters at the far end.

Three of the tables were occupied. An elderly, raddled man and a faded-looking woman—obviously off the streets—drinking red wine. A group of four men who looked like bargees, eating sausages and bread before going back to work for the night. And then, at the farthermost table, almost in the shadows of the back of the café, a large middle-aged fat man, a heavy, flop-bosomed woman, and a buxom young one with a pale face and large dark eyes.

The fat man knew right away that the newcomers were from the police. His kind seem to have a nose for officials. He didn't get up to greet them. Instead, he and his family continued to eat their bread and sausages. Only the younger woman looked startled. The elder one sat listlessly there, her elbows on the table, her fingers feeding the pieces of roll into her mouth.

"What do you want?"

Everybody looked up as the fat man finally called out to Littlejohn, who, with Cromwell at his heels, slowly crossed the room. The bargees started to whisper among themselves. The elderly soak was half-drunk and the girl was trying to persuade him to leave with her.

"Monsieur Henri Valdeblore?"

"Yes."

The fat man tried to look casual and sucked his teeth to prove it. Then he jerked his chin in the direction of two vacant chairs at the table. The marble top was splashed with wine and gravy and the plates contained a mixture of hot sausage, sauerkraut and fried pototoes. The detectives sat down.

"Well?"

"You were a friend of Mr. Samuel Cheever, an Englishman?"

The atmosphere at the table changed instantly. Valdeblore relaxed. He'd obviously expected trouble from another source. Now that he'd found out the newcomers were English, his fears evaporated. The younger woman's face lighted up and she settled down to hear some news for which she seemed to be waiting. Even the old woman looked up and smiled.

"Yes. We were in the first war together. We were good pals."

"He was here five or six weeks ago?"

"Yes. What of it? He was going on to Paris on business. He stayed here three days."

Valdeblore threw a glance in the direction of the younger woman, who flashed a look back at him which only meant one thing. This was Cheever's French woman, as Mrs. Cheever called her.

"This is my wife, and my daughter, Rosalie. We were all good friends of Mr. Cheever."

Valdeblore took a cigarette from a crumpled blue packet, lit it, blew out the match, broke it in two, and cast it away.

Rosalie couldn't wait for news.

"You are on holidays here? He sent you to call on us with a message?"

Whatever people in his home-town thought of Sammy Cheever, here was someone who was fond of him, to say the least.

The boozer and his light of love were on their feet ready for off. She had to hold him up as she led him to the door. Valdeblore rose and went and collected their bill. Then he pushed them out into the rain. On his way back, he picked up a bottle and glasses from the bar.

"Have a drink. This'll do you good on a cold, wet night."

He poured out Calvados for all five of them. The mention of Cheever had converted the hostile reception into a social gathering.

"How is Sammy?"

The girl with the pale complexion almost held her breath waiting for news. She was handsome in a vulgar kind of way, scantily covered in a blue woollen jumper and skirt, with a lot of her bosom visible below the low-cut collar. The bargees at the table nearby kept turning and eyeing her.

"He's dead."

For a moment, you could have heard a pin drop, and then Rosalie screamed and beat the marble top of the table with her clenched fists.

"No! It's a lie! You're trying to trap us into something."

"I'm sorry to say that it's true. He was found drowned in the Etang de Vacarrès, not far from Arles."

The younger woman couldn't believe it. She gasped and gurgled until the elder intervened.

"Come along, love.... I'll take you to bed.... Don't take on so...."

It was obvious the Valdeblores were completely knocked out by the news. Rosalie made no reply to her mother.

"When did it happen? He was here.... Then he went to Paris.... How did it happen?"

"We don't know. That's why we're here. To find out."

Valdeblore raised his stricken eyes, liquid from the drink he'd already absorbed.

"We don't know any more about it than you do. He went off to Paris in good spirits. Laughing and merry, he was, then. He promised Rosalie he'd come back with a present for her. That's why she was so anxious for news of him. Instead...."

"Yes."

"But why?"

"I don't know."

Rosalie had got out of control again. She sprawled across the dirty table, her hands clawing at the marble, her hair in her empty plate.

"Take her away."

Valdeblore was getting impatient with the scene. The old woman gently forced the girl to her feet and almost dragged her away, through the door at the back, beyond which, as it opened, they could see a staircase in the gloom and another passage leading to the back quarters.

"Now, what's all this about? Why did you come?"

"We're from the police."

"From his own town ... Francaster?"

"No. Scotland Yard."

"Ah! It's something important then?"

"Cheever might have met with an accident and got drowned. On the other hand, what was he doing in the Camargue, miles from anywhere? He was supposed to be going to the Riviera and stopping off at Mâcon. He was in France buying antiques, or so he said."

"He told me the same. I believed him."

Four more men entered and Valdeblore had to leave Littlejohn and Cromwell to attend to them. He served them with a bottle of wine and they began to play with a grubby pack of cards.

"Did he mention anything about going to a place called Pont de Veyle?"

A show of interest appeared in Valdeblore's dark, bloodshot eyes and his puffy face grew animated.

"Yes, he did, come to think of it. It was about a little picture he had."

Cromwell produced the miniature from his side pocket. He had brought it in case of need and valued it so much now that he feared to pack it in his luggage. He unwrapped it from the piece of black velvet, which his wife had provided.

"This it?"

"That's right."

"Why was he making all the fuss about going to Pont de Veyle? We know the woman in the picture was connected there at one time and left the place. But why was Cheever so excited about it?"

They all looked quietly at the exquisite picture of the plain woman in her lace cap and Paisley gown. It was out of place, lying there on the marble table-top of a cheap bistro. She seemed to take a hold of people in different ways. Cromwell for the beauty of the painting itself, Littlejohn for the delicacy of the artist's workmanship, Valdeblore because, somewhere, he smelled money in the affair. What had attracted Sam Cheever, the twister, the dealer, the old-clothes man?

Valdeblore sat back, drained his glass and filled-up all round. His paunch was escaping over the edge of his trousers, the top three buttons of which were unfastened. He wore a waistcoat, greasy with food droppings, and was in his shirt-sleeves.

"It's a thing I could never understand, this collecting of antiques. There's money in it, of course. According to Sammy, there are any number of crackpots ready to pay big for old stuff which I, personally, wouldn't give house-room. The miniatures, for instance, now...."

"What about them?"

"That one you've got there. It's a picture of a wealthy woman, according to poor Sammy. She was a member of a big family. They lived at Pont de Veyle, he said, and that was why he was going there."

"But she's probably been dead nearly a hundred years."

"That's not it. Sammy had got in touch with a rich American who collects those sort of pictures. But, he doesn't want them of anonymous people. He wants to know who he's buying, and the more aristocratic, the better. As Sammy said, the American is willing to pay for history. He's a catalogue of his collection and he's proud of it. The finest in the world. Worth half a million pounds. His house is full of these things...."

He tapped the miniature with a grubby forepaw.

"So Cheever was going to Pont de Veyle for more history?"

"Yes. He'd got a paper showing the pedigree of the lady. But that wasn't enough. He wanted to find out all about her and her life. He was going to start at Pont de Veyle. He told me the American had an agent in London who said a full story would make the picture worth two hundred dollars, at the very least. Sammy said that wasn't to be sneezed at, especially as it was only part of what he was in France for. He was going to buy more miniatures, too."

Cromwell tapped Valdeblore on the arm.

"You said...."

He forgot he was speaking English and as Valdeblore looked puzzled, he turned to Littlejohn.

"He mentioned a pedigree, sir. Could you ask him where Cheever got it from?"

Valdeblore knew the answer to that one, too.

"It was with the picture. Cheever showed me and told me about it. When he bought the little picture, it was dusty, so he took it from the frame. Between the back, which, as you see, is an old letter, and the picture itself, was a thin piece of paper. Cheever said that was often the way they did; they put the name of the sitter behind, between the picture and the back. The piece of paper was, Sammy said, the lady's pedigree. Her family tree...."

Cromwell managed to follow Valdeblore's easy, resonant French, which he spoke slowly out of regard for his visitors.

"The paper wasn't with the picture when I bought it, sir."

Valdeblore knew that.

"Cheever had it in his pocket-book."

"His clothes and pocket-book were not found. In fact, the body was not recognisable after being in water for a month and all the birds and vermin about and at it. It was identified by the false teeth fixed in the jaws."

Valdeblore winced.

"Poor Sammy. This is a bad blow to all of us, especially Rosalie. Sammy was a friend of hers in the old days after the first war when I brought him here. She was a little girl then. She married and her husband was killed in the last war. When the war ended Sammy came to see us again. He was a great comfort to Rosalie. They were always good pals. There is a child, a boy of five...."

Valdeblore shrugged his shoulders as though nothing were wrong, except that Cheever had died before his time.

"Cheever's son, you mean?"

"That's right. Cheever would have married Rosalie if he hadn't had a wife already in England. She was an old baggage, Sammy used to say in his comical way. So Rosalie didn't mind. He used to come and see us often. Twice a year. On his way to buy antiques....."

Cromwell shook his head.

"I don't understand this, sir. You'll have to tell me what it's about later."

He smiled as he thought of Sammy Cheever, a Don Juan in his blazer and home-made French!

The old woman was back. Or at least, that was what Littlejohn thought of her in his mind. An old woman. Although, judging from Valdeblore, she couldn't have been much more than sixty. She looked years older than that. Fat, grey, worn and bad on her feet. They'd had a bad time with the gestapo in the war. Rosalie's husband had been in the underground and the whole family had been under suspicion after he'd been caught at it and shot. Even Madame Valdeblore had been tortured. Valdeblore told the two detectives as he drank glass after glass of Calvados.

"Poor Sammy! What a bad end! And him so cheerful and fond of Rosalie."

Tears ran down the old woman's cheeks and off the end of her nose.

"I put Rosalie to bed and gave her two sleeping powders in some milk. She didn't know I put them in. She'll sleep.... Little Sam was asleep through it all."

Little Sam! He'd been called after Sammy Cheever! Well, well. This was indeed something which had slipped through Mrs. Cheever's net!

Mrs. Valdeblore turned her sad, almost lifeless eyes on Littlejohn.

"Are you staying the night in Mantes?"

"No, Madame Valdeblore. We're getting the 22.48 to Paris."

He looked at his watch. Half-past nine. The night seemed long. Outside it was raining. The bargees had left and all that remained was the group of card-players, drinking their wine and making their calls excitedly. The atmosphere was thick with smoke and the effects of that and the Calvados made Littlejohn feel he was in some kind of misty dream world.

Two more customers; a young fellow and a girl. They entered nervously and ordered a meal. Mrs. Valdeblore went out by the door in the back and returned very shortly with two more plates of the same old stuff: sausages, sauerkraut, greasy fried potatoes. She sat down with the men again.

"I forgot to ask you…. Have you had a meal? You can have one here with pleasure."

"We dined before we came."

Littlejohn lied in a good cause. He felt he couldn't face the 'ordinary' of the *Butte Verte*. He sat with his elbows on the table, his pipe between his teeth. Cromwell was lolling back in his chair, hardly able to keep his eyes open. And the Valdeblores, too, were gazing ahead with grief-stricken eyes, their hands in front of them on the marble top, fingers spread, like two crooks being searched. It might have been a picture called *Ennui*.

"And that's all you can tell us, Mr. Valdeblore?"

The café-keeper jerked.

"Yes, that's all there is to it. He simply left us to go to Pont de Veyle and find out who the lady was and to buy some more antiques. Now, he's found in the Vaccarès. What was he doing there? I ask you. What was he doing?"

Valdeblore started to cry, alcoholic tears, Calvados tears.

"He was really our son-in-law, mamma, wasn't he? The father of our little grandson, Sammy. Our only grandson."

The old woman began to cry, too, and they had it out together. They sat there, sobbing, sniffing and looking at one another pathetically. Littlejohn could imagine them, night after night, lolling there, drinking, bored, brooding, and now and then attending to a customer or two. When some old man got obstreperous or had taken too much, Valdeblore would chuck him out and then return to his table. And so it would go on, till one of them died of cirrhosis of the liver or something else horrible, and then Rosalie would carry on....

The taxi driver put his head round the door.

"Have you forgotten me? How much longer? You'll have bought the cab in fares if you keep me waiting much more."

Valdeblore gave him a drink and then said good-bye to his visitors.

"Give my love to the Midi," he said as they parted. "I was born in the hills above Grasse and so was the missus. I don't suppose we'll ever see them again. Come back and tell us what happened to Sammy."

He slowly returned to his table and his ennui again. The young lovers were still there, their meal over, looking into each other's eyes, oblivious of the sordid little place they were sitting in together.

The card-players were half-drunk, shouting their calls at the tops of their voices.

"*Pique ... et encore pique! Et voilà ....*"

The cab took the two detectives through the dark streets to the station, and there they caught the train to Paris.

CHAPTER IV
ETANG DE VACCARÈS

It was raining at Orly airport when they left Paris, and, as usual, the air cleared over Lyons. By the time they reached Marseilles, the hot spring sun was shining. The light sparkled on the waters of the Etang de Berre as they turned to land at the Marseilles airport at Marignane. Beyond stretched the blue Mediterranean. Already, both Littlejohn and Cromwell began to feel sweltered in the heavy suits which had barely kept them warm at home.

At the airport they had the red carpet out for them with a vengeance. The case of Sammy Cheever was a queer one, if it really could be called a case at all. Sammy might have tumbled in the Etang de Vacarrès and drowned himself. Local information stated he couldn't swim a yard. On the other hand, what was he doing there, so far from his planned route? What was left of the body proved nothing at all. Any sign of foul play had been eradicated by water, rodents and birds. As for complete absence of clothes or personal effects; the Camargue was infested with gypsies, any one of whom might have stripped the body and thrown it back.

The case was, therefore, unofficial as far as the English police were concerned. Just an investigation to keep quiet the M.P. for Francaster, who continued to ask the same question over and over again. *What happened to Cheever?*

So, to enlist as much off-the-record help as possible, Littlejohn had telephoned Marseilles and forewarned his good friend Commissaire Clovis Audibert of his pending visit. Cheever had died within the jurisdiction of the Prefect of the Bouches-du-Rhône, centred at Marseilles. Audibert was a member of the Sûreté there and in close touch with the departmental police. He could make things very easy for the English detectives.

"Looks as if they're expecting somebody very important," said Cromwell to Littlejohn, and glancing round the 'plane to see if he could spot some foreign potentate or ambassador, or perhaps even a film-star who might merit a royal reception.

A squad of airport policemen, smart in their uniforms and spotless white gloves, marched to the 'plane and lined-up on each side of the gangway as it came to a halt. Three men in plain clothes accompanied them, anxiously peering to find the V.I.P.

"I'm afraid it's us they're after," said Littlejohn, and Cromwell turned the colour of a beetroot.

"You're kidding, sir."

"No. It's a way they have here of showing you're welcome."

Before anyone else was allowed to leave the 'plane, Audibert entered, embraced Littlejohn, shook hands with Cromwell, and led them off. Cromwell eyed the man from Marseilles with approval. Plump, short, with delicate hands and small feet, he looked like a respectable lawyer rather than a policeman. In spite of the southern heat of the day, too, he wore a dark suit, rather old-fashioned in cut, and spotless white linen. An elegant, scholarly-looking man, thought Cromwell, and very different from the other member of the reception committee, now wringing Littlejohn by the hand and talking twenty to the dozen in very rapid French. A little, swarthy man, dressed in an almost white synthetic jacket and trousers, with a belt and shoes of snakeskin, and a red carnation in his buttonhole. Littlejohn introduced him as Dorange, Inspector Jérôme Dorange, of the Sûreté at Nice.

At first, Cromwell felt disappointed. Littlejohn had always spoken of Dorange as the best detective he'd ever met. Then, he noticed how one or two people on the airport were eyeing the man from Nice, some with respect or deference, others with what looked like terror.... Perhaps there was something about the little fellow after all, even if he did look as though life were a perpetual holiday.

They passed along the line of saluting policemen, who then marched solemnly back to the police-post.

On the way into the airport they passed a flower stall. Dorange took two red carnations from a bunch lying ready for someone to take home or present to his mistress, and placed one in Littlejohn's buttonhole and another in Cromwell's. The sergeant was bewildered and couldn't understand it at all. Later, Littlejohn told Cromwell that Dorange's entire family, with the exception of Jérôme, were in the Nice flower trade and that his constant stream of buttonholes was probably a form of propaganda!

The third member of the reception party was Inspector Pignon, an officer who spoke excellent English. His rank in the French force approximated closely to that of Cromwell in the English police, and they got on well together from the start. After a couple of *Pernods* and several glasses of *Châteauneuf du Pape* at the ensuing lunch, they might have been pals all their lives and showed each other photographs of their wives and families and made arrangements for visiting each other's homes in the near future. What if

Pignon did have five children and a mother-in-law to look after? After four glasses of red wine, Cromwell felt he could somehow fix the lot of them up in his four-roomed flat in Shepherd Market.

Meanwhile, the other three were discussing *l'affaire Cheever*. Audibert had all the papers from the files of the French police. They had, of course, not ignored the idea of foul play. Indeed, they had suspected some gypsy or other might have done away with the unknown victim for his money. As a rule, the *gitanes*, however, did not stoop to murder. Picking pockets or pinching geese, yes. But murder for plunder, never. The Arles police, who had taken over the case of the body in the Vaccarès, had had a round-up of suspects, but nothing had come of it. It looked like a case for the unsolved files. Another insoluble mystery, perhaps a suicide. It was always happening in the Rhône valley. The Avignon and Arles records were full of such cases.

Now, however, the unknown body had a name, address, history, and a mysterious itinerary connected with it. The French police were interested again.

As for Dorange, whose hunting ground was far away, his arrival was easily explained. Audibert had merely told him over the 'phone that Littlejohn was coming to Marseilles, and the man from the Riviera had chartered a private 'plane and joined the party.

"Littlejohn's methods interest me. They are so like my own. I have a lot to learn...."

Dorange passed cigars all round, lit one himself, and emptied his glass.

"Besides, a holiday will do me good. Especially in the Camargue in the spring."

A good-looking woman sitting alone a couple of tables away, smiled at Cromwell and gently raised her glass at him. He turned the colour of the wine he was drinking, but felt all pleasant inside. The holiday feeling, that was it! Littlejohn was just the same. The carnation, the wine, the cigars, the general atmosphere of good fellowship. Very different from the reception at Francaster…. He shuddered as he thought of the rain there, the sombre buildings, the starchy Superintendent, the lights on in the middle of the day. Here the sun was shining, the sea calm, his colleagues overflowing with exuberance and goodwill. He felt a little better disposed towards Sammy Cheever for bringing all this about.

A police sergeant deferentially approached the table and whispered something to Audibert.

"The 'plane's ready, my friends. We're flying to Nîmes. It's the nearest proper airport to Arles."

They all rose and Cromwell, when nobody else was looking, bowed and smiled at the lady who had saluted him. She waved her hand.

"*Chic,* that's it," said Cromwell to himself. He almost rubbed his hands. This was a bit of all right! An investigation which was running like a picnic. *"Bien, bien,"* he said aloud, his French improved and lubricated by the *Châteauneuf du Pape.*

The 'plane steered a course across the Crau and the Camargue, purely for the benefit of the English visitors. They flew low over the maze of goods yards, petrol-refineries and pipelines, market gardens and vineyards which cover the west side of the great port, and crossed the stony wilderness of the Crau. Then, the delta of the Rhône. Locked between the capricious river and its tributary, the Little Rhône, stretched a vast triangle of lagoons, bogs, lakes, salt grass and sandy flats with Arles at its apex. It was the Camargue. Here Cheever had met his death. Anything more remote and unseemly for a shady provincial second-hand dealer from a little town in England could not be imagined.

Pignon, sitting beside Cromwell, described the scenery as they passed over it. He even lent the sergeant a pair of binoculars he'd brought specially for the occasion. He was himself a native of Provence—Beaucaire, in fact, near Tarascon.

"You remember Tartarin, no doubt?"

Cromwell nodded, in spite of the fact that he didn't know whom Pignon was talking about. He thought Tartarin must have been some desperate criminal and imagined his going down in police files like an earlier Dominici.

"We are a race apart here. We call those from the north *franciot* or *franciman*. We are of the kingdom of Provence."

Cromwell nodded sagely again. He looked down over the Rhône and the wide Camargue. Hardly a soul about. It reminded him of the sand dunes at St. Annes-on-Sea where he'd once had a case, and the stony beaches looked like parts near Portland Bill, where he'd once arrested a forger on his way to Weymouth where he hoped to get out of the country.

Suddenly, a herd of little black bulls appeared and then a cluster of strong stocky horses, off-white in colour, with long tails. Pignon grew lyrical again.

"The bulls of the Camargue and the famous horses, my friend. The bulls are bred for the bull-rings at Arles and Nîmes.... We are bullfighters in Provence, I can assure you."

Cromwell, who hadn't much patience with bullfighting, grunted as he kept his eyes glued to his glasses. But Pignon wasn't going to be silenced.

"With us, in our part of the country, it is an ancient religion. The Mithraic cult of the bull, the ritual of sacrifice."

Cromwell was just about to remind his friend that bullfighting was supposed to be illegal in France—or so his

book of French law said—when his binoculars picked up
a large building like a fort, standing desolate and isolated
on the seashore. A large Roman tower with three bays, solid
buttresses, long red parapets, visible from the air.

"What's that place below?"

"The fortified church of Les Saintes-Maries-de-la-Mer.
A famous place of pilgrimage. We will go there. It is quite
near the Etang de Vaccarès…. That's the large stretch of
water inland there on the right."

Desolation indeed! What a place for Cheever to finish
up in! A vast lake, miles in length and breadth, bordered
with sedge and rushes, and, as Cromwell looked, flocks of
birds rose at the sound of the 'plane, hovered restlessly, and
then went to ground again. He grew excited. His hobby was
bird-watching.

"Why! They're flamingos!"

"That's right."

Pignon stuck out his chest. He was a large, dark man,
with a hatchet face, a broad forehead with receding hair,
and quick, brown protruding eyes. The essence of good
temper and sociability.

A mounted figure in a ten-gallon hat, riding a white
horse and holding a trident aloft, came in sight.

"A fisherman, eh?"

Pignon was indignant.

"It is one of the *gardians*, the cowboys of the Camargue."

"What's the trident thing for?"

"Prodding the bulls…."

Cromwell gave it up! They were nearing Nîmes, leaving
the old walled, landlocked port of Aigues-Mortes behind
on the left, and the 'plane banked and quickly came to rest.
Another car, and they were soon in Nîmes.

It was late afternoon, the heat was stifling, and over Nîmes hung an atmosphere of indescribable tension and expectancy. They passed the great Roman amphitheatre with huge brightly-coloured posters at the entrances. A mighty shout arose from the arena and, outside, even passers-by in the streets jumped excitedly and rushed to ask for news. Audibert and Pignon craned their necks at the windows. Dorange smiled ironically and thought it as well to explain.

"These western Provençals are bullfighting mad. On the Riviera we have something better to do."

Audibert smiled sadly and shook his head, like one who pities another's ignorance or incapacity for enjoyment.

"It was once a religion. It is in the blood."

Dorange was still smiling.

"I suppose this afternoon in Nîmes it is a *Mise à Mort*."

And he went on to explain to Littlejohn how, now and then, they imported a bullfighter from Spain and killed a bull or two.

"Of course, it is illegal. But very probably the Chief of Police and the local magistrate are among the audience. Tomorrow, the promoters of the *Mise à Mort*... the killing... will be fined ten pounds and, then, off to arrange the next *Mise à Mort*."

The picnic continued. They drank several *Pernods* in a café and watched the crowds going home from the bullfight. Pignon promised to take Cromwell to see one in Arles. "Just a little one.... Not a *Mise à Mort*, if you don't fancy it."

They even made a detour to show Littlejohn and Cromwell the aqueduct at Pont du Gard and the sights of Tarascon, and Beaucaire, where Pignon was born, as he'd said before and said again about a score of times on the way. He left them looking at the castle and the river whilst he went to see his aged aunt who still lived in the old home.

Littlejohn couldn't settle down. It wasn't like work at all. Just the old holiday feeling over again. The town of Beaucaire was bathed in a sunny glare which dazzled him. People seemed to be walking about like shadows. The Rhône slid idly by like a shining ribbon. Littlejohn mopped his forehead and followed Dorange and Audibert, whose ideas of a stroll seemed to consist in nipping skilfully through the traffic and passers-by.

They had a drink in a little café with a green awning, and then Pignon returned and they all said they'd better be getting along. A man in the street jumped as he recognised Dorange and then he took to his heels and vanished down a dark alley. Sammy Cheever and his miniature seemed miles away. At the other end of the earth, in fact.

They were all smoking cheroots provided from Dorange's inexhaustible store when they reached Arles. Along the dry and busy main road and then, the city gates. Cromwell's guide-book advised motorists to get out and walk, as the streets of the town were narrow and dangerous. The police-car took them at high speed, hooting pedestrians out of the way and menacing the handcarts slowly making their ways here and there in and out the alleys. A narrow, melancholy-looking town, full of tall old buildings. Pignon promised to show Cromwell round very soon. They drew up in the Place du Forum, where, at the hotel *Nord-Pinus*, rooms had been booked. Littlejohn and Cromwell shared an enormous chamber complete with bath and all a man could desire in the name of comfort, and dedicated by a plaque on the door to the poet Mistral. Cromwell threw back the shutters and there, among the trees, was Mistral himself, in bronze, sombrero cocked at a jaunty angle, stick in hand, just as if he'd walked in from his old village of Maillane and was ready to recite his own poetry.

The holiday still went on. Audibert was leaving for Marseilles after dinner. There were things to see to. After all, crime didn't stand still just because they'd been having a little jollification. Pignon would remain attached to the English police and Dorange would stay until to-morrow. One of the Commissaires of Arles, Inspector Marion, would meet them over dinner and talk things over.

Marion arrived a bit late. He excused himself. That afternoon they had fished the dead body of a pedlar from North Africa out of the Rhône. The usual. A knife wound in the back. They'd got the murderer an hour later. Marion spoke as though such things happened every day and were as quickly disposed of. He was a fair-sized stout man, a real son of Provence; dark, sleek, little black moustache, and brown sparkling eyes. They sparkled more at the sight of the excellent dinner. The landlord was a big friend of his. He'd laid it all on.

Littlejohn, over coffee, recited his commission to Marion all over again.

A little second-hand dealer from Francaster had vanished during a holiday on which he was due to visit the Riviera in search of antiques. On the way he'd stopped at Pont de Veyle, near Mâcon. The police at Mâcon had made sure he'd stayed there for one night. Then he'd vanished. Next thing, his body was found in the Etang de Vaccarès.

"Ah, yes. The false teeth. I remember."

Marion took out his notebook.

"...Body quite impossible to identify. The birds and rodents had made it unrecognisable. The teeth you, Superintendent, were able to trace."

He bared his own gleaming teeth and then peeled and ate an orange.

"Yes. The M.P. for Francaster has taken the matter up in parliament, and we've been asked to make tactful enquiries from the police here."

Marion seemed puzzled. He wanted to know what it had to do with parliament. In France, when there *was* a government, they'd too much to do to bother with men who drowned themselves in foreign parts.

"Drowned himself?" Littlejohn explained about the miniature, the visit to Mantes, the enquiries in Pont de Veyle. Why should Cheever want to drown himself? Besides, from all accounts, he wasn't that sort. Scotland Yard wished to be quite sure there hadn't been any foul play.

Marion consulted his notebook again.

"The body was discovered, as I said, on the north bank of the Etang de Vaccarès, not far from Méjanes. The main road from Arles to Les Saintes Maries forks at Albaron; one fork to the Saintes, the other to Méjanes. A casual tripper would continue to the Saintes, unless, of course, there was something on at the bullring at Méjanes. Your Mr. Cheever had got a fair way off the beaten track."

"Who discovered the body?"

"A *gardian* on patrol saw it and gave the alarm. Such things don't often happen in those parts. Most unusual, in fact."

"Had Cheever been seen in—in Méjanes, did you call it?"

"No. We enquired everywhere. Nobody had seen isolated strangers around. After all, it was Easter, and the tourists hadn't begun to come in great numbers. Also, the gypsies were few. We checked on those, too."

Littlejohn produced a photograph of Cheever. It was a good one, taken at the door of an old hall he'd bought for demolition. He was dressed-up in his blazer and flannels, too, just as he'd been when he made his unfortunate trip to France. Sammy was trying to look like the squire of the place, sticking out his stomach and smiling benignly, and managing to look like the visiting captain of the local sports club.

"So this is Cheever, eh? Hardly the kind who'd get himself murdered for, say, international spying or for the sake of his fat pocket-book. On the other hand, he might have been a small-time drug smuggler or something such."

"No, no. I don't think that. He's probably interfered in some private affair that didn't concern him. Perhaps a bit of blackmail, or he'd unearthed some secret he wasn't to be trusted with."

"I'll take this picture, if I may. We'll have it enlarged and circulate it again."

"I didn't get it until just before I was leaving. His daughter took it some time ago and the Francaster police managed to unearth it. I thought it would be quicker to bring it with me."

"Of course. We'll see what we can do with it."

"Is the spot where Cheever was found just wilderness or is it cultivated?"

That seemed to tickle Marion.

"Cultivated? The Vaccarès section of the Camargue? Impossible. It's full of salt. It is a zoological station for the most part, but Cheever was found on the *domaine* of Monsieur Denys de Berluc-Vidal. He is a *manadier*, that is, an owner of flocks of bulls and of Camargue horses, which roam and feed on the surrounding land."

"Does Monsieur de Berluc-Vidal live there?"

"Yes, nearby, in the manor, the Mas de Vidal. He was in residence at the time and Cheever's remains were carried there until we arrived to take them away."

"And none of the servants or others of the *mas* ever saw the stranger?"

"As I said, there was little of him left to recognise. Now, with a proper picture of Cheever to help us, we can try again. Someone might have seen him."

Night had fallen and the rest of the party had been listening with such interest that time had not counted. Now Audibert, who had a long trip by road to make, rose to say good-bye. They saw him off and then Marion departed too, promising to call for Littlejohn and Cromwell next day and take them over to Méjanes and the Vaccarès to the spot where Sammy Cheever had perished.

"It may bring something to light, though it's very doubtful."

"Why?"

"The people of the Camargue are a secret lot. Loyal to one another. If a stranger has interfered in their affairs and got himself in trouble for his pains, none of them will help. The *gardians* are a brotherhood. They call themselves, in the language of Provence, *nacioun gardiano*, the nation of *gardians*. They are fanatically loyal to one another and to their employers. We shall have a difficult task...."

The streets lights glittered among the trees of the Place du Forum and the old town was silent. Now and then the rowdy voices of some revellers; otherwise, the place seemed dead. Far away, the noise of traffic passing on the main road, leaving the town aside. A café or two open, but deserted.

With the departure of the sun and a chilly wind shaking the trees, the town seemed forlorn and melancholy. It even affected the little party sitting in the dining-room, still finishing the last of their wine, chatting about one thing and another. Dorange was telling Littlejohn about his father and mother, who were friends of the Superintendent and his wife, and giving an account of their farm, where roses were grown in their thousands, just above Nice.

Pignon and Cromwell were comparing notes about their families again. The French Inspector, too, had been filling-in the gaps of previous talk between Marion and Littlejohn, much of which Cromwell had not understood.

There were one or two other clients dining, and these were getting to the end of their long meal. The landlord came to the Superintendent's table now and then for a friendly word and to ask if all was well.

The door opened and a woman entered, clad in a heavy tweed coat and an expensive little hat. Cromwell turned to look at the newcomer, gasped, and changed colour. It was his *chic* lady of the restaurant at Marseilles airport! She showed no sign of recognition. It was as if, in her case, too, the vanishing sun had taken away her smile and her joy. She looked tired and annoyed. She was giving orders to the waiter as the police left the room and the man seemed very anxious to please; in fact, obsequious. The landlord himself appeared and greeted the woman with courteous respect.

Dorange proposed a walk round the town and another nightcap before retiring. It suited the rest. Littlejohn suggested to Cromwell they might put on their raincoats. Now, their heavy suits seemed too light for the keen air. Cromwell went to their room, returned with the coats, and found his friends had gone into the Place du Forum to wait for him under the stars. The landlord was in his office. Cromwell went in.

"The lady who just arrived, monsieur. I think I've met her before. In Marseilles. Could that be so?"

"Of course. She gets about quite a bit. Her car is in the square. A fast one. Not much of a journey to Marseilles in it at the speed she travels."

"Her name?"

The landlord smiled a bit archly at Cromwell.

"She's charming, isn't she? Mademoiselle Yvonne de Berluc-Vidal. Daughter of M. Denys de Berluc-Vidal, a wealthy *manadier* of the Camargue."

Cromwell held his breath. Berluc-Vidal. The *domaine* on which they'd found Cheever's body.

The landlord was talking still.

"They spend a lot of time here, although they are aristocrats with properties elsewhere. They own a villa at Cap Ferrat, and a large estate near Mâcon, at Pont de Veyle."

CHAPTER V

CAMARGUE

As Cromwell stepped out of the hotel next morning for a breath of fresh air, a slatternly gypsy woman, carrying a dirty baby on her hip, told him the child hadn't had a decent meal for three days. Cromwell was covered with blessings in exchange for a hundred franc piece. He looked around and saw the square was full of gypsies.

"It's May 23rd," said Pignon, joining him and reproaching him for paying blackmail. "To-morrow is the feast-day of les Saintes-Maries and gypsies come from all over Europe to celebrate it and to pick up what they can on the way."

Over breakfast, it was explained by one and another that a body of early Christian refugees, including two Saint Maries, and a black gypsy servant, Sara, had landed at Les Saintes and the two Maries and Sara had been buried there. The gypsies claimed Sara with a vengeance and invaded the place in May and October. Littlejohn and Cromwell were advised to leave wallets, watches, and even sleeve-links behind at the hotel.

They took the road over the Rhône out of Arles and almost right away found themselves on the good highway which crosses the Camargue to the coast. The land at the start was well cultivated and under rice and vines, with men working in the paddy fields, their heads swathed in cloths to keep off the mosquitoes and flies. Then, as they approached Albaron, sixteen kilometres from Arles, the country deteriorated into barrenness.

A vast stretch of desolate flats, tufted with coarse salt grass, intersected by shallow streams and canals, dotted with pools and lakes, on which the light produced fantastic effects. Reeds and rushes hid many stretches of water from the eye and provided cover for water-fowl of all kinds; ducks, herons, cranes, bittern. Great settlements of flamingos nested there, too, rising and pursuing a brief, measured flight and then returning to their breeding grounds again. Cromwell, the eager bird-watcher, made a few notes, but showed no inclination to descend and pursue his hobby. The hot sun blazed down from the azure sky and made them all listless with its heat. The upholstery of the car was scorching and the air, in spite of the speed of travel, was stifling and like hot wool.

Now and then, a herd of little, sturdy black bulls would wander across the road or, here and there, a group of white horses grazed on the poor salt grass.

At times, on a patch of better land, appeared the thatched huts, the *cabanes* of the cowboys, with walls of local clay, plastered and whitewashed; high, deeply-pitched roofs of rushes, with round gable-ends and a cross on the eastern point of the thatch. Where the dry land was more extensive, a large dwelling, a *mas*, belonging to a *manadier*, or cattle boss. It was at one of these that the police cars drew up. The Mas de Vidal.

A low, sprawling house, built in a clump of wind-bent trees. A long drive, an extensive single-storeyed, white homestead, surrounded by *cabanes* and with a large corral of split logs. Something was afoot in the corral, judging from the noise and cheering going on and the jeeps parked in the yard, but before the police could investigate, a man, obviously of authority, approached.

A slim, well-built man, bordering on sixty, but strong-looking, sure of himself, authoritative. A heavy, intelligent face, with a broad forehead, from which his thinning grey hair was brushed back. A powerful Roman nose, firm mouth and heavy lips, with a small grey moustache. He wore riding clothes of an expensive cut, a white shirt, black tie, and a broad brimmed hat. He had the clouded grey eyes and burned complexion of one who might have been in the colonial army, and carried himself like a cavalryman. Marion knew him and greeted him with restrained deference. And then he introduced him as Monsieur Denys de Berluc-Vidal.

Monsieur Vidal didn't seem very interested. His eyes kept straying to the corral.

"Come and see what is going on here and then we'll adjourn if you wish, and talk."

He led them to where a crowd, *gardians* and others, were gathered. Among the spectators, Cromwell saw Yvonne de Berluc-Vidal, his friend of the day before. She was wearing riding habit, but as their eyes met, she showed no signs of recognition.

In the corral itself a dozen or more small, strong little black bulls had been herded. An open fire burned, and branding irons were heating in it.

"The *club-taurin*, the bull club, from Albaron is here to-day. They are capturing the bulls for branding. The difference between the members of the *club-taurin* and my own *gardians*, is like that between your own professional and amateur footballers in England," Berluc-Vidal told Littlejohn. "One is professional, the other sport. If the professionals didn't give the amateurs a chance now and then, there would be no fun. Look at that fellow ... ."

A youngster, obviously showing-off in front of some of the local girls, having singled out a bull he proposed to throw, seized it by the horns after stalking it stealthily, was dragged along the ground several yards and then tossed into a corner, unhurt, rubbing his limbs.

"The bulls are clever. They inherit the manner of evading men. That is what makes them famous in the bullrings of Nîmes and Arles. Otherwise, they'd just be turned into beefsteaks ... ."

At last a bull was mastered by the united efforts of several clubmen, branded, and released.

"They now bear my own mark and are turned adrift to feed on the Camargue until needed. We breed them mainly for sport in the ring."

It was obvious that what was becoming a boring spectacle for Littlejohn and Cromwell, was intensely fascinating for their French colleagues. Marion and Pignon hung over the corral, cheering and goggling, men who knew all the fine points of a game which was in the blood. Dorange stood with his elbows on the log fence, a cheroot hanging from the corner of his mouth, his eyes shining, looking undecided whether or not to try a hand as well.

For Littlejohn, the holiday feeling had vanished. So had serious thoughts of Sammy Cheever. If things went on like this, they'd never get to the bottom of Cheever's death. He felt parched and impatient, as though the hot salt air had sapped all his vitality away. His work was being held up by trivialities whilst the M.P. for Francaster was leaping up in the House every other day. *What about Cheever?*

"You look hot and unhappy, sir."

It was said in English by a tall, well-knit young man in his early thirties, who, from his likeness to Denys de Berluc-Vidal, must have been his son.

"I am Raymond de Berluc-Vidal."

Blue mocking eyes, a ready ironical smile, an easy courteous manner. He was well-groomed and clean and might easily have been a guest at an American dude-ranch.

"I'm baked and tired already, sir. It must be the change of air."

"Come indoors, then, and quench your thirst."

Everyone else, except Cromwell, who was receiving a lecture on branding by Pignon, seemed fully occupied by events in the corral, so Littlejohn went. He followed young Berluc-Vidal into a large room, cooled by patterned red tiles and thick white plastered walls. The wall facing them as they entered held three deep arches, the middle one containing a vast fireplace and the others, one on each side of it, alcoves for pottery and books. A gracious place. Fine antique furniture scattered about, including two enormous Provençal grandfather clocks and a finely carved walnut bread-cupboard hanging in one corner. On the mantelpiece, mounted trident-heads as ornaments, and vases of exotic marsh flowers. Over the centre of the chimney-piece, the head of a magnificent Camargue bull with golden medals of merit hanging from a silk cord slung between the horns.

Berluc-Vidal produced glasses and red wine. He filled up and handed one to Littlejohn.

"Good health, Superintendent Littlejohn."

Raymond de Berluc-Vidal stood leaning against the upright of the fireplace arch. He was just short of six feet and dressed in cowboy clothes; long narrow trousers, with suede riding-boots and spurs, a checked cotton shirt open at the neck, and he carried a broad-rimmed black hat.

"You speak English well, sir."

"I went to school there for two years. Then, I went studying ranching in Canada and the United States. This your first visit to the Camargue?"

"Yes."

"I'm glad that duty has induced you to come. I'm sure you will enjoy it. You're here on the matter of the dead body we found in the Vaccarès?"

"Yes."

"I can't think how we can help you, sir. It was merely found and brought here as an act of decency. Nobody had seen the man before, and what was left of him gave us no idea of who he had been or what he was like."

"Inspector Marion has a photograph of him now. Perhaps that will help."

Raymond offered Littlejohn a cigarette and lit one for himself as well.

"Another glass?"

"If you please. This is excellent wine. Is it local?"

"Good heavens, no, sir! We don't raise that kind on the Camargue. The local wine is a bit strong and rough. This is from our vineyards in the Burgundy district. It's really Mâcon, from our *domaine* at Pont de Veyle."

"Pont de Veyle?"

"Yes. Ever been there?"

"No, sir. But I've heard of it."

"From whom? Excuse the inquisitive questions, but it is a small place and few people know of it."

"Cheever, the drowned man, had it on his itinerary for visiting. He went there on his travels and that's the last place he was traced to before he was found here."

Berluc-Vidal sat down in a wooden armchair with scarlet cushions. The whole place reminded Littlejohn of a Spanish or a Mexican ranch. Sumptuous, tasteful, cultured....

"That's funny. How did he come to do that? There's nothing of interest at Pont de Veyle for a tripper from abroad. It's a flat, damp country, flooded at times by the river Veyle, and on the edge of the Dombes area with its hundreds of little uninteresting lakes."

"Cheever had an interest. If you'll excuse me, I'll call in my colleague, Cromwell, who'll be able to tell us more."

Cromwell, under the burning sun, in his heavy suit, albeit he had shed his waistcoat, wasn't listening to Pignon's tale, a vivid description of the Arles bullring. He had discovered what had so interested him about the girl on the other side of the corral, the one who had smiled at him at Marseilles airport, and refused to recognise him since. It was her resemblance to the woman whose portrait he held in the miniature, still in the side pocket of his jacket. She was better looking, but that probably was due to the differences in their dress and style. Yvonne de Berluc-Vidal wore tight-fitting riding breeches, almost like jodhpurs, but obviously modelled on those of the *gardians* here. She was tall, too, and dark; slim, with long legs and small, almost imperceptible breasts. The cowboy get-up suited her, and her short black hair strayed from under a broad brimmed black hat. And the shape of her face, the fine bone formation, and the high-arched delicate nose were those of the woman in the picture, who had left Pont de Veyle more than a century ago.

Littlejohn emerged from the house and joined Cromwell.

"Excuse me, Pignon, but I'd like a word with Cromwell indoors. We won't be long...."

Cromwell followed, was introduced, drank wine, and felt better.

"And now, old man, do you mind showing Monsieur Raymond the miniature you have with you?"

Cromwell frowned. He wondered what was coming next. He carefully took out the picture, unwrapped it, and passed it across to Berluc-Vidal.

As soon as the young man saw it, he started, looked up suspiciously at Cromwell, and threw his cigarette purposefully in the empty fireplace.

"Where did you get this?"

It was said so harshly that Cromwell reared, too, and looked ready to answer just as offensively.

"It's mine. It belonged to the late Samuel Cheever, and I bought it from his widow."

His voice was like ice.

"Where did Cheever get it?"

Cromwell looked across at Littlejohn, who nodded.

"Bought it in an antique shop in Cannes."

Young Berluc-Vidal sighed, looked relieved, and then smiled.

"How strange! It's of great-aunt Clotilde. As the note on the back remarks, she left Pont de Veyle more than a century ago and went to live God knows where."

"A strange thing that Cheever should buy it and fetch up here, get himself drowned, and that the picture should be brought back, after all this time, to you and the nearest relatives to the lady in the picture."

"You're right, Superintendent. But it can have nothing whatever to do with the death of the fellow. How could it?"

"I'm sure I don't know."

Embarrassment was beginning to enter the conversation.

"I'd like my father to know about this, sir."

"Very well."

"Let's go and find him."

Denys de Berluc-Vidal was still watching the last of the branding and turned as the Englishmen and his son entered the yard again.

"Where've you three been? Ah ... a drink. We'll all go inside for another. Find Yvonne and bring her."

Raymond went across the yard to gather in his sister.

"Whilst we're waiting, would you care to take an aerial view of the Camargue, Superintendent? No, we've not got a private 'plane here, but are you any good at climbing telegraph poles?"

It sounded a mad idea, but Littlejohn was ready to try anything once. Berluc-Vidal led him to a spot behind the house, where, planted in the ground, a large pole rose skywards, with rungs nailed to it at regular intervals. It was indeed like the telegraph poles at home, laddered to enable the linesmen to mount them.

"This is known in the local language—one never speaks of Provençal as a dialect—it is known as a *guinchadou,* a ladder we mount to spy out the land and especially the state of our flocks, herds, and horses. Up you go. There's a splendid view from the top."

He was right. Littlejohn mounted without any difficulty and looked around him. He could see as far as the sea at the Saintes with the huge church dominating all, and back to Arles where the towers and buildings stood out like figures against the backcloth of the pitiless blue sky. Below stretched the vastness of the Camargue, with the Etang de Vaccarès quite near, on which he could see great flocks of flamingos, white-breasted and rose-winged, preening and cleaning themselves and feeding their young with scooping gestures of their strange beaks in the mud and water.

The whole immense delta was visible, flat, marshy, forlorn, with clumps of trees, ponds, bogs, the desolate loneliness relieved here and there by wandering herds of bulls and horses, or flocks of sheep, scarcely discernable in the far distance. On either hand, miles away, the two rivers; the great Rhône towards Marseilles, and the Little Rhône on the Nîmes side, where far off, the Nîmes uplands relieved the vast stretch of prairie.

A group of *gardians*, on white horses, entered the yard and, releasing the bulls from the corral, drove them ahead into the open, piloting and thrusting them along with the help of the long tridents they carried, three shallow metal prongs mounted on the end of a long pole. These men might have been imitating their Hollywood counterparts; and yet, they were not. They were shod, for the most part, in gumboots for use in the marshes, and sat relaxed and happy astride their Camargue mounts, on their wooden saddles like small armchairs, with reins and harness of plaited horsehair. Some of them grinned up at Littlejohn and waved their ten-gallon hats at him.

The rest, with the exception of Yvonne de Berluc-Vidal, had gathered indoors and it had been arranged that the whole party of police should stay for lunch. Dorange, as usual, was interested in the bill of fare. He had already sampled and passed commendation on the wine of Pont de Veyle.

Denys de Berluc-Vidal was as moved and surprised as his son when Cromwell produced the picture of Clotilde de Montvallon. He was a bit less reticent in explaining matters, too.

"I am a Montvallon on my grandmother's side. She married a Vidal, later changed by marriage to Berluc-Vidal. Clotilde, in spite of her staid expression and dress in the picture, was not without spirit. In fact, she vanished from Pont de Veyle on the date stated. She ran away with the painter, a fellow called Lepont, and was never seen or heard of again. You say you got the picture from the dead man's belongings, and he'd purchased it in Cannes? It gave me a shock to see it, I admit. There was, I believe, another and larger one of her, but, it is said, her father put his foot through it and threw it on the fire when she eloped with her artist. What will you take for the picture? Its obvious place is with her family, here or at Pont de Veyle."

Cromwell flushed and his jaw set stubbornly. But Littlejohn was quick to his rescue.

"I'm sorry, sir. The picture is police evidence and we can't part with it yet. It may contain a clue to the whole mystery of Samuel Cheever's death."

"Why?"

"He left for Pont de Veyle to find out all he could about Clotilde de Montvallon. He had, I believe, a customer for such works of art, who, however, would not buy them without a full history of the subject. Cheever, we were told, made his trip to Pont de Veyle to obtain such information."

Dead silence. An atmosphere of antagonism was growing.

"I may claim it then when the case is ended?"

"I don't know, sir. Presumably, in the course of its career, this miniature was sold by your relative, or someone who acquired it after her death. It eventually arrived in an antique shop in Cannes, where Cheever bought it. It doesn't belong to your family any longer."

"I will pay a fair price for it...."

"We will see...."

"I must...."

The argument was interrupted by the arrival of Yvonne, who had changed into a blouse and skirt and looked more

fresh and charming than ever. There was a round of introductions. Finally, she faced Cromwell, and smiled at him as
though they were meeting for the first time. She gave him a
cool firm grip and said she was glad to welcome him to the
Mas Vidal.

"Haven't we met before, mademoiselle?"

"Last night, at the *Nord-Pinus*. You were dining there, I
think."

"Yes; and at the airport at Marignane, just after we'd
arrived."

She looked bewildered.

"You were lunching there?"

Cromwell was feeling hot about it. It looked as if he'd
made a gaffe somehow, but he couldn't say why.

"No. I wasn't anywhere near Marseilles yesterday."

Cromwell looked her straight in the eyes and knew she
was lying. But there was, in her glance, a fearful appeal,
beseeching him not to pursue the matter further.

"I'm sorry," he said. "No, it wasn't you. Somebody very
like you, though, but not so dark."

He turned quickly to look for Littlejohn and found
Raymond de Berluc-Vidal at his elbow, with a look of dia-
bolical anger changing to one of relief as his sister smiled
at him again.

CHAPTER VI
THE ANCIENT COWBOY

"He must have been a very important man to have brought out so many eminent police officers."

Luncheon was finished and they were all—about a dozen, all told—sitting over coffee and brandy. The meal had been memorable. Excellent eel soup, barbecue steaks and rice, after a hors d'oeuvre of tomatoes, peppers, green olives, sausage and fish. Then, fruit and goat's cheese. All washed down with the fulsome red and white wines of Mâcon from the vineyards at Pont de Veyle. It was Denys de Berluc-Vidal who turned the general conversation back to the murder of Cheever.

Littlejohn removed his cigar.

"On the contrary. A very insignificant small-town shop-keeper, and hardly respectable at that. A broker, a second-hand dealer in oddments, and not above a shady trick when opportunity arose. The trouble is political."

"Ah! A friend of one of the ministers in the government!"

"Not even that. Just that the Member of Parliament for Francaster is anxious to earn his votes at the next election. He's showing the electors how anxious he is for their welfare. He keeps asking in Parliament, 'What's happened to Cheever?'"

This gave Marion an opportunity to open his brief-case and produce the enlargements of the snapshot of the victim. He handed out half-a-dozen copies, like a gambler dealing cards.

Cheever in his blazer, standing on the steps of his second-hand orphanage, later sold at a profit as a Borstal institution. Stomach thrust out, cigar held aloft between first and second fingers, a smirk on his fat face. The squire of the place!

There was a brief silence and then all the photographs were passed back to Marion. Dorange intercepted one and put it in his pocket.

None of the Berluc-Vidals had seen the man before. There were five of the family present. In addition to father, son and daughter, the mother and sister of Denys were also there. Now over eighty, thin and aquiline like an old bird of prey, Madame Etienne de Berluc-Vidal was wheeled-in in an invalid-chair attended by her middle-aged and unmarried daughter, Solange. Solange looked more than ever like the woman in Cromwell's miniature. These were a haughty couple who let it be understood that they were merely present out of courtesy and did not, as a rule, dine with policemen. Solange, a highly-strung, nervous woman, was fully occupied in attending to her mother, who wielded an ebony stick with a crutch handle. In addition, there was a small pug dog, which ate sitting on the Widow Berluc-Vidal's invalid chair when he wasn't trying to climb on the table after victuals. The meal ended, the pair excused themselves on the score of the widow's health, and departed.

They dined at a long plain-wood table, of the refectory type, sitting on ladder-backed chairs, probably the work of local craftsmen. The manager of the ranch joined them, too, a grey-haired giant who was obviously deeply interested in Mademoiselle Solange and who could hardly eat for looking at her. He leapt to his feet to open the door for the widow and Solange as they left and followed them out to see the wheel-chair safely on its way. Nothing was said about it by the family. Everybody at Mas Vidal sympathised with him except the widow, who refused to countenance the courting of her daughter by what she called a cow-hand. So the love affair was apparently in suspense until the old woman died.

The police were next conducted to the Etang de Vaccarès and shown the spot where the body of Cheever was found. The trip was made in jeeps, of which there seemed to be as many as there were horses on the ranch. Monsieur Denys himself drove Littlejohn; Raymond took Cromwell and Marion; and, for some reason, Dorange had contrived to get Féraud, the ranch manager, all to himself in a third vehicle. The party set out across the narrow track which led to the étang.

The road undulated across the flat marshy plain, and the jeeps kicked up a thick dust wherever the dry land occurred. At other times they ran through shallow pools or across bridges beneath which some canal or brackish stream dawdled almost unmoving between thick banks of reeds. Now and then, small sheets of water glistened in the sunshine, reflecting the blue of the sky in the deep parts, but among their reeds and shallows aglow with oily iridescent mud, the air was alive with insects, the wings of which kept up a persistent faint strumming and the men had to smoke all the time to keep them off.

Everything quivered in the bright, intense sunlight and the earth exhaled a damp, mouldy smell under the relentless heat. Here and there the grass had been completely roasted away and thistles and reeds stood like white dried-up skeletons.

Monsieur Denys explained to Littlejohn that he owned thousands of sheep in addition to horses and cattle, here and in the nearby Crau. But with the parching away of the pastures in summer, they had all been sent by train to the high alps beyond Gap, more than a couple of hundred miles away in the north, until autumn.

"They used to travel all the way by road, on foot. Some still do. The old paths of this annual migration, *La Transhumance,* as we call it here, are still used and marked on the maps, as they were hundreds of years ago. Our alpine pastures are really not far from Pont de Veyle. Less than a hundred miles. I visit them later in the year."

They were at the Etang de Vaccarès, a vast sheet of water, pale blue under the sun, and in spite of the stillness of the air, sparkling and gently rippling in tiny waves. The approach to the water-side was of fine grass, covered with small flowers found only in those parts. Cromwell gathered many of these and pressed them between the leaves of his official note-book, ready for sending to his little daughter, who studied botany at school and who wrote to him every day.

Unlike the rest of the journey, here they were on velvety elastic turf dotted with isolated shrubs, which bore the mark of the mistral blowing to the sea and which twisted towards the south like silhouetted bent figures fleeing across the flat wilderness. Flocks of ducks, divers, herons and flamingos ceaselessly rose in flight and then returned. A long triangle of wild geese, flying low, spotted the assembled jeeps, the leader with a wild cry stretched his neck and increased height, and the echelon turned and went back over the sea.

The party dismounted and Féraud, the head man, led them to the spot where Cheever's corpse had been discovered. At the edge of a sandy spit of land lay a small thicket

of reeds, tamarisks and rushes. It was in the middle of this
that the body had been found.

To Littlejohn, the affair looked more than ever one of
murder. If not, what was Cheever doing there at all? With the
exception of the wild horses and bulls grazing on the juicy
grass of the lakeside, there was not another living thing in
sight, not, of course, counting the birds, which seemed to be
in a state of ceaseless agitation. Even if Cheever had decided
on suicide, why choose this, of all places, and, instead of
making for deep water, why fling himself in a bath of half-
baked mud?

"Who did you say found the body?"

"A queer fellow who spends his time rounding up horses
for one *manadier* and another. An old man who never keeps
a job for long. When he's earned enough money to retire on
for a month or two, he sacks himself. When the cash runs
out, he hires himself again. He can always get work, he's a
skilled *gardian*, and knows the Camargue like the back of
his hand."

"And he came and reported what he'd found to you,
Féraud, and you brought help?"

"That is so, Superintendent."

Féraud looked at Denys de Berluc-Vidal to see if he
approved of his talking so much, but the *manadier* was lighting a cheroot and didn't seem particularly interested.

Marion took Littlejohn and Cromwell to the water's
edge. They were ill-provided for an excursion to the muddy
scene of the crime. Besides, what good could it do? Any
clues would already be at the bottom of the water or deep
in the mire. The smell of baking slush hung over the place.
Littlejohn almost felt sorry for Cheever fetching up and
dying in such awful loneliness in a country which seemed
doubly foreign, for this was a land all of its own.

Dorange and Féraud had been conversing aside and Féraud was now pointing along the bank of the lake, where a flock of white horses with flowing tails and long manes were grazing. Among them, on horseback, was a figure wielding a long trident, driving them before him in the opposite direction from where the jeeps were parked. Dorange and Féraud entered their vehicle and made off in the direction of the newcomer, pursuing a jerky career on the close grass of the verge. They reached the man, engaged him in conversation, and then turned to rejoin the party. The man rode beside them, keeping up with the speed of the jeep, set in his saddle like a born rider, his horse's tail and mane flying in the breeze he was creating. They joined the rest of the party.

The newcomer on horseback was a cowboy of the old school. None of the modern Hollywood get-up for him. He was bearded like the Ancient Mariner, with long greying whiskers reaching to the top of his chest. A fine head, covered in a soft black felt more like a priest's than a ten-gallon; a long hawk-like nose; regular features, baked brick-colour by the heat and netted with deep lines; and strong ivory-coloured teeth showing when he smiled. He held his head high, quite unimpressed by the presence of the wealthy rancher. He seemed to spurn even rubber-boots, for his legs were covered from ankles to below the knees in old-fashioned leather leggings. A soiled red waistcoat, a white shirt open at the neck, and a thin sky-blue jacket completed his get-up. He held the traditional trident in his hand.

Denys de Berluc-Vidal and his son didn't seem too pleased to see this arrogant tramp of a cowboy, mounted in front of them, holding himself like an independent free-man in the saddle.

"Good day, Davso."

"Good day, Monsieur Denys ... and all gentlemen."

A raucous voice and difficult to understand, too. The man spoke French mixed with Provençal idioms which Littlejohn couldn't follow. The strong, stocky little horse, his nostrils heaving from his run, his wild eyes red, stood as proudly as his master, eyeing the jeeps with disdain.

"This is the man who found the body."

Dorange spoke, half explaining the reason why he and Féraud had so suddenly made off.

Marion took charge.

"These are the English police, Davso. They are anxious to know what happened to their countryman. The man you found in the étang...."

"In the mud, you mean."

"In the mud, then."

Davso seemed to have a peculiar sense of humour. He smiled to himself as he corrected Marion and smiled again frequently as he told his tale.

"And, by the way, speak in French, not Provençal. The Englishmen understand French, but the other...."

Marion shrugged and Davso imitated him impudently.

"So much the worse for them, sir. All the same, I can speak all in French. I'm an educated man, you know. I read a lot."

Dorange intervened. He spoke to Davso in his own language, that of Provence, and what he said obviously shook Davso considerably. Later, Dorange told Littlejohn he'd threatened to take Davso to Marseilles for questioning if there was any delay or insolence. Davso, who'd never in his life travelled beyond Arles, was scared to death at the idea of Marseilles, where, he'd heard, strange diseases from the East prevailed. He was careful of his health and dreaded death. Féraud told them that his 'education', as he called it, was gathered from old medical books and leaflets for quack medicines which he diligently collected.

"What did you wish to know, sirs?"

Davso's eyes were now fixed on Dorange, like those of a bird on a snake.

"You found the body here?" asked Littlejohn.

"Yes, sir. It could hardly be called a body. The rats and birds had almost picked it clean. You'd think to see all the lovely birds round here that they wouldn't hurt a fly, sir, wouldn't you? Look at those flamingos, there, feeding their young, or any other flamingo's young, for that matter. They don't care whose chicks they feed don't those flamingos...."

He looked at Dorange.

"Right, sir. I'm coming to it. I saw the body because of the flies. Place was black with them. It was stuck in the mud. He either fell in or was put in when the water was higher, but we've had no rain for weeks so the level of the lake has gone down and left the mud. He'd not sunk in, you see. It's only shallow here. All the same, but for the flies, as I said, all traces of him would soon have vanished."

"Had you seen him about before?"

"I couldn't say, sir. When I found the remains, they were in no condition to identify. I never knew what he really looked like."

Dorange produced the enlargement from his pocket.

"That's the man. Ever seen him before?"

Davso studied the picture carefully. He even turned it upside down in an effort to appear serious and helpful.

"No. He looks a wealthy man. Perhaps he was waylaid and killed for his money."

Poor Cheever would have been pleased had he known! He'd taken-in one person at least, either by his blazer, or his cigar, or could it be the way he thrust out his stomach?

Questions now came thick and fast from Dorange, whose mind always worked rapidly.

"Did you ever see anybody else about here?"

"When?"

"Within the last six weeks. It's six weeks since the dead man left England. Give him a week or two to get into the condition in which you found him. Say, over the last month."

"There've been quite a few people here."

"What! In a lonely place like this? And at this very spot?"

"There's always somebody about."

"You mean *gardians?*"

"Yes, sir."

"I'm talking about strangers. Where do you live? Where's your *cabane?*"

"Two miles along the edge of the lake. You can see it on a clear day from here. Now, it's too hot. There's a bit of a mist...."

"Have you got a ladder there... a *guinchadou?*"

"Yes."

"I bet you're always climbing up it, when you're at home, a lonely inquisitive chap like you."

Davso bared his strong teeth.

"Well, yes. Not so much goes on around the Vaccarès that I don't see."

"Or on the Camargue, either, from what I can see of you, you old rascal. Come on, now. You know what I mean. Haven't there been any suspicious strangers around here in the last month?"

Denys de Berluc-Vidal had been showing signs of great impatience and now could contain himself no longer.

"It's time we were getting back. No good will come of questioning this man. He is eccentric and ignorant and will only tell you what he wants you to know. And that will, as likely as not, be far from the truth. With Davso, lying comes like breathing."

The ancient cowboy merely smiled again. He didn't seem in the least put-out by the character Berluc-Vidal had given him. On the contrary, he looked proud of it, as though the local aristocrat had written him a good testimonial.

Dorange wasn't satisfied.

"You'll excuse my talking, Littlejohn, won't you? Perhaps I can handle this better. I want to set your feet on the right path before I leave for Nice.... This is a God-forsaken place, and no mistake."

He looked round at the vast wilderness and mopped his streaming face. Then he addressed Berluc-Vidal.

"I'm sorry to detain you in this heat. I won't keep you. Kindly drive back to the ranch and we'll join you there. Littlejohn and I will stay and I'll drive the jeep back. No...no...I won't hear of any other way. You are busy, I know, Monsieur Denys, and are only staying out of politeness. Please leave us and we'll follow quickly."

In no time, the vital little man from Nice had cleared the field, Cromwell and all, and saw the other two jeeps off on their way back to the *mas*. Only Davso, Littlejohn and Dorange remained.

"Now...."

There was an unpleasant flavour in Dorange's voice.

"Now. Tell me whom you saw—a stranger—about here lately."

"A few bird-men studying the wild life. We get a lot, as you will know. There are also poachers on the government bird-reserve, but, of course...."

"Come along, Davso. Tie your horse behind the jeep and we will take him back to the *mas* for attention during your absence."

"What do you mean, sir?"

The man was like a cornered rat and ready to turn nasty. He gripped his trident and waved it angrily.

"Nobody's going to touch my horse, or me. Take care. I may have a grey beard, but the young men of the Camargue know better than to try conclusions with me."

His voice trailed away. Davso was looking down the barrel of a blue automatic which Dorange held at an angle pointing at his head.

"You either answer my questions truthfully, my friend, and at once, or we take you and your horse along with us. The horse will stay at the *mas*, as I said, and you and I will go to Marseilles."

"I haven't said I wouldn't answer; and nobody can say that Davso doesn't tell the truth when he speaks."

"Did you see anybody suspicious round here during the last month? And I don't mean poachers, bird-watchers, fishermen, or horse-thieves. I mean unusual men.... In other words, someone bringing a body here to hide it in the Vaccarès...."

Davso nodded.

"I saw a man three weeks... or maybe a month since. All days are the same to me. I was up my ladder and I spotted him wandering round here, practically where you're standing, sir. He hadn't a body with him. He was just alone. He wasn't poaching, because he'd no gun. And he wasn't fishing."

"Because he'd no rod and line. Get on with it!"

"And bird-watchers are usually calm, slow-moving men, who have all day to spare. This man just came and went."

"Was he walking?"

"No, sir. He had a car. A motor-car, like the one there...."

Davso pointed to the empty jeep beside which they were standing.

"You're sure he wasn't a gypsy. There are plenty about."

"Now, there are. It's the feast at the Saintes to-morrow. But he wasn't a gypsy. No; I'd swear he wasn't."

"Why?"

"Well…. There's something about a gypsy, sir. If he's after something, he sneaks about. If he's not, he has an air about him…. The way he walks…the free-and-easy. You understand, sir?"

"I do. This chap. How was he dressed?"

"That's it. Not like a gypsy. He wore a black suit. Or that's what it looked like from my ladder, and I can see a long way from it. It's two miles from here but my eyes are as good as any telescope."

"We'll assume they are. Can you make out colours so far away?"

"On a clear morning on the Camargue, sir? Why, I could see the bullfighter's red cloak in Nîmes from here on such a day."

"Monsieur Vidal was right when he said you were a liar. You were nearer than that. You weren't up your *guinchadou* at all, Davso. You were somewhere about where we found you to-day, or nearer."

Davso's eyes grew furtive and afraid. If the jeep hadn't been there, he'd probably have made a bolt for it and galloped away. As it was…. Dorange still swung the neat service revolver at his side.

"Now tell me what the man was like."

"I could only see him from a distance…. Where you met me. It's true. I swear it. I saw him. He was dressed in a black suit and carried his jacket. You see I'm telling the truth. How could I think about him carrying his jacket if I were telling lies? Eh?"

"Was he tall or small, or what?"

"Medium, I'd say."

"And just spying round?"

"That's all. One minute he was here, looking at the lake; the next he'd gone. I'd just turned to look at the horses and when I looked again, the car was driving away towards Méjanes."

"And that's all?"

"I couldn't tell you more if I tried, sir. It's all."

"And there's been nobody else lately?"

"No, sir. It's too far away at this time of year for casuals or campers or picnickers."

"Right."

"Is that all, sir? Can I be getting on with my work now? I'm herding the horses for Monsieur Manille."

"Just one more question. Who paid you to keep your mouth shut about all this?"

"Nobody, sir. I've tried to tell you everything and it's not fair or right of you ... ."

"Stow it! It's been the devil's own job trying to get a true word out of you, and I doubt now if you've told the truth or all you know. Who paid you to keep your mouth shut?"

The old man's lips grew thin under his beard and his face assumed a stubborn angry look.

"Nobody."

"I know the way you *gardians* have of hanging together. But this is a case of murder. Somebody killed the Englishman and threw him in the Vaccarès ... or rather hid the body where they didn't think it would ever be found. You came across it, told the *gardians* of the Mas Vidal, and they came and took it away. Then, somebody sought you out and paid you to keep your mouth shut about anyone you'd seen around here at the time of the crime, or when the body was brought and thrown in the lake. *Who paid you to keep quiet?*"

"Nobody."

The revolver was levelled again with a steady relentless hand.

"Get off your horse; tie him to the jeep. You're coming with us."

The old reprobate sat there, began to curse in his own language, and his beard grew flecked with foam. He looked ready to have a fit.

"I'm waiting."

"I'm not coming."

With a quick gesture, Dorange seized the man's boot, and with a smart jerk, dragged him from the saddle. As he fell, he seized his arm and held it in a firm lock. Littlejohn didn't need to interfere at all. The little man from Nice was quite up to the occasion.

"Now. To the jeep.... March...."

Davso tried to break the grip, winced, and then stood still.

"I promised not to tell."

"Promises and lies to a man like you? What are they?"

"I keep my promises."

"Come along, then. You may be in Marseilles for some time, but I'm sure Monsieur Vidal will look well after your horse."

"Blast him! Why did he get me into this? Here I was, all peaceable, doing my work, minding my own business. Then I find a body. A man who finds a body ought to see that it's reported. It's his duty to see that it gets a decent Christian burial. Well, isn't it?"

"Yes. What of it?"

"I reported it. Then, Monsieur Denys arrives one day and asks me a lot of questions, like you did. I answer them truthfully, like I did yours. Thank you, Davso, he says, and gives me a few *écus* for my trouble. That's all. I thank him, and he goes."

"After telling you to keep your mouth shut. To keep your mouth shut, or he'll have you driven off the Camargue?"

"So he's told you, has he? I've never lived anywhere else but here. In the same *cabane* even, for nearly thirty years. And in one on the same spot before that. I'd die if I was driven off. And all because he says he can prove I shot a duck now and then on the government reserve."

"So, to put it bluntly, then, Monsieur Denys told you to say nothing about the man you saw rambling about here?"

"That's right. That's all it was."

"Why did he want it keeping secret?"

"He said he didn't wish the whole place swarming with police. It's quiet and peaceful here and we've our work to do, he said. And once the police get around, they won't leave things alone till the whole Camargue is in an uproar. And, after all, he said, it wasn't as if the man had been murdered. He'd probably got lost, fallen in, and died. Or else committed suicide ...."

"And that's all?"

"Yes. I swear it."

Dorange released the man's arm.

"All right, you old rascal. Get on your horse again and be off with you."

"I can go?"

"Yes."

The *gardian's* even teeth shone through his beard again. They couldn't tell whether he was smiling with satisfaction or good will. He mounted nimbly and took the horsehair reins in his hands.

"By the way, sir, you'll do me the favour of not telling Monsieur Denys what I told you. After all, I did you a good turn in speaking truthfully about what happened. Don't let him know, or else he'll make it hot for me."

Dorange slapped the horse on its hindquarters and the wild pair cantered off. Davso rode magnificently. Man and horse seemed carved from one piece.

They turned to see the last of him as the distance between them increased. He had stopped among the wild horses and was talking to them and feeding them, like tame things, with pieces of bread from his saddle-bags.

Chapter VII
The Stranger on the Marsh

Littlejohn seemed to be moving in his sleep, in a dream in a strange land. He had felt it before in the vast Breton moorlands and in the barren heights of High Provence. The great flat landscape, dotted with the cabins of the cowboys, the limitless stretch of the wilderness, the merciless heat of the sun. There was not even a cloud in the sky to relieve it; only a waste of burning blue overhead and the hot air below, which seemed to have substance and was heavy about him, like hot lather.

Soon, the Mas Vidal came in sight, surrounded by a little village composed of *cabanes* and with, in the far distance, the great tower of the church at Les Saintes, blotted on the skyline like a huge two-dimensional shadow. The roads to the coast were crowded with gypsies, on their pilgrimage to the feast of their saints on the morrow. Every type of vehicle. Old traps and carriages, which might have been stolen from some abandoned junk heap; horse-drawn caravans, some of them with goats tethered to them and trotting along in the blistering heat, their cries sounding above the rumble of wheels. Donkeys, mules, old jeeps. Now and then, a fairly new car. Motor vans and waggons, lorries, trailers. Some of the motor vehicles were even without tyres, for, it is said, that among their own race, even the gypsies dare not leave anything movable lying about.

There were people of all kinds, too. Including the gypsy-king, resplendent in coloured sash and headcloth, and long moon-shaped ear-rings. He was riding in an ancient Provençal high-cart with a hood, like that of a perambulator, elevated to keep off the sun. He was shouting with rage and nobody dared approach him. Skilled in all the tricks of his kind, he had, nevertheless, had his pocket picked in Arles.

Now and then, one or another of the pilgrims on foot—mainly slovenly women carrying bundles or babies behind a mule on which their husbands were riding—would pause as if to ask the occupants of the jeep for alms or help. Then, seeing Dorange, they suddenly changed their minds.... The man from Nice was always genial, smiling, sociable, and yet must have carried with him wherever he went an aura which was the terror of lawbreakers and wrongdoers.

At the *mas*, the party had gathered again in the large dining-room and were drinking beer or *anis* with lumps of ice floating in it. The old lady was taking a siesta and Solange had joined the rest. Away from her mother she was changed and agreeable. Talking animatedly with Féraud, she was obviously as much in love with him as he was with her. They looked in each other's eyes and gently touched one another now and then. Their emotions might have appeared superficial, but ran deep. Soon, preferring to be alone, they quietly withdrew to the next room. When Littlejohn and Dorange entered, they encountered restraint from Denys de Berluc-Vidal. He gave them a questioning look and asked them stiffly what information Davso had given them.

"Exactly nothing, monsieur," said Dorange. "He is a rascal who will only sell what he has and knows. He gives nothing."

Dorange poured Perrier in his *Pernod*; the drinking water from the deep well in the yard was brackish and unpleasant, even when filtered.

Denys regarded him silently for a moment and then bared his even white teeth.

"They are all that way. It is not money, but loyalty."

"Loyalty to whom?"

Denys shrugged.

Cromwell was holding a cord with a tassel at each end and a red cockade almost like an English general-election rosette.

"They've been giving me a lecture on bullfighting, sir," he told Littlejohn. Lubricated by two glasses of *Pernod*, he was talkative. By his side sat his friend, Yvonne de Berluc-Vidal, examining a medal.

"This," he continued holding up the tasselled cord, "this is slung between the bull's horns and this cockade is hung on the middle of the string, with the tassels hanging from the horns. Like this...."

He held the lot aloft.

"The bullfighter has a steel comb, called ... called ...."

"A *raset*," prompted Yvonne, "And the bullfighter is a *raseteur*."

Cromwell produced a *raset* with four teeth and brandished it, looking ready to accept a challenge to partake in the bullfight at Arles on the morrow.

"Then, all it consists of is snatching the rosette ... the ...."

"*Cocarde*...."

"And the tassels...."

"*Glands*...."

"From the bull's horns with the comb. The high-scoring *raseteurs* win trophies, and the best gets the golden cockade."

Denys de Berluc-Vidal interrupted.

"But the best bulls are those trained to avoid having their cockades and tassels pillaged. They see with their horns as well as their eyes. If, after a quarter of an hour, the assembled *raseteurs* in the bull-ring have failed to score, the bull has won, and himself receives the *cocarde d'or*. A bull such as *Le Romain*, there."

He indicated the mounted head of the bull over the fireplace.

"... He was never beaten in his best years and won innumerable trophies and cash prizes."

Yvonne showed them the medal she was holding. It was itself a *cocarde d'or*.

"This was one of *César's* trophies. He is still alive; the grandson of *Le Romain*. If you care to keep the rosettes, the tassels and the *cocarde* as souvenirs, please do so."

Cromwell, flushed and content, accepted, and put them carefully away to take home.

An hour passed in talk of horses, cattle, bullrings and the Camargue, which were in the very blood of the locals and which seemed to be an unending topic. The arts of branding, or *ferrade*; the ritual of the arrivals, *les arrivées;* and departures at the bullrings, *la bandide;* horse dressage and breaking, *desbrandage;* separation of bulls from the herd by means of the trident or *ficheron,* and known as *le triage....* They were all scientifically discussed and it seemed that life on the southern Camargue was one long round of sport.

The afternoon was ending and already signs of dusk were appearing. Littlejohn looked through the large window facing the west and saw the sun low over the horizon, a ball of orange fire. The sky was a mixture of purple and gold and mirrored in the forlorn little lake at the back of the *mas,* where the waves broke into innumerable iridescent rainbow tints. It was as though somewhere there was a great destructive fire and these were its reflection. A flock of cranes flew across the water and descended among the reeds and two flamingos, beating their great wings, sailed sadly past like film subjects seen in slow-motion.

His reverie was disturbed by the rattle of horse hooves in the yard outside. Somebody in a hurry! The rider dismounted and they could hear his running footsteps, then his voice, excited and shrill, talking to the maidservant, a young girl, dressed-up for the occasion in the white cap, shawl, and coloured skirt of the Arlésiennes. She entered and, unable to contain her news, spoke it to the company in general.

"Davso is dead. He has been killed."

The *gardian* was brought in to tell his tale. He wore a battered slouch-hat, a velvet jacket, coloured neck-cloth, and narrow trousers tucked in gum-boots. A strong man with a strong face.

He had, returning past Davso's cabin, seen the old man's horse wandering about unattended. He had dismounted and found Davso lying at his very door, dead. He was still warm. His skull had been smashed. A dreadful wound.

The jeeps were out again and the police officers, with the Berluc-Vidals, father and son, and Féraud, the *baile,* or head cowboy, went over the same ground again to the Etang de Vaccarès.

This time, the vast spreading wilderness looked more ominous. The stillness and heat were oppressive, the insects more aggressive. The twisted trees and stricken salt-grass seemed to move gently as though alive, yet there was no breeze. The cabins dotted here and there were deserted and forlorn, and the streams and drainage canals over which their road lay gave off noisome vapours, full of miasmas, making the English wish to spit and clear their throats of what tasted like the plague.

When the Etang de Vaccarès came in sight it might have been of molten metal. The orange sunlight, reflected from the west, fell across the tiny waves of the lake, giving it almost the appearance of boiling gold. The tall vegetation of the banks was silhouetted in spectral shapes and the birds had chosen this hour for their quarrelling and shrill squawking, and provided an unearthly background of mournful noise.

The *gardian* who had found the body rode ahead, admirably astride his horse, the pair of them moving like one. He still carried his trident, without which none of them seemed to stir very far. The jeeps followed, tossing their occupants about as they sped along the rough road after the horseman. They passed the scene of Cheever's death…. Poor Cheever, who was almost forgotten already.

Davso's cabin was built in traditional style, the rush thatch falling away in parts, the walls, once white, now soiled and neglected. It stood on the shore of a small tributary of the Vaccarès and a drainage canal of still, slimy water flowed, like a sewer, past the front door. An ague-stricken spot and if, as he said, Davso had lived there all his life, he must have been a physiological phenomenon.

They didn't need to look far for the old cowboy. He was stretched on his back, arms and legs spread like those of one crucified. His head was on one side and his open sightless eyes looked straight at the setting sun. His hat lay on the ground a few yards away.

Littlejohn and Dorange knelt and examined the body without moving it. There was no need for that; the story of Davso's death was plain to be seen. One side of his head had been smashed in by a fearful blow and there was blood oozing from the wound, and matting his long grey hair and beard. The mouth was wide open, as though, seeing death upon him, he had uttered a frightful cry. The glazed eyes were staring as if they had recognised, at last, the fate Davso had always feared, his own end.

The body was bleeding in the chest, too, from three deep gashes, about three inches apart and Littlejohn, pressing his finger around them, felt the wall of the chest had been smashed in by some heavy instrument. Dorange knew at once how it had occurred.

"He was probably taken unawares, perhaps by some intruder who came upon him from his cabin. He was knocked from his horse by a powerful blow of a trident.... The three wounds in the breast are from the prongs. Then, before he could recover himself, he was beaten on the head by the same weapon. One blow from such would be enough...."

Davso's horse snorted and shook his head as the insects pestered him. He was tied-up to a tether-post by the side of the cabin door, which stood open.

Pignon and Féraud were sent back to the ranch to telephone for a doctor and a *juge d'instruction*, the magistrate who would be in charge of the case, from Arles. As they left, the rest of the party entered the *cabane*. Dorange took an old hooded cloak of heavy cloth from behind the door and went out and covered the body with it. The cowboy took the horse to a small lean-to, and they left him bedding down, grooming and feeding the beast, which is natural with every good *gardian*.

A single-roomed hut, illuminated by a small window at the far end. This was too dirty to admit light and they left the door open. They would have done this in any event for the air was noisome and dank.

The place was a shambles. This was not due to ransacking; but its natural state. In one corner, a dirty camp bed, with a mass of soiled canvas, shawls, sacks and rugs piled on the misshapen straw mattress. A rough wooden cupboard, with its doors wide open, revealing food and drink, a conglomeration of old jars, bottles, tins, dried fruit, olives, stale bread, old cheese, emitting an aroma which added its share to the fetid stench of the whole cabin. A battered chair or two, a bucket full of dirty soapy water, and a sack which served as a towel. A rickety wooden table with the remains of a meal scattered on it. Bread, cheese, a half empty tin of beans, some boiled rice....

Hanging from a nail driven in the wall, two large eels, already past their best. Then, a long shelf containing bottles of all kinds, some empty, some partly full. Quack medicines, pills, lotions, oils, tablets, for a multitude of ills. Davso seemed mainly concerned with rheumatism, malaria, the ague, the kidneys, the intestines, the stomach, the lungs and the spleen. There were several bottles, all, except one, empty and obviously regularly used, of *Duvivier's Prescription of Life*. This conglomeration greatly interested Cromwell, who was somewhat of a health faddist, albeit a sane and reasonable one, himself. On the same shelf as this strange materia medica, a pile of booklets, leaflets, old newspaper advertisements, all on the same topic, health through quackery.

"I'd think the best way to do away with old Davso would have been to poison his physic," remarked Dorange dryly.

But what attracted the attention of them all was the old wooden chest in the middle of the floor. It could not have been, by any stretch of imagination, described as a strong box. It was made of a mixed lot of timber, old boxes, matchwood, and even driftwood, and would easily have yielded to a pair of pincers or a claw hammer. But it had probably served as a treasure-chest for Davso in a land where—remote from gypsy paths—everyone was honest and minded his own business, especially if he was a member of the *gardians,* one of the Brotherhood of St. Georges.

The box, however, had been rifled. Its contents were strewn about the floor, as though the intruder had been searching for something in particular. And, being disturbed by Davso, had turned and killed him.

The policemen turned over the odds and ends in the chest and on the floor around. The searcher had only skimmed off the top of the contents when he had been startled. A lot more advertisements for patent medicines and a bottle of brandy and one, a small one, of laudanum. Then some family papers, concerning marriages, deaths, first communions and terms of military service. An old gun-metal watch with the glass broken, two brass signet rings and a wedding-ring of the same metal in a cardboard box. A lot of little devotional cards such as are given to good children who regularly attend church. Two faded photographs of old people on pieces of tin, and some coloured ribbons.

In the chest itself, Davso had kept his Sunday best. An extra pair of trousers, a shiny velvet jacket, a soiled white shirt, a pair of dirty rubber pumps. A box containing *cocardes,* obviously won by Davso in the bullrings of past days. And then the *raseteur's* comb he had used. At the very bottom, a woman's dress, after the fashion worn by Arlésiennes for centuries. White bonnet, coloured skirt, scarf, bolero.... Perhaps his mother's. There was a pocket concealed inside the skirt, and there they found an old wallet. This must have been where Davso had hidden special treasures; the heart of the box.

The wallet held a few hundred-franc notes and five gold pieces. But it was the envelope lying loose between the two sides of the wallet which interested the searchers most. It was of the pass-book type issued by banks for containing statements of account, and was dirty and obviously dried after immersion in water. It was even marked *'Private'* in English in the top left-hand corner. It contained seventy-five notes of one thousand francs apiece. These, too, had suffered from water and had been dried-out. On the flap of the envelope was embossed the name of the sender. *Home Counties Bank.* And across the embossing, by means of a rubber-stamp, *Francaster,* to complete the address. Davso must have pillaged the remains of the body before giving the alarm; and he must have concealed the clothes and wallet containing the money, which, alone, he had kept.

It seemed, somehow, to bring the ghost of Cheever into the picture again, right into the squalid *cabane* so far from home.

There was little else to help them. No footprints on the hard earth floor; the objects thrown from the box were too dirty and man-handled to be much use for fingerprinting; and, although Marion went up and down inside and out until he looked ready to collapse with fatigue, nothing turned up to inspire him. He did find a gun, an old pinfire, with a few cartridges of the old-fashioned kind, in one corner. One barrel had been fired and was still foul, with the empty cartridge still in the breach. He thought of Cheever, and then decided that it seemed a silly theory to pin on a poacher like Davso.

Marion stayed behind, with the *gardian* who had found the body, until help arrived from Arles. The rest returned to the *mas.* It was rapidly growing dusk and, during their stay in the *cabane,* the cold mistral from the north had started gently to blow. They could hear it making the reeds and shrubs rattle around the Vaccarès and the water being lashed and whipped up into little waves.

It was going to be a cold, perhaps a terrifying night for the stranger, the murderer, on the Camargue.

CHAPTER VIII
THE PLACE OF THE MONKEY

Littlejohn drew back the curtains of his bedroom facing
the sea at a small, first-rate hotel on the Croisette at
Cannes. Dorange had personally deposited the pair of them
there the night before and spoken to the manager about
them. The result was a room with a view, reasonable prices,
and treatment meet for royalty.

The situation on the Camargue the previous night had
been embarrassing. After the discovery of Davso's dead
body and their return to the Mas Vidal, an atmosphere of
restraint, to say the least of it, had crept in. The "nation
of *gardians*", the knights of St. Georges, wanted no outsid-
ers investigating their private affairs. If one of them had
been murdered, it was their business to arrange matters in
their own way, find out who had done it, and decide how he
should be dealt with. They didn't say as much at the *mas*, but
Denys de Berluc-Vidal implied it by his manner. Dorange
and Marion had to take him aside and put him in his place.
The Arles police were almost members of the brotherhood
and Marion made it quite plain that he was staying there
until the case was solved.

Littlejohn and Cromwell were another matter. They
were, from the start, mere foreigners, visitors, sightseers,

93

interested in the lonely death of some wandering Englishman or other who had fallen in the mud of the Vaccarès. Berluc-Vidal said it in as many words during the picturesque quarrel and exchange of insults which went on between the French police and himself. High words apart, however, the Englishmen had no official standing and, remaining there, they would only become nuisances to Marion and lay themselves open to certain indignities. Dorange advised them to leave it to the local police, and they were glad to do so.

When Denys de Berluc-Vidal learned that the two English detectives were leaving, his manner changed. He even said he was sorry they were going, which they took as a mere courtesy in the course of saying farewell. He invited them to return the stay at the *mas* for as long as they liked.

"... When all this trouble is over and we can ride around the *domaine* and watch the *brandades* and bullfights with an easy mind...."

Dorange left with them and Marion, busy interrogating everybody in the vicinity, promised to keep them in touch with developments. A police car was placed at the disposal of Dorange, and he, Littlejohn and Cromwell started for Arles.

It was almost dark and the headlamps cast long blinding rays across the desolate wilderness on each side of the main road. Everything was silent. Here and there a cabin with a light showing through the window. Strange animals exaggerated in sizes and shapes by sudden illumination. A hamlet, shut up for the night; the lamps of a *mas* flickering through the trees; stretches of dark water lighting up with an unholy phosphorescent glow as the headlights struck across them. They could make out clusters of wild horses and bulls, standing mute, astonished, as the beams from the car caught them by surprise.

As they neared Arles, the road changed. The country-side to right and left was cut off frequently by tall reeds and rushes growing from below the level of the causeway, and the monotonous stretches of rice in the paddy-fields rose, a pale blue-green, from the mists which hung across the submerged soil. An odd car or two passed, and countryfolk on bicycles hurrying home. Once or twice they came across gypsies, encamped where it was dry and firm.

Littlejohn, caught-up in circumstances which, though obviously closely connected with the work he himself had to do, found his plans thrown awry. Not only were the natives of the Camargue unlikely to help a stranger in investiga-tions which might involve the guilt of one or more of them, but also, the local police had become concerned with a crime which might easily have been caused by the visit of the English detectives to Mas Vidal. It seemed better, there-fore, for Littlejohn to work on the flanks of the case, try to follow the path of Cheever during his stay in the South, and perhaps from such sources find out the circumstances which had led Cheever to his wretched end. There were two places concerned with Sammy's itinerary. Pont de Veyle, where he had probably struck the trail of the squire of Mas Vidal, and Cannes, where he had first bought the miniature which had started all the trouble.

Dorange was on his way to Nice, where urgent business awaited him next day. It seemed best to go with him and drop off at Cannes. So here Littlejohn was, looking from his bedroom window at eight in the morning.

The view helped to dispel the gloomy memories of the previous day. The sun was shining and the sky was a dome of untroubled deep blue, without a cloud. Across the bay the Lérins islands were dimly visible through a morning haze of heat. The promenade was almost deserted. A man feeding the sparrows, another exercising a dog, a third riding past on a bicycle, cluttered up with fishing tackle, on his way to the pier. Cromwell, recognisable in the distance, taking his morning constitutional, his shoulders well back, his walk brisk and optimistic. It was obviously hot already in the open air. People were having breakfast on little tables scattered on hotel terraces, and, on the private beaches between the promenade and the sea, rolls and coffee were being served to early birds in bathing costumes and bathrobes.

And the sea…. As blue as the sky, stretching untroubled until it disappeared in the distant mists. Early bathers were plunging about or peacefully lying on their backs, drifting here and there. Little boats and pedal-craft bobbed about on the water and yachts with white sails spread skimmed across the skyline. A luxury liner riding at anchor just off the coast and ready to leave for the East; not far from it, an American destroyer with busy motor launches shuttling to and from the port for provisions and depositing white-clad sailors on leave. The whole stretch between the Esterel and Cap d'Antibes, with the mountains behind Nice just visible in the distance, was like a scene on a coloured postcard.

The two of them ate breakfast on the hotel terrace facing the promenade. A string of cars came and went before them, the ordinary, workaday models punctuated now and then by the appearance of magnificent turnouts containing film-stars, millionaires with one or more elegant women, or else an eastern potentate in a turban. An Algerian with a hopeful face and a fez indicated to Cromwell over the wall of the terrace that he would like to enter into negotiations about the sale of a carpet he was carrying draped across his shoulders.

One thing was certain. Littlejohn had brought his light shirts and flannel trousers; Cromwell in his excitement at the trip had forgotten his, and was still wearing his heavy dark suit. Already the air was buzzing with heat. They would have to do some shopping. Cromwell wondered if his expenses-sheet from Scotland Yard would be an appropriate document to use for the purpose.

Work! Littlejohn shuddered. A day, or perhaps more, hunting for antique shops and asking questions. *Did a little fat chap in a blazer call here last year and buy this...?* And then they'd produce the miniature of Clotilde de Montvallon. Some of the shopkeepers would be polite; others would think they were trying to sell something and give them short shrift. Littlejohn groaned.

"You all right, sir?" said Cromwell, who, in harsh and limited French, had just got rid of the carpet pedlar.

"Quite, old man. I'm worried about your get-up. It's too hot. You'll be having a stroke."

"I've been thinking the same myself."

He almost asked about the expenses-sheet, but decided not to spoil Littlejohn's day but argue it out with the cashier at the Yard later.

Littlejohn drained his cup and rose slowly. The holiday feeling was upon him again. He felt he could sit there all day grilling in the heat, watching other people enjoying themselves, admiring the marvellous blue sea, counting the heads of the tycoons, rajahs, and the rest of them, as they passed, just visible over the terrace wall.

The manager made a low obeisance as they set out to work, casting, at the same time, a wondering eye on Cromwell's heavy clerical-looking attire. Dorange had told him Littlejohn was world-famous and that the manager would personally answer to him, Dorange, in case of any complaints. The manager's eyes were like those of a faithful spaniel and Littlejohn told him that last night's meal, his room, and the breakfast had all been excellent. For the rest of the day, the staff commented on the light-heartedness of the boss.

Round the corner and down the nearest side street, to a men's outfitter's Littlejohn remembered. They fitted Cromwell out with light trousers and summer underwear, slipped a white shirt of fine poplin over his head...and he looked a new man. Littlejohn thought he only needed snake-skin shoes and a belt, like Dorange, to get himself mistaken for a French detective. All Cromwell's heavy wear was par-celled up and the manager of the shop promised to see them delivered at their hotel. There was a special discount on a very reasonable bill. It didn't take Littlejohn long to find out the reason. The manager showed him the morning paper.

MURDER IN THE CAMARGUE

A GARDIAN IS BEATEN AND STABBED TO DEATH WITH A TRIDENT FAMOUS DETECTIVES ARE ON THE CASE

And in the text, it mentioned that Dorange and his English friend, the famous English Superintendent Littlejohn, of le Scotland Yard, were concerned in the case.

"It is a pleasure to be of service to a friend of Monsieur Dorange."

Littlejohn wondered what else they could get cheap by mentioning Dorange's name. It was the Open Sesame to the Côte d'Azur, and even far beyond!

"Is there anything else, monsieur?"

The manager shook hands with the pair of them and seemed reluctant to see them go.

"Yes. You might be able to help us, as a local man. Do you know an antique shop in Cannes where the proprietress, an elderly lady, owns a monkey and keeps it in the shop?"

It seemed a ridiculous question, but there was nothing like trying.

The manager burst into smiles and waved his arms joyfully about as though it were a great joke, perhaps a practical joke they were playing on him, these English and their queer sense of humour.

"But, certainly. Next door. Madame Labourel. You wish to see the monkey? It is said to be very intelligent."

"Not exactly. We want to see Madame about some antiques. Will she be in the shop now?"

"Certainly. I'll take you and introduce you. She will give you special terms, if I tell her to do so. She is usually rather expensive, you know. These holidaymakers.... Plenty of money...."

He shrugged to give them a rough idea of how much money the visitors to Cannes usually had to spend. Then he led them into the street and next door, walking on his toes with a jaunty swagger and swinging his hips to show what a pleasure it was.

A large shop with three great windows, tastefully exhibiting very nice-looking old furniture, ornaments, clocks, glass and china. There was an Aubusson carpet on the floor and Madame herself was seated in a Louis XIV chair, polishing a Limoges enamel, which she gently laid down in a bed of cotton-wool when the ebullient outfitter approached her.

A good-looking woman of past sixty, with a mop of beautiful close-cut white hair. Her features tapered from high cheek-bones to a small delicate, pointed chin. The dark eyes were bright and shrewd and a finely arched nose set-off a clever face. The hands which fondled the enamel were small and white, as white as her complexion, which was like marble. A beautiful woman in her time, and she remained seated, like a queen among her treasures.

"Good morning, Monsieur Bossi."

Bossi! What a name! But Madame and the outfitter didn't seem to see anything strange about it. Monsieur Bossi kissed her hand. Perhaps the furniture, tapestries, and old clocks which, at the moment, all started to strike eleven, made him feel courtly.

"These gentlemen are friends of Monsieur Dorange, of the Nice Sûreté."

Madame's eyes went as hard as iron and her little mouth tightened. It was like mentioning Walsingham to Mary, Queen of Scots!

"Superintendent Littlejohn and Brigadier Cromwell, of le Scotland Yard...."

Cromwell missed it, but Littlejohn's eyes twinkled, caught those of Madame, she smiled, and the ice was broken.

"You are on police work, Superintendent?"

A gentle, cultured voice, too.

"Not exactly. I want your advice on a small matter, if you can spare the time, madame."

"I've all the time in the world...."

Whereat there broke on the shop one single raucous shout, which made the outfitter jump and even Madame turn pale pink. They had been so busy with introductions that they'd forgotten the monkey, which stood gripping a crutch-like pedestal, marking time in a rage with its shrivelled old feet, glaring at Cromwell, and making as if to fly at him and tear him apart.

"Silence, Quintilien! Or else...."

The monkey glanced at the inner door through which he was exiled when he misbehaved, swore a more respectable oath, and hung his head.

"I must apologise for Quintilien. He is old and moody and takes dislikes to people."

The cunning old eye of the monkey again fixed itself on Cromwell and he made a noise like a snort and then another like the emptying of a bottle.

"I think I'll be going now the introductions are made," said the outfitter, who was obviously not on the monkey's friendly list, either. And, with assurances of his profound respect and willingness to serve the two detectives in any way whatsoever, he tripped back to his shop, followed by a scorching farewell yell from the monkey.

"And now, gentlemen...."

Cromwell produced the miniature and handed it to Littlejohn.

"Ah..." said the old lady when she saw it. It was an anxious sound, but no more.

"You sold this miniature to an Englishman last year, madame?"

"Yes. It is a very fine one and genuine, I assure you."

"I'm not challenging that. But the man has died. I may as well tell you, madame, he was murdered. His trouble seems to centre round this picture. Not content with buying it from you at what, I believe, was a fair price...."

"It was very cheap. I will take it back at more than he gave me for it. I have buyers for such things again now. When he was here and made an offer, I let him have it at very little profit. I needed to keep up my turnover. Things are not so good as they were with the English, with whom we once did the bulk of our trade, now restricted officially on what they can spend."

"Can you tell me anything about the miniature?"

He passed it to her and she took it gently. Her eyes lit up as she looked at it.

"It is very good to look upon.... A delicate little piece of work."

"Did you take it to pieces before you sold it, madame?"

"Yes. It has since been opened again. I took off the back to clean the picture and the frame."

She felt it between her thumb and finger.

"Something has been removed. There was a paper inside, with an account of the woman in the picture. It was wrapped in a thin gold-beater's skin. It was often done with portraits of this kind, and gave some story, some interesting detail of the person."

"Did you read the statement?"

"Yes."

"What was it? A pedigree ... a family tree?"

"No. As far as I can remember, it was an account of her death. Very sad, too."

"Do you remember what it said?"

The woman eyed him up and down and then smiled again. It might have been a smile just to herself. She might have been satisfied that here was a cultured and sympathetic listener; or it may have been that he was a personal friend of Inspector Dorange. Whatever it was, she seemed satisfied.

"I cannot remember the woman's name or where she came from ...."

"They are on the old letter which was used for the backing of the picture."

The old lady put on a pair of gold-framed spectacles and examined the back.

"Clotilde de Montvallon ... Pont de Veyle .... That is it. I remember. She eloped with the artist .... His name is on the picture. Lepont .... That's it. They eloped. She was having a child. Her father, I seem to remember, was a hard man who would not have hesitated to kill Monsieur Lepont. So, loving one another, they fled. The date was 1838 .... I'll tell you why I remember. Everyone remembers 1838 in Provence. It was the year of the great cholera, which swept the whole countryside and killed people off like flies. I have some contemporary engravings in the chest, there. Marseilles...a shambles...."

The monkey again interrupted with a string of chatter, levelled at Cromwell, and was silenced by the same threats as before.

"The child was born. In an hotel at Manosque, where the couple were living. If you know the story of Manosque during the cholera...oh, monsieur...dreadful, appalling. The woman died, and the man, sure he would die, too, sent the child south to the mountains, where it might be safe. The document with the miniature was presumably the last letter of the child's father, tucked behind the picture, which must have accompanied the child and the nurse, or whoever took him—it was a boy—to safety. The letter stated that the cholera area was sealed off—a kind of quarantine. The picture was the means of identifying the child, who was to be sent to his grandparents at Pont de Veyle as soon as communications were restored. I think whoever took him away must have died, too. Or perhaps she sold the picture, or someone else came by it and sold it. At any rate, instead of getting to Pont de Veyle, it went astray and eventually came in the market and I bought it."

"May I ask where, madame?"

The woman hesitated and the monkey chattered to himself, eyeing Cromwell murderously.

"This is most unusual, Superintendent. We dealers are not in the habit of divulging our sources of trade. It is not to our advantage, as you will understand. Competition is keen for good things and one does not...."

She shrugged and threw out her hands in a gracious, appealing gesture.

"All the same.... You are not a dealer, are you? You are a friend of Monsieur Dorange and anxious to help the course of justice."

Littlejohn smiled and nodded.

"I bought it in the old part of the town.... Yes, in Cannes. There was a sale of remnants in a tenement house, just off the Rue Clavel, 22 *bis*, Rue Belle-de-Mai. There were some odds and ends of old furniture the property of a deceased tenant who owed a lot of rent. They sent for me. The land-lord is a wealthy local man who knows a good thing when he sees it. He prefers to sell such as antiques rather than in an auction sale. You understand? There was an old wardrobe there. It was the only thing of value. It had been painted over in white and was in dirty condition, but it was Napoleon I, and there was mahogany under the paint. I made him an offer. He agreed. In the course of examining the piece, I took out the drawers, as is my custom. They were full of filthy rags and odds and ends. The dead man must have been very poor... on his beam ends, in fact. Behind the drawer, I found the miniature. Also in filthy condition. It must have lain there, lost, for many, many years."

"And you cleaned it up and sold it to Mr. Cheever?"

"Cheever? Ah, the funny little upstart who bought it. He thought himself a clever one, to be sure. Yes...."

"With the letter in the back?"

"Of course. It belonged to the picture. It was no use to me. The cholera of 1838. There must have been thousands of such cases. As I said, it swept over Provence like the breath of death, killing everybody in its way. The story of Clotilde de Montvallon is one of thousands. I left it with her picture. But I did not tell the little bantam-cock about it. Let him find out, I thought...."

Her eyes grew spiteful. She and Cheever must have had a rather unfriendly tussle about the deal. Littlejohn wondered how the monkey had taken it.

"An unpleasant little man, but his money was good."

She rummaged in a desk and produced a business card.

SAMUEL CHEEVER,

OBJECTS D'ART, FRANCASTER.

Cheever and his objects d'art! And his home-made French!

"...Quintilien took an instant dislike to him. He hurled abuse at him and even flew at his wife, who was with him, and bit her. Well, I suppose Monsieur Cheever found the letter and it has not done him any good. He did not, I hope, die of the cholera."

"No. His dead body was found in the mud of the Vaccarès."

"God help us! So that is the case. It was connected with the one in the paper this morning."

"That's right. By the way, did he call on you again a month ago?"

"Come to think of it, he did. He wanted to know where I had bought the miniature or if I could tell him more about the woman in it. It seems he had markets, which were very valuable, for this kind of thing, but he must have a history and full details of the subject of the miniature. As he was in the trade, and it was doing me no harm, I told him."

"Do you know the name of the man who died; the one who owned the miniature?"

"No. There is a concierge, a horrible old woman, who will tell you all about him for the price of a drink."

"Thank you, madame. By the way, my friend here has purchased the miniature. It will be in excellent hands."

"I'm sure it will, in spite of Quintilien's rudeness. It is Monsieur Cromwell's tie. Quintilien cannot bear red. Like a bull."

"Au revoir, madame."

"Till we meet again. So pleased to see you both."

It made them jump. This was the first time she had spoken English and it was said with a flawless accent.

They went into the street, which, after the cool depths of the shop, felt like a furnace. The monkey screamed hot abuse after Cromwell. Littlejohn didn't mention the tie. After all, it was a nice one, a present for his birthday from Cromwell's eldest daughter, whom he called his little sweetheart.

CHAPTER IX
RUE BELLE-DE-MAI

They walked on under the sweltering sunlight. It was so dazzling that it affected the sight and they seemed to be progressing through a warm mist. The hot stones of the side-streets between the promenade and the main shopping quarter burned like an oven-bottom. They threaded through a pandemonium of cars, lorries and trade vehicles of all kinds, jumping here and there to avoid being mown down, irritated and dazed by the heat and the incessant blaring of impatient horns.

A rush of smart cars, bicycles and scooters, and they were in the Rue d'Antibes. Huge, elegant shop-windows displaying expensive clothes, jewellery, confections, bric-à-brac.... An ice-cream there cost three times as much as anywhere else!

They followed the old antique-dealer's directions, turned one corner, then another, saw the railway station in the distance. A narrow street full of food and souvenir shops and a blind man selling lottery tickets. Then, another world....

The wealth and fashion of the Croisette, the huge white hotels, the blue sea, seemed hundreds of miles away. Narrow lanes and alleys, tall aged buildings, tenements, small tradesmen, junk shops, old houses with filthy walls and rotting as they stood. The blue sky was just visible above, like the relieving sight of daylight at the top of a tall chimney. Between the sky and the hot squalid pavement, a network of washing-lines slung from one side to the other and a jumble of telephone and electricity wires almost as thick as a spring mattress.

The Rue Belle-de-Mai was no better than the rest in spite of its attractive name. Littlejohn and Cromwell were met by a torrid noisome blast of air as they turned into it. They had to pick their way gingerly over a plank which spanned an open drain, for the workmen were repairing a sewer.

Each building had its own special smell. Tenement houses emitting the odours of garlic and ill-kept sanitation, alternated with little shops and intersecting narrow alleys. A greengrocer's hidden in a dark recess gave off the flavours of stale vegetables and rotting fruit. A warehouse dealing in 'products of Provence' cast out an aroma of rancid olive oil and pickled olives. In a yard with tumbledown double doors, two men were skinning a dead horse which had been there some time.

And yet, this had been a respectable quarter in days past. As the detectives slowly climbed the steady incline to the top of the town, they passed what must have been the houses of gentry in better times. Now and then a shield or coat of arms showed over a great neglected doorway. The head of a stone satyr or a nymph, corroded with the weather and misuse, stared down here and there and, if they happened to be accessible to passers-by, they had been ornamented by obscenities or indecent additions. Once or twice, the double cross of de Gaulle appeared, its dirty white paint still visible after all the years.

22 *bis* was one of such places. A fine old house with a heavy door surmounted by a shield and crest, divided into

seedy hovels and emitting a noisome stench, a mixture of hot oil, garlic and stale slops. Cromwell's nose twitched and he began to pick his way like a cat unwilling to wet her feet.

An old woman with white hair screwed back from a face netted with wrinkles and with bright eyes like shoe-buttons set in her spiteful features, was sitting on the top step of three which rose to the door, peeling potatoes and dropping them in a bucket. She was comparatively clean and wore a rough black jumper and a large soiled white apron. She looked up at the two men as they halted.

"This is 22 *bis*...?"

"Yes."

With this laconic reply, she rose, crossed the street to a small workmen's café, dumped the potatoes there, and then returned.

"What do you want?"

She recognised them, with the sure instinct of her type, as officials of some kind, but knowing from Littlejohn's speech that he was a foreigner, could not properly size them up.

"Are you the caretaker?"

"Yes."

Her little sloes of eyes challenged them to find anything wrong with her.

"Do you recollect a tenant called Lepont.... He died last year."

"Nobody of that name lived here. And tenants are always dying. It's nothing to do with me."

"He might have been called Montvallon, then.... He lived here and couldn't pay his rent. He died bankrupt and they sold his furniture...."

The old woman cackled this time.

"They all die ruined. Most of the tenants are behind with the rent. The broker's men wear out the pavement in this street. We have a furniture sale every other day."

They weren't getting anywhere. Cromwell looked bemused. The heat, the smells, and the fact that he couldn't understand a word of the old woman's local patter were getting him down.

Littlejohn took a five hundred franc note from his pocket. The woman's eyes lit up with greed.

"This wasn't the broker's man. The landlord brought up an antique dealer, Madame Labourel...."

"Why didn't you say so, then? You mean Monsieur Rivaud, perhaps.... He was on the fourth floor and was a bit above the usual. He didn't leave much in the way of furniture, but what he had was good, or so they said. I wouldn't know."

The note changed hands and vanished from sight. The old woman looked around to be sure that nobody was watching the transaction.

"You'd better go up and see Devard the tailor on the fourth. Rivaud's room was opposite his and they were pals. Used to get drunk a lot together and, no doubt, Rivaud told him all his secrets in his cups. He never told me anything. A mystery man, I called him. He'd seen better days and didn't like to talk much. He used to think himself a cut above me. Well.... I've outlived him and I shan't die without a sou to bless myself or be buried with. Go on up.... You'll find Devard in."

They lit their pipes to begin with and entered in a cloud of tobacco smoke to antidote the smells emerging from the house. A spacious hall with a door on each side. Good doors, too, although almost completely without paint by now. The old decorations, filthy and damaged, were still visible.

Bosses, ribbons and *fleur-de-lys* motives…. The remains of a faun's head in relief. Obscenities scribbled on the walls. The staircase was broad and had a fine handrail and wrought ironwork. Littlejohn wondered why the obviously avaricious landlord hadn't dismantled and sold them. Perhaps the job would cost too much.

Their footsteps echoed on the broad staircase, with its shallow, graceful treads now rotting away. Repairs had been effected by nailing on pieces of old packing-cases. At the head of each staircase, a landing, and as they climbed upwards, the well of the stairs narrowed and deteriorated. Looking down the giddy depth to the ground floor, Littlejohn could see the caretaker, her neck bent at a right-angle, looking up, watching their progress. Behind the doors of the tenements, hoarse, quarrelsome voices and the smells of cooking. On the landings, outside the doors, empty wine bottles, garbage cans full of rubbish, a bottle of milk, a long loaf of bread.

The fourth floor was next to the top. Obviously the servants' quarters in days gone by. A window, almost opaque with dirt, at one end of the landing overlooked the house-tops of Cannes and gave a distant view of the backs of the great hotels, with a streak of the sea showing like an oasis down an alley off the promenade. Someone on the fifth floor above emerged, threw a large bundle of clothes—it might have been laundry or useless old rags—down the well of the stairs, and it landed with a thud almost at the feet of the watching concierge, who picked it up and shuffled off with it.

They knocked at the door which the old woman had told them was that of Devard, the tailor. There was a brief silence and then, as though operated by silent mechanism, the door opened and a man stood looking at them. The first thing you noticed about him was that he was almost a dwarf and he had a huge dome of a head fringed with shaggy white hair. A snub nose and a loose mouth. He was in his shirt sleeves and had a tape-measure round his neck. He needed a wash.

"Monsieur Devard?"

Another pause.

"Yes."

He, too, recognised the official type and hesitated, wondering what his visitors were after.

"We want to speak to you about your former neighbour, Rivaud. You remember Rivaud?"

Devard listened without moving a muscle or an eyelid and then spoke nervously.

"I knew him. What is it?"

The woman in the opposite flat, probably the one once occupied by Rivaud, put out her head. A slattern with a rough mop of bleached hair and wearing a loose wrapper with nothing on underneath it. She eyed Littlejohn and Cromwell impudently up and down.

"May we come in?"

The tailor opened the door wider and with a sweep of his arm indicated that he was willing.

A large room with another at the back behind a closed door. The window was shut and stuffed with rags to keep out the draught. The place was mainly occupied by a large table for cutting-out. A suit of cheap material, a dish of pins, a large tailor's ruler, scissors, a pressing-iron.... Another small table of plain bare wood, with a bottle half-full of cheap red wine and a glass, and a long roll of bread beside it. An iron stove in front of the fireplace, cold, and with the ashes of the last fire heaped beneath it. A gas-ring burning to heat the tailor's iron. The only other articles were a large rough wooden cupboard, an armchair leaking horsehair, and a divan in one corner. Two large cats were asleep on the divan and the place stank of them. That, and the smells of human habitation, fetid air, drains, alcohol, stale tobacco.

Devard shuffled noiselessly here and there.

"Please excuse me …. My soiled appearance embarrasses me, but I have been very busy. Worked all night to finish a job. What is it you want to know about poor Rivaud?"

Littlejohn took out a thousand franc note and passed it to Devard.

"I appreciate you are a busy man and I am willing to pay for your time and information. First of all, was Rivaud your friend's real name?"

The tailor climbed on the work-table, sat himself cross-legged on it, made himself comfortable, and tucked the bank-note in his waistcoat pocket.

"Why do you ask?"

"Because you are the only likely man alive to know. We are over from England investigating the death of an antique dealer who bought a miniature once owned by Rivaud."

"But Rivaud died more than a year ago …. Nearly two years, to be exact."

"The Englishman bought the miniature from an antique dealer."

"Ah … the Labourel woman. I'll bet he paid a rare price for it, too."

"Did you ever see the miniature?"

"Only when the landlord—blasted old bloodsucker—called with Madame Labourel. Rivaud had an old wardrobe. He said it had belonged to his family. A great curved piece, with narrow legs and feet and a great belly, like a fat woman. I kept my eye on them and saw them looking at it. Then they took out the drawers and I saw Labourel discover the little framed picture on the bottom of the wardrobe. It must have fallen out of one of the drawers some time. I never saw it before, and there wasn't much I hadn't seen of Rivaud's. We were pals."

"It was a picture of a woman called de Montvallon. Do you know the name?"

The tailor's eyes flickered, and to give himself time, he scrambled from the table, poured himself a good drink from the bottle of wine, and drank it off in one.

"You'll excuse me not offering you some refreshment, sirs. I've only one glass and you won't want to use my dirty one."

"Do you know the name de Montvallon?"

"Yes. It was the name of some of Rivaud's relatives."

"Who wasn't called Rivaud, either, but Lepont?"

The dwarf sharply turned his head.

"Who told you?"

"Never mind. It's true?"

"Now he's dead, I can tell you. He always confided in me. As I said, we were pals. *Copains.* He took on the name Rivaud, because he didn't want anybody to know his real name."

"Why?"

The tailor gave Littlejohn a look full of cupidity.

"This is valuable information? Perhaps the lawyers...?"

"Oh, very well. But I want a full tale now. Otherwise, you'll have to tell it to the French police."

Littlejohn passed across another note.

"Please don't think I'm not being co-operative. But these are the secrets of a dead man. I alone know them."

"Get on with it, then. Why did Lepont call himself Rivaud?"

"Because he hated the name of Lepont. His grand-mother was a lady.... One of the aristocrats, he used to say.

Of course, everybody tells the same tale. You could say the same of me. All my family haven't little button noses like mine. They've got big aristocratic Roman ones, have my family... the wealthy ones who live in Paris...."

"What about Rivaud?"

"His grandmother was a Montvallon and ran away with a chap called Lepont, an artist. She died of the great cholera and left her husband with a kid. Rivaud used to say that if his grandfather had had any guts, he'd have gone back to the Montvallons and let them have the baby boy to bring up.... That was Rivaud's father, you see. Instead of which, he turned to drink, dragged the kid up anyhow, and then died and left him with as good a taste for the bottle as he'd had himself."

"What age was Rivaud's father when Rivaud was born?"

"I was waiting for that! Just turned fifty. He sowed his wild oats all his life and then, at fifty, he married a young woman with a bit of money. Alfred—that was my friend, Rivaud—was born and his mother died of it. The old man lived to be seventy. How he did it, I could never guess. An old soak and a libertine. He died and left Alfred penniless, except for the wardrobe I told you of. Alfred's father tried a time or two to get money from the Montvallons, who lived somewhere in the north... Bourg-en-Bresse or Mâcon, I forget which, but they chucked him out on his neck. He'd nothing to prove it and they must have thought him a sponger."

"How old was your friend Rivaud when he died?"

"A year or two past sixty. He was a delicate, refined sort of chap. You could see he'd got aristocratic blood in him."

"What did he do for a living?"

"He'd done all sorts of things. He said he'd once been to sea, but the life was too rough. He was a bit consumptive. He ended up as an artist. He must have taken after his grandfather, who he said, was a painter in his time. Alfred used to paint flowers and fish and birds on the local pottery. You know the kind of thing. *Souvenir de Cannes.* He had a job at Vallouris, the pottery village, at one time. Then he did work here in the town. He never kept a job for any length of time."

"He drank?"

"Yes. He never had money for long. He was ill for quite a time before he died. I did what I could. Then they took him to the local hospital. Too late. He died. Lungs...."

Cromwell looked bleakly at Littlejohn. He'd been able to make out most of the tale and it didn't amount to much. Alfred Rivaud, or Lepont, had been directly related to the Montvallons of Pont de Veyle, and to the Berluc-Vidals. But what of it? That didn't account for the death of Cheever. It had no connection at all.

"Did you have a visit like this one from another Englishman about a month ago? A man who asked the same questions?"

"Come to think of it, I did. It seems he'd bought the little picture they found in the bottom of Rivaud's wardrobe. He said he collected them and he was writing a book on them and wanted a complete history of every one of them. He'd bought the picture from Labourel, he said, and she'd given him the address here."

"You told him all that you've told me?"

"Yes."

"I suppose he paid you for it."

"A matter of fact, we went out for a drink together. He was a sociable man and although his French wasn't half as good as yours is, we got on all right."

Cheever had obviously taken the tailor out and got him half drunk and talkative. A much cheaper way of doing things than by way of cash.

"Did Rivaud ever go to see his relatives at Pont de Veyle and ask for help?"

"No. He always said he'd die in the gutter rather than do it. The way they treated his father, he said, was enough for him."

"Coming back to the miniature.... Did you ever see it before the day the antique dealer found it hidden in the wardrobe?"

"No. Never knew it even existed."

"Did Rivaud?"

"I don't think so. I never heard him mention it. Many a time, we'd get talking about his grandmother, who died in the cholera. He seemed fond of the memory of her. You see, she was the only decent relative he'd ever known of. His mother died in childbirth. That was all his father's fault, I believe. He was drunk and sleeping it off when he should have been going for the midwife. Where was I? Yes, Alfred's grandmother. He talked a lot of her, and I'm sure he'd have shown me her picture, if he'd known he had it."

The tailor had taken another drink and the bottle was empty. He was still thirsty and looking uneasy for more. There was nothing else useful in his repertory, and the room was growing more and more stuffy and unpleasant.

"I've got to go an errand now. I've been idle long enough. So...."

Devard couldn't stand it any longer. He must have his bottle by hook or by crook. He must have been a pretty sight every evening after his day of tailoring and tippling. Soon, he'd land up like Rivaud had done and the landlord would be round selling up his odds and ends for arrears of rent.

"That's all I have left to remind me of poor old Alfred. He used to have it in his room. It was his mother's. It's all the sharks left when they sold him up."

He showed them a small Dresden figure of a woman, without a head, and hiccupped into his dirty hand.

Outside, even the smell of the street, with its open sewer and the carcase of the horse, which the knackers were now loading on a cart, was better than the tailor's abominable room. The annoying thing, too, was that the journey had availed them nothing. A bit of news about a distant relative of the Berluc-Vidal family; a second account of how the miniature was found; the story of how Sammy Cheever had visited Rue Belle-de-Mai and paid far less for his information than Littlejohn. What had it to do with the death of Cheever? Apparently nothing.

Littlejohn and Cromwell wandered back through the fish and the vegetable markets. Cromwell noted down the prices of eggs, chickens, butter, cheese and fruit in his book. He intended to tell his wife all about it when he returned and to supplement his discourse with statistics. He even found himself almost saddled with a live hen and in the course of his quarrel with the woman selling it and Littlejohn's extricating him from the transaction, the hen laid an egg, much to the delight of everybody around.

Back on the promenade, they were in another world again. Impossible to believe that the squalid Devard was plying his needle and cotton and drinking himself to death in a filthy tenement, and that Rivaud had died of tuberculosis in the same place, almost a few yards away. A man in uniform and a yachting cap, with a half-naked actress on his arm, crossed the gangway of a huge yacht and the sailors almost bowed two-double to receive him. There was a diversion going on on the Croisette whilst a film company shot some scenes. The director was yelling orders through a microphone, and speed-boats and girls in bathing-costumes were waiting for the word "Go", as soon as the leading man and lady were ready. These two were busy supplying autographs to teen-agers and the leading lady was allowing holidaymakers to take snapshots of her, clad in a bathing-costume which might just as well not have been there at all.

It was past noon, and the hour of the *apéritif* had gone. All the same the discouraged pair of detectives wandered into a café near the town casino and ordered drinks. Cromwell, now becoming an habitué of the Coast, eagerly called for two *Pernods*. They talked about the case which seemed to have died on them.

The main question was, Cheever had got himself murdered. Why? Who would want to murder him?

Had it been Davso, and had he killed him for his money? In that case, what was Cheever doing in an isolated spot like the Vaccarès?

Or again, had the Berluc-Vidals been involved in it? Cheever had turned up with a miniature of their great aunt. What was the use of that? You couldn't blackmail anyone by just proving that a relative far distant, and a century or so ago, had run away with an artist and died of the cholera.

"Could it be a matter of family money?" asked Cromwell. He was on his second drink and his eyes were bright. His question remained unanswered because an enormous procession had started to pass. It consisted of five brass bands and about a mile of Catholic Youth parading in connection with the local rally.

"What were we saying when the procession started?"

"Could Cheever have been poking his nose in matters of money? Suppose, on the strength of Clotilde's death and disappearance, some other part of the family got the money. And now, along comes Cheever with proof in the document he found behind the picture, that she had a family... Alfred, in fact, who might make a claim."

"But that was concerned with a hundred years ago. And Alfred is dead."

"Yes, that's right. We're stumped, aren't we?"

Everyone seemed to be on the way to lunch. Families passed, parents struggling to keep children in order, people crowding in the restaurants for meals.

"Perhaps we'd better take a trip to Pont de Veyle. It's quite a distance and the expense-sheets will look a bit sick. All the same, Cheever broke his journey there and we may get some idea, some clue, as to what happened later. We'll go to-morrow."

"What about the rest of the day?"

The rest of the day! Littlejohn felt like sitting back and letting the sun soak right into his bones. On the quay just opposite, men clad in white trousers and thin sleeve-less jerseys were pottering about with boats; a horse in a straw hat to keep off the flies and hitched to a landau with a kind of awning over it, with tassels dangling, slept as he waited for a fare; on the promenade the film company had gone to lunch and now maroons were being fired to start a yacht race. More expensive convertibles, their hoods full down, and loaded with jolly holidaymakers, kept swishing past. The asphalt was almost boiling and, at the fountain opposite, a man was swilling his head under the jets. And Cromwell was eager to work all afternoon!

"Let's talk about it over lunch, old man. We'll make our way back to the hotel."

The menu seemed to hang visibly in front of Littlejohn like a lot of objects levitated by a conjuror. Hors d'oeuvre of all kinds of queer interesting things, livened up by scar-let prawns; kidney vol-au-vent; Châteaubriand garni; fruit salad *au marc;* and one of those special Provençal cheeses.... Washed down with Châteauneuf du Pape....

"I could just manage a nice plateful of steak and kidney pie, followed by apple tart and custard, and a pint of beer," said Cromwell nostalgically. He looked pained when Littlejohn laughed, not in ridicule, but ironically at himself. They went back through a maze of shady sidestreets, where it was easy to keep out of the blistering sunshine. The shops were closed. All except Madame Labourel's antique shop. There was someone inside, arguing with her in the cool recess behind the windows. Littlejohn looked twice, as the figure seemed familiar. A little dapper man, gently caressing an exquisite Dresden figure as he talked. With his free hand, delicate in gesture and restrained in movement, he was emphasising a point. He turned as Littlejohn glanced through the window, looked surprised, and waved delightedly.

It was Commissaire Audibert of the Marseilles Sûreté.

Chapter X
The Dwarf's Story

They did not dine at the hotel after all, but at a small restaurant in a side-street, where Audibert seemed very well-known. So much so that it brought out the proprietor, in his white chef's hat, from the kitchens. He and Audibert discussed the menu whilst the rest of the diners waited for their next courses. It was only when the conference was over that Audibert started seriously to explain his presence in Cannes.

"I didn't wish the pair of you to be pursuing a forlorn enquiry, without some assistance from your friends here. It would not be right of us to leave you to your own resources when a little help here, a little there, would make it so much easier. Besides, I regard the owner of this place as the best chef in France. My personal opinion, of course. He was once in an hotel in Marseilles.... I come to see that his standard is not falling away whenever I can."

Audibert, dressed in his black suit and spotless white linen, looked as cool as a cucumber. With his small hands and feet, his gentle fastidious ways, his air of scholarly calm, he might have been a family lawyer or a judge, instead of a police inspector.

"There was another matter, too. You remember, at our first meeting, you mentioned the miniature which the late Cheever bought here in Cannes, Littlejohn? The monkey, too…. You remember?"

"That's right."

"I telephoned Cannes and asked about the shop and its proprietor. I wanted to know if they had any files or recollections of the owner."

Hereupon a procession emerged from the kitchen bearing food and wine. The rest of the customers, having been warned in whispers who the guests were, exercised patience, showed good humour, and even enquired concerning the courses, which they approved or criticised according to taste.

Mushrooms. *Champignons maréchale.* These had been dipped in egg and breadcrumbs, fried in butter, and were served with asparagus tips and truffles. They drank white Graves with them, Château Haut Brion.

Cromwell, who had seen all kinds of fungus on sale in the fruit market, including some which, he thought, was very like that which flourished on the rotten tree-trunks of his father's garden long ago, tackled the dish cautiously at first, but soon overcame his scruples and wired-in with a will. There was no further talk of crime until the table had been cleared for the next course. Even then, Audibert was called into the kitchen for his opinion on the components of the dish.

"I thought I had better come over to Cannes, call on the antique dealer myself, and then take you both to lunch. I was just about to telephone your hotel, when you saw me through the shop-window."

"And, apart from the excellent meal, has the trip been worth while?"

"Certainly. I had a good talk with the old lady. She doesn't own the place. She looks after it for her nephew, who is too busy merely to sit in a shop all day selling *objets d'art*. He has a fast speed-boat down at the harbour here. Sometimes the boat vanishes for days at a time. The police always keep an eye on local craft which make strange voyages. For example, to North Africa, where drugs, jewellery, foreign currency and the like are obtainable."

"And you think the nephew...?"

"Whose name is Casimir. An adventurous sound about it, hasn't it? You were saying...?"

"You think the nephew might be involved in our Cheever case?"

Audibert absent-mindedly ran his finger along the edge of the book he had placed at his elbow. He always carried a book with him, in case he was bored or had time to spare. This one was *La Bête du Vaccarès*, by Joseph D'Arbaud. He afterwards gave it to Littlejohn, who knew a lot more about the Camargue after reading it.

"Maybe. You see, Cheever's death might have been due to several things. Pure theft, for example. He might have been knocked down and killed for a mere handful of notes in his pocketbook. Or again, he might have angered someone and been killed in a fury."

"But why in the Camargue? What was he doing there?"

"You know as much as I do about that. There was no sense in taking his dead body to the Vaccarès merely to hide it there. He could just as easily have been buried anywhere. So, you see, the miniature does enter the case. Cheever was found dead a little more than a stone's throw away from the home of the nearest surviving relatives of the woman in the portrait. Which brings me to the picture itself. Have you got it with you?"

Cromwell produced it from his side pocket and carefully unwrapped it from its velvet covering. Audibert gently held it in his hands and examined it closely. Then he took from his pocket a jeweller's glass, screwed it in one eye, and scrutinised the object back and front.

"You have had it out of the frame, sergeant?"

"Yes, sir. There's the glass, then the picture on a thin sheet of ivory, a cardboard backing, and the lot simply fixed in the frame. There's nothing else behind. The antique dealer did say, however, that there was a document wrapped in goldbeater's skin with it when Cheever bought it. It was between the cardboard backing and the ivory. Cheever must have removed it and it was either stolen or lost with his belongings in the lake. It's vanished."

"You know what the document was about?"

"The antique dealer, who'd read it, said it concerned the history, elopement and death of the woman in the picture. She ran away with the artist and died of cholera."

Audibert pursed his lips and nodded his head.

"Ah...."

The second course was arriving.

Tournados Rossini. A common enough dish in junketings at home, but not like this one. Small steak fillets, with a slice of *foie gras* on top, served on fried toast. Audibert explained the ritual of first dipping the *foie gras* in milk, then in flour, and finally tossing it in butter in a frying pan for a few minutes. The sauce was of truffles simmered in port wine with the gravy of the meat.... As the chef reverently served the dish, his wife poured out wine in large goblets. *Romanée Conti.* Cromwell had never tasted wine like it and, as the meal progressed, he grew sad, thinking of the poor lady in the miniature who had died of the cholera. Audibert did not refer to the matter again until the course had ended.

"I hope you did not pay too much for the picture, my dear Cromwell."

"Five pounds, sir."

"Five thousand francs.... Not too bad. But you could hardly describe it as a bargain. Monsieur Lepont was not much of an artist. An amateur. Forgive me. I see you are fond of your little souvenir. And sad to think of the lady dying so tragically. But, I'm sure you want to know the truth about it, don't you?"

"Of course, sir."

Cromwell would normally have felt crestfallen and ashamed of being taken-in, but the working of the *Romanée Conti* had suddenly changed. Now, instead of instilling sadness, it was making his heart glad. He wanted to laugh outright. So much so, that he had to keep a tight hold on himself and remind himself of the dignity due from him in a foreign place, to prevent his tittering and guffawing. Little Cheever, the twister in his phoney blazer, being himself swindled. And then all the fuss, and finally his death for something which perhaps was a fake itself.

Audibert was handing him the glass and he screwed it in his eye firmly after many attempts.

"You will see the rather inexpert way the brush has been used. Observe the obvious trail of the bristles all over the ivory. The background, for example, shows every stroke of the brush. The drapery, too, is the same, and the features of the woman. Even the face, which has been touched here and there with black to emphasise the points. As a whole, it doesn't look too bad. But in detail, it is mediocre. A good miniature is smooth, the brushwork invisible, the whole, although so delicate and calling for such fine work, should have the smooth appearance of a first-class modern colour print. You follow? I wonder if Monsieur Lepont really was an artist at all, or just an amateur who used his small talents to get into the presence of the lady and seduce her. But this is not helping us find out who killed Cheever.... By the way, I spoke to Marion at Arles this morning. They are still baffled by the murder of Davso. Not a clue, not a sign. So, much may depend on your own case of Mr. Cheever. The solution of that may bring the other solution in its wake.... Ah...."

Another course. Small mountain strawberries, soaked in Armagnac, served with whipped cream. It reminded Littlejohn of the days when he and his wife, investigating the death of another travelling Englishman in High Provence, had eaten so much of the delicious fruit at the *Hôtel Pascal.* He wished Letty were with them, instead of in Edinburgh, acting as a delegate from some women's society or other.

A long pause in Audibert's discourse this time. He was taken in the kitchen again to supervise the making of coffee. He detested it made in any other way than his own. Finally, he emerged, carrying it himself in a plain earthenware jug. The rest of the customers enviously inhaled the aroma and indicated that if there was any left, they would be delighted.... A bottle of Grande Champagne Cognac was placed on the table and Audibert returned to business.

"What was behind the miniature? Was it a sad history? Was it something which would enable the little Cheever to blackmail the family of the lady in the picture who left Pont de Veyle a century ago? I think not. Did it, then, contain a map or information about family treasure and indicate how it might be found? Your famous *Treasure Island,* in fact, a translation of which I am at present reading to my children every night before they retire. Again, probably not. Hardly anything so romantic and melodramatic. What then?"

Cromwell shook his head. Littlejohn lit his pipe and waited patiently, now and then sipping his brandy. He liked this neat little man with his tidy brain and his quick grasp of events. Although a police officer and trained in the procedure of the law, he also brought to his task the breadth of a well-stocked and philosophic mind.

"There might still have been something behind the miniature which, when he got it home and opened the back, made your Mr. Cheever wish to return and find out more about the picture and those concerned with it."

Littlejohn nodded.

"Yes. In the cavity behind the picture, so innocent-looking, one could hide quite a number of small but valuable things. Dope, for example.... Or even diamonds."

"Exactly, Littlejohn. If so, Mr. Cheever somehow got hold of an object, a miniature, he should not have done. Let us say that, by mistake, he found himself in possession of this thing with drugs hidden in the back. Perhaps drugs smuggled in from North Africa, where the traffic is intense."

"You have asked Madame Labourel, at the antique shop, about it?"

"Yes. One could hardly expect her to tell the truth. She said that when she herself opened the picture, it merely contained the account of the elopement and the death from the cholera."

"Did she tell you how she obtained the miniature?"

"Yes. From the belongings of a man now dead, a man called Rivaud, in the Rue Belle-de-Mai. I telephoned to the local police from the shop and asked them to find out anything they could about Rivaud, his manner of life, and his death. I will now get them on the telephone and hear what they have to say. I told them I would ring after lunch."

He quietly drank the remainder of his brandy and then, after asking them to excuse him, went again to the premises behind the restaurant to telephone.

"You've got to hand it to the French police, sir," said Cromwell, now mellow and wise-sounding after his old brandy. "They don't let the grass grow under their feet, do they?"

Audibert reappeared, threading his way through the maze of tables like a nimble little ballet dancer.

"They've been to the Rue Belle-de-Mai. They learned at once from the concierge that the two of you had been there questioning Devard, the tailor who lives opposite Rivaud's old quarters. Devard was out, but our men soon laid him by the heels. He was dead drunk in his favourite bistro. He'd come into money from somewhere ...."

Audibert placed his hands on his knees, looked Littlejohn in the face, and gently smiled.

"I admit, it was the only thing you could do, Littlejohn. When you've no authority, money loosens the tongue. Our men soon loosened Devard's. They sobered him by putting him under the tap. They pressed him to share with them the information he'd given you. But they were in a better position to insist on the truth. He seemed to be under the illusion that *you* had sent them round after him. I gather he told you that Rivaud's real name was Lepont. He'd abandoned it because he despised his father and his father's name. Well, it was all a pack of lies. He confessed he'd made it all up to give you your money's worth."

"Is that so? Well, I wonder, then, how he knew all about the family names, the cholera, the way Clotilde died. I admit I mentioned the Montvallons and the Leponts, but I said nothing whatever about the cholera. *He* told *us* that. And it tallied with what Madame Labourel said was in the account found behind the portrait. Can it be that Madame Labourel has been playing some game and given Devard a tale to tell us?"

"I don't know. But one thing has come out. Rivaud was never called Lepont. His father's name was Rivaud, too. Our men have been through his papers and details of his death. Your Monsieur Rivaud was born Rivaud, in Cannes; his father, a drunken railway out-porter, was also a native of Cannes. His mother, née Fugier, was a washerwoman. None of them had any claim to aristocracy. That's all so far. Our men are still working on Devard. They have obtained his papers and are tracing his antecedents, too. If you care to do so, we'll go down to the Cannes police now and see how they are getting on."

"This is a hell of a case!"

Emboldened by his potations, Cromwell expressed a candid opinion, gravely rose from the table, stretched himself to his full powerful height, and admitted that it had been a hell of a meal, too. He paused to make a note of the menu for later discussion with his wife, congratulated the proprietor, and solemnly walked out into the deserted street. Everybody has sought shelter indoors from the sun. A stray cat, and a dog dragging a stolen string of sausages. His friends joined him. The holiday feeling weighed more heavily than ever on Littlejohn. He felt a longing for Dorange. Audibert was a fine chap, but too detached, too sober and invulnerable. Littlejohn was in the mood for sitting on the promenade, under the awning of some pleasant café, Dorange at his side, one of the little Frenchman's cheroots in the corner of his mouth, a glass of *Pernod* at his elbow....

A police car drew up, the driver saluted Audibert with great respect, and they all tumbled in and were swished along the Croisette to the *Hôtel de Ville*.

Devard was in a small room filled with the fug of French tobacco. He was being questioned and he looked a wreck.

His tie had been removed and his jacket was draped on the back of his chair. He had received the water-cure for his drunkenness and now was enjoying the tobacco cure for his reticence. He raised his sad eyes when the newcomers entered, and he sprang to his feet and tried to get at Littlejohn, only to be intercepted and almost carried back to his chair.

"I only tried to help him. What if I did make up a thing or two? He was paying for information and I'd not much to give. I made it up to give him his money's worth. It's cruel of him to put the police on me like this. I never did anybody any harm."

"Tell us the truth, then, and you can go. Otherwise, we look like being here all night."

The sergeant interviewing him took out a pipe and started to fill it from a blue packet.

"I've owned up that Rivaud wasn't Lepont, haven't I? I admit I made it up."

"Who told you about the woman in the picture dying of the cholera, though?"

Audibert took over. There was no bullying in his manner. Just a kind of paternal tolerance, of sorrow at being involved in putting Devard to such inconvenience.

"I made it up."

"You didn't, you know. Madame Labourel had already told the English officers the same tale. Had you been in touch with her, and had she told you what to say?"

"How could I? I never set eyes on her after she bought Rivaud's old wardrobe."

Devard's head and face had been wet from sobering cold water. Now they began to be soaked in sweat. He was obviously becoming terrified.

"Have you anything you wish to ask him, Littlejohn?"

Littlejohn fingered his pipe and felt like lighting it, but
the room was so full of smoke it seemed cruel to inflict further suffocation on the miserable little tailor, now almost
kippered by it.

"Did you tell Cheever the same tale you told me, Devard?"

"Yes."

"Are you sure? You were drunk, I take it, when he started
questioning you. Were you sober enough to stick to the
truth, or rather stick to the tale you made up for me?"

"Why not? I might get drunk, but I retain my discretion.
I don't go shooting my mouth all over the place when I've
had a drink or two."

"You had a long talk with Mr. Cheever?"

"We spent most of the afternoon together. He was good
company."

"Did he mention having visited Pont de Veyle?"

The dwarf's round eyes flickered.

"Yes."

"You remember the name of the place?"

"Yes. I've a good memory."

"Even though it's a place that isn't well-known and it was
only mentioned once to you?"

"Yes. What are you trying to make me say?"

"What had Cheever been to Pont de Veyle for?"

"Enquiring about the family of the woman on the picture. He said he'd got to have a full history to sell the picture at a good price."

"And what did they tell him?"

"He didn't say. Why should he? I wasn't concerned."

"Are you sure?"

The rest of the men in the room looked baffled. They
wondered what Littlejohn was getting at. All except Audibert,
who spoke to the sergeant in charge of the enquiry.

"How long are they going to be getting hold of this fellow's papers?"

"They've gone to his room for them and then they'll just check them up in the records of the *Hôtel de Ville*."

As if in answer to the question, a policeman entered with a file, which he passed over to the sergeant, who, after looking it over and raising his eyebrows, handed it to Audibert.

Littlejohn was still quietly questioning Devard.

"You seem to know so much about the Montvallons and Pont de Veyle, one would think it was you, and not Rivaud, who was the Lepont. Am I right?"

The dwarf was on his feet again in indignation. The sergeant pushed him back in his chair.

"Behave yourself."

"This is interesting, Littlejohn."

Audibert turned over the pages of the file.

"Here are Devard's papers. And here is the police file. Only the name isn't Devard. It's Augustin Brassard. And under that name, he was arrested and tried three years ago for smuggling. Casimir Labourel was charged with him at the same time. They got off on an alibi. I'll bet it was faked."

"So, it looks as if he's a confederate of Labourel's and has been coached to tell this cock-and-bull story about the miniature. Well, Devard?"

"I'm not saying anything."

"Oh, yes, you are."

Audibert approached him and gently tapped him on the chest. It was like the manipulator of a marionette jerking the dummy to make it function.

"Oh, what's the use! I'm sick of this. I want to go home. If I tell, can I go home?"

"We've told you that already."

"Well, Madame Labourel asked me to tell the tale to the Englishman. He'd paid quite a price for the picture and he was keen on a story about it. So, they said they wanted to give him his money's worth."

Littlejohn intervened.

"Had Cheever the miniature with him when he called on you?"

"No. He'd left it with his luggage. I think he said it was at Mâcon. Have you finished with me now?"

"Where did he say he was going to from here?"

"He asked the best way to get to a place called Méjanes, near Arles. I told him to enquire at the railway station. I knew the name, but I'd never been there. Can I go now?"

"Oh, shut up. You'll go when we think fit." The sergeant-in-charge was getting fed-up.

"Did Cheever tell you why he was going to Méjanes?"

"No. He was going on business."

"Did *you* sell the miniature to Madame Labourel?"

"No ... I ..."

He was sweating again and, seeing that they were getting on a tender spot and something important was forthcoming, the sergeant rose, took Devard by the lapels, and shook him.

"Now, look here. Tell us a proper tale here and now, or else I'll chuck you in the cells and leave you overnight to cool off."

Devard licked his lips.

"If I talk, you won't take it out of me? I mean .... "

Audibert intervened again.

"If it's anything illegal, you'd better tell us, and we'll give you the benefit of any help you volunteer."

Devard mopped his sweating brow with his sleeve.

"It was this way…. As I said before, Rivaud was an artist. We started a little business. We painted those little miniatures, or rather Rivaud did. I got a fellow I knew to make the frames. We cooked them up to look old. We even pasted old letters and things on the back to fake the age."

"And the one in the case…? The miniature of Clotilde de Montvallon was a fake? You made it between you? Do you mind showing it to him, old man?"

Cromwell, crestfallen, produced his little treasure.

Devard hardly looked at it.

"That's one of 'em. Even to the writing on the back. I cut the old paper out of a book belonging to my father, and we mixed some paint to look like faded ink and copied some old writing. It made the picture look real good and antique."

"And you sold it to…?"

"Rivaud had it when they took him to hospital. I tried to find it, but couldn't. Instead, Madame Labourel came across it when she was rooting in the old wardrobe. I had to let it go and behave as if I never saw it before. We'd sold her one or two at her shop and I couldn't very well blow the gaff and say they were fakes. Now could I? I just had to let it go."

"So, this was painted by Rivaud and cooked-up to look genuine?"

"That's right."

"And what about the tale of the elopement and the cholera?"

"It was written in rusty ink on a loose sheet in the back of an old book of my father's. Part of the family records. It was wrapped in some parchment sort of stuff, so we left it where it was and we stuffed it inside the frame behind the picture. We'd intended telling whoever we sold it to that it was there, just to prove the age and that the whole thing was genuine. Much good it did either of us. Him dead, and me not able to claim a sou for it, and in the hands of the police into the bargain. That's everything, and God's truth. Can I go now?"

They let him loose.

"Better keep an eye on that fellow," said Audibert to the local sergeant after the dwarf had gone. "His fear of someone has stimulated his imagination. I've never heard such a pack of lies."

Chapter XI
The Abbé Caseneuve

"The whole thing's a mess...."

Cromwell withdrew a small bag of tea from the teapot, thrust it back again, and then began to pound it with his spoon. He had insisted on tea. He always fled to it when a problem got on top of him. It comforted and inspired him, he said. The manager of their hotel had assured him that he was completely at Cromwell's service in the matter of tea. They imported it from England for those who liked it that way. "What part of England?" Cromwell had asked when the brew arrived and he'd inspected it. All the same, he had to admit that it was good.

Littlejohn and Dorange were at the teacups, too. Dorange, with his customary courtesy, pretended to enjoy it. He smacked his lips over it, at the same time casting a longing eye on the *Pernod* being consumed by a man on the next table.

Audibert had gone to see Madame Labourel again. There was something fishy about the antique shop and he was determined to get to the bottom of it. He had instructed the local police to pull-in Madame Labourel's nephew, Casimir, and to give him a good grilling about the way he'd been spending his time of late. Littlejohn had felt it would only embarrass Audibert if he and Cromwell went once again to the antique shop. So, with a promise to look up Audibert as soon as they returned from Pont de Veyle, they had made for their hotel. Dorange was waiting for them there. Whenever Littlejohn was within a hundred miles of Nice, Dorange seemed to regard himself as his host, and behaved accordingly.

"You look down in the mouth, Cromwell, my friend. What is it?"

They told him about the miniature and how it seemed that the little twister Cheever had, even from beyond the grave, lived up to his reputation for shady dealing.

Dorange drank all his tea in one gulp, like a child who takes his medicine quickly to get it over.

"Cheever said it was genuine and was anxious to get its history and sell it to Americans. Then, on seeing it, Berluc-Vidal wished to possess it. He must, therefore, have recognised the picture. Devard tells a tale, changes his mind, and says he and Rivaud faked the miniature. Our friend Audibert, a very clever man and of good taste, pronounces it second-rate. It is time we had the views of someone who understands these things."

"You mean, an expert in a museum or art gallery, sir?"

"Exactly, my good Cromwell. One of the greatest experts on miniatures in France...in the world, in fact. Monsieur l'Abbé Caseneuve, of Apt. We will go to see him."

"I seem to have heard the name Apt before. Where is it, Jérôme?"

"Forty kilometres, twenty-five miles, west of Manosque. You know Manosque?"

"I'll say I do. I shall remember the St. Marcellin case as long as I live."

Dorange looked at his watch.

"Four o'clock…. It will take us just short of four hours. I will drive you over, we will stay the night there, and tomorrow, you can get the train for Mâcon and Pont de Veyle and I can return to Nice. Agreed?"

Time and space seemed nothing to this vital, good-tempered Niçois. Everything else went by the board when there were friends to help or cases to solve.

"Is there a comfortable inn there?"

"We will stay with Monsieur l'Abbé. He is my uncle. My mother's brother. He has no church to look after. He is an archivist for the Holy Church and has living quarters in the old bishop's palace at Apt. I must telephone the police at Apt to warn him we are coming. He refuses to have the telephone installed…."

Dorange's driving was like his intellect, rapid. Cannes, Fréjus, Aix, Manosque, Apt. They flew through the countryside at an average of sixty miles an hour, Cromwell, sitting in the back of the car, reading the speeds, dividing by eight and multiplying by five, and then mopping his brow. Now and then, a policeman held them up, saluted, grew red, and made some fatuous remark when he saw Dorange at the wheel.

"Glad to see you, sir…. What's the weather like in Nice, M. le Commissaire…?" One at St. Maximin was struck dumb altogether and stood gaping and saluting, until Dorange thrust one of his famous cheroots in his mouth and drove away.

It was dusk when they climbed the hills to Apt, set in its fruit trees, chestnuts and oaks under the towering Luberon. It was only then that Cromwell remembered where he'd seen the name before. His little girls had, last Christmas, given him a box of sugary preserved fruits for a present. It was marked *Bonnieux, Apt*. He rubbed his hands. He could eat preserved fruits until the cows came home.

They drew up in the middle of the broad town-square. Beneath a low wall ran the River Coulon, almost dried up and yellow with the effluent of the ochre works. The last swallows were flitting about under the plane trees and men were playing bowls in the half-light. Thence, down narrow side-streets to another, smaller square, in which odd lamps were already lit and glinting through the leaves. Two elegant fountains, each with a small stone child astride a large dolphin, from the mouths of which jets of water poured into basins with a gentle splash. Behind the fountains, the large graceful palace of the last of the bishops of Apt, the bells of whose basilica, the cathedral of St. Anne, were now chiming the hour of eight. Dorange shepherded his friends up two flights of stone steps to a terrace with an iron balustrade overlooked by tall windows, and rang the bell of the front door. It tinkled in the hall beyond and then there was silence. There were no signs of life in the great building and the windows were shuttered.

Shuffling feet from the far distance and then the door opened. A little woman dressed in black, like a pew-opener, with a small pointed chin and shortsightedly wearing a pair of gold-rimmed oval spectacles, stood in the doorway. She raised her head and thrust out her neck, like a hen drinking, in order to see who was there.

"Good evening, Monsieur Jérôme."

Her face creased in smiles as she thrust it up to be kissed.

"Good evening, Félicité."

"Monsieur l'Abbé is expecting you."

She switched on the light and they entered the vast hall, with heavy doors leading off it, and followed her up the fine staircase to the first floor. Everywhere, the smell of age; parchment, old stone, dust, and aromatic timber. Félicité entered the room without knocking.

Half a room and half a workshop and office at the back of the building. The shutters were drawn to keep out the mosquitoes and the place was lighted by a single large electric table-lamp. By its light an old man was scrutinising what appeared to be architectural plans of some kind. Books on shelves in every available place, on the walls, piled on the floors, and heaped on chairs. A large stove, the pipe of which pierced the outer wall, glowed on the hearth, beside which were two old armchairs, a small dining-table, and a stool on which a large sandy cat was asleep on a cushion.

The old priest laid aside his spectacles, slid from his high stool and came to meet them. A fine humorous face, with a generous mouth, long nose, and bright dark eyes. The thin grey hair, worn long at the back, swept from a great broad brow, with bushy eyebrows. He embraced and greeted Dorange in French and then spoke to Littlejohn and Cromwell in perfect English.

"Scotland Yard.... Well, well. I remember it, though I was never inside. I'm afraid all my time, when I come to England, is spent in South Kensington or in Manchester Square at the Wallace collection.

"I've also been to Welbeck Abbey, Belvoir Castle, Montagu House.... All about miniatures. Giving and begging for opinions about this one and that one, or merely to stand and stare at them in wonder.... The art of the miniature is the most beautiful and the most personal of them all, from the illuminated manuscripts and missals of days long gone down to the portraits of the heroes and beautiful women of our own times. But, there I go.... Come inside. It has grown chilly since the sun set. Félicité, may we have some wine while you prepare the meal...?"

He was a small, chubby man, dressed in a soutane and spotless white bands. His general appearance was elegant and clean and his small fine hands well-kept. 'A prince of the church,' thought Cromwell, who didn't know much about it, but who always remembered the Abbé Caseneuve afterwards as the finest Frenchman he'd ever met. The little priest even seemed to overawe his ebullient nephew.

"Jérôme," he said, "you suggested all of you might stay here with me. You know better than that. There are only two bedrooms. My own and Félicité's. Our English friends will, therefore, sleep at the mayor's house. It is all arranged. You can share my room. A mattress on the floor...."

"Yes, uncle," meekly replied the terror of all the criminals of the Midi.

Until dinner time, they left alone the business which had brought them there. Instead, they let the abbé talk about his hobby. He took them into the next room, which, instead of books, was this time draped in prints, pictures and miniatures of all shapes, styles, and sizes. In one corner, stood a large safe, which the priest opened, revealing a treasure of priceless enamels, ivories, large and small paintings....

"Some belong to the church, some I have bought, though very few. The rest have been given to me by my friends, many of them in England, including Sir Tollemache Sinclair, who had a magnificent collection and an even more magnificent knowledge of the subject."

He unloaded many of the contents of the safe, carrying on a running commentary.

"Here are some Fragonards—he was from Grasse, you know. Carle Van Loo, Raspal ... Peter Adolphe Hall—charming!—Rosalba Carriera, a woman .... But you are interested in the English ones...."

Heavy opaques of Bernard Lens, Holbeins and Hilliards on the backs of playing-cards, a Samuel Cooper on cardboard, and on ivory, Cosway, George Engleheart, Ozias

Humphrey, Andrew Robertson.... The abbé praised and explained them, pointing out their merits and defects. Cromwell felt that his own modest little picture was quite outclassed.

"... Many, of course, give Richard Cosway first place. He is easy of touch, graceful, delicate, but I'm sure that, faced with the subjects of the miniatures in the flesh, you would never have recognised them. A flatterer, if a skilled one. I prefer John Smart... sturdy, honest John. Or else... look at this robust, full, fleshy one by Andrew Robertson....'

"Dinner's ready and getting cold...."

Félicité stood looking at them over her spectacles. She was used to this kind of thing.

They ate a chicken done on the spit. Where the spit was, or the kitchen, for that matter, the visitors never knew. Like Félicité's virgin bedchamber, it was secret and inviolate. Sauté potatoes, and the crisp little truffles which are found in the hills above Apt. They drank a rose wine from Tavel. And then followed, from Cromwell's point of view, at least, a perfect Christmas party of the products of Apt. Sugared fruits, almonds, jellies, nougat, marrons glacés, jam....

Cromwell mentioned his own recent present from his daughters.

"I'm inundated with them, Cromwell. So many of my friends here are in the trade, one way or another, and are always sending me little presents. It seems that if I approve the samples, the rest of the world will follow suit! You must take a parcel of them home with you. Advertise the delicacies of Apt for us. And a bottle of lavender essence for your wife. We make that here, as well."

Then, over coffee and brandy, the local *marc*, they turned to Cromwell's miniature, the business which had brought them there.

L'Abbé Caseneuve took it to the light, turned it over delicately in his small hands, examined it under a lens, then carefully took the ivory from the frame. He handled it all like a watchmaker scrutinising the intricate inside of a valuable timepiece. Then he gave his verdict.

"My dear Cromwell, you have nothing to be ashamed of in this little work of art. You have not been 'done', as you say in England. It is perfectly genuine. The date is right. About a hundred years ago. The ground, the *guache*, is hard and dry. In no circumstances would it be thus if, as your man in Cannes said, he or his friend had faked it during the past few years. The back has been considerably tampered with and there isn't much there to guide us. It would need microscopic study to identify clues from there, and we don't need to take so much trouble. I also know of Joseph Lepont, the artist...."

He rose and took one of the folios from the shelves. It was a handwritten dictionary or encyclopaedia of art.

"I have collected this at various times in my life. One day perhaps it will see the printer's.... Really, Jérôme, you must learn English. It's an awful nuisance talking to my friends here in their own language and you hardly understanding a word. It wastes time carrying on a bilingual conversation all the time."

"Yes, uncle."

"Well, see to it, my son. A clever man like you ought to know half a dozen languages, instead of French and all the local dialects between Lyons and the Mediterranean."

"Provençal isn't a dialect, uncle."

"Now don't begin that argument again, even if you are a *félibre*—a Provençal laureate. Let us attend to the work in hand."

"Very good, uncle.'

The priest thumbed through his scrap-book and finally found what he was seeking.

"I was saying, Lepont, of Mâcon, was a landscape painter on fairly large canvasses. I've seen some of his work. In the case of this little miniature, he was obviously painting in an unaccustomed medium. He may have loved this young woman or have been doing someone a favour in making her portrait. He was not used to the fine brush technique of small ivory. The work is good. I've no doubt that, unlike your English Cosway, he made a true, unflattering likeness. No frills, no suppression of the blemishes. He just lacked the smooth technique, that is all. He seems to have vanished. He wasn't heard of again after 1838."

"He ran away with the lady in the picture and died of cholera in 1838, sir. Or that's what we've gathered in the course of our investigations."

"Did he, indeed? Then that explains it. Your little find, however, is most pleasing. Perhaps Lepont's lack of smoothness was due to emotion or to constantly desisting from his work to embrace the sitter. Whatever it was, it is most interesting. One might almost say, historic. A very desirable item indeed for your collection."

The abbé paused with a puzzled expression on his face.

"But one thing I cannot understand. This miniature has great character and is a most important collector's piece, both historically and intrinsically. It is the kind of thing the French antique dealer usually keeps in the room behind his shop for sale to initiates, special collectors, who will treasure them, not to little casual vulgar dealers who seek bargains, as seems to have been the case of your unlucky Cheever. I know Madame Labourel, of Cannes. A woman of good taste who would be reluctant to deal in treasures with upstarts, although miniatures are not her speciality. Her nephew, who owns the shop, would, however, know a good thing. I am baffled."

They had another session among the abbé's treasures, until the cathedral clock struck twelve. Cromwell, especially, was fascinated. He tried hard to acquire some of the knowledge which cannot be conveyed in words, but which arises from a lifetime of experience.

"We are keeping M. le Maire and his wife out of bed, I'm afraid. I will take you over and introduce you whilst Jérôme prepares his mattress on the floor...."

The priest was reluctant to break-up the party and shepherded his friends away with diffidence.

"You'll find me in your bed when you return, uncle."

They crossed the silent square, in which everything except the tinkling water issuing from the mouths of the dolphins seemed petrified in a sleeping world. The lights shone through the trees, the houses were shuttered and dark, the old bishop's palace, haunted by the squabbles and ambitions of past prelates, looked down solidly and scornfully on it all.

The Mayor and his wife received the two detectives like honoured guests and the abbé left them together. As he wished them good-night, Cromwell drew the priest aside and taking out the miniature in its velvet wrapping pressed it in his hand.

"It will be better if you keep this, sir. It will be more at home in your collection."

There was a pause, and Cromwell wondered if he'd offended the little man. The Abbé Caseneuve thrust the parcel back in Cromwell's pocket.

"I am very touched, my son, but you must take this with you. I have hundreds of them and this is...it is your one ewe lamb, to quote the scriptures. One day you will have

two, and then three, and then four.... A whole collection.
And if you like Apt, come to see me again. In fact, come in
the summer or autumn and bring your family. We will fill
you and your wife and the little girls with our sugar plums.
We will open two more rooms for you in the old episcopal
palace. Let me know in good time. Jérôme never gives me
enough time; always in a hurry...."

After a morning of seeing Apt, the detectives left for
Manosque again, Cromwell carrying a large parcel of deli-
cacies for his family. They parted from Dorange there; the
French officer making for Nice, and the Englishmen for
Lyons and Mâcon.

A melancholy twilight settled over everything as they
neared Mâcon. Unhealthy mists rose from the great plain
of Bresse, alive with poultry, looking like a vast farm-yard.
The innumerable ponds of the Dombes marshes glowed in
the setting sun. Cromwell, as ever, passing his time between
the guide-book and *Comment-ça-va?*, now and then read pas-
sages to Littlejohn, who snoozed over a book, watching with
amusement Cromwell's delighted reactions to the lovely
land of France.

"It says here, 'There are ten thousand ponds in the
Dombes, extending from ten to two hundred acres each,
and all full of fish.' They drain the ponds, put the fish in
tanks, and send 'em all over France."

Hereupon, a man in the opposite corner, who had been
dying to start a conversation, opened out in full spate, obviously about the fish, and he and Cromwell's complete con-
versational guide, *Comment-ça-va?*, kept the sergeant busy
till they pulled up at Mâcon.

Audibert had promised to let the police of Mâcon know
of any developments in the cases, and the Scotland Yard
men called right away at the police station there.

There certainly was a message.

Féraud has confessed to murder of Davso.
Please meet me at Arles to-morrow. Wire time.

Audibert.

They consulted time-tables and finally Littlejohn sent a reply arranging to get the train arriving at Arles about two in the afternoon next day. By this time it was dark. They had seen nothing of Mâcon.

"It means getting our business done right away, and leaving first thing in the morning."

"There's nothing much at Pont de Veyle, sir," the inspector at Mâcon told Littlejohn. "The crossroads; a bridge over the River Veyle, a tributary of the Saône; a few houses; an inn at which you won't want to stay the night; and the big house, two miles out, a sort of château that belongs to the Berluc-Vidals. Pont de Veyle's only a mile or two away. We'll lend you a car and I'll see that you have rooms at a good hotel when you get back."

"I'm very grateful for your help, inspector."

Littlejohn didn't know quite what he was after. Certainly he hadn't bargained for a night trip to Pont de Veyle. "You aren't missing much not seeing it in the daylight, sir," the inspector at Mâcon had told them. "It's marshy and misty there, the Saône's often in flood and makes it one big lake, and when it dries up, it's just flat meadow-land full of henhouses."

All they wanted to know was, had Cheever been to Pont de Veyle and what had he done there? The best place of call was probably the inn. They asked the driver to drop them there.

Le Chapon Gras. The Fat Capon. They might have expected that in the Bresse country. A small place, with one large room. Iron tables and chairs here and there and a long seat covered in what might have been moleskin running round the room. A dim light over the bar, little variety in the way of drinks. Everybody seemed to be drinking red wine or local brandy.

An unsavoury looking lot, too. A postman with one eye, a man with a wooden leg, two or three yokels, and two tables filled with not very prosperous hen-keepers playing cards and making their calls in thick, loud voices.

The landlord was standing at the bar, half asleep, but he awoke when Littlejohn and Cromwell entered. He wasn't used to their kind and wondered what was going on. A fat man, dressed in trousers, shirt and braces and with espadrilles on his feet. His paunch hung out of the top of his trousers like a pneumatic tyre.

"Yes?"

"Two brandies, please."

"We haven't any Cognac. Just the local..."

"That will do."

They paid him and he didn't say another word, but just kept giving them sidelong looks.

"We're English, landlord. Do you get many Englishmen around?"

"No. This isn't a health resort."

Another pause and another brandy apiece. The cardplayers had stopped their noise and were listening suspiciously. The man with the wooden leg stumped off.

"Have you had an Englishman, a man wearing a blazer—a jacket with a coat-of-arms on the pocket—here during the last month?"

"You from the police?"

"Yes. English police. The Mâcon police told us to call on you."

"Well, English or French police, it's all the same to me. They've nothing on me. I'm well within the law...."

He was half-drunk himself and swanking in front of his customers.

"Nobody denies it. All I asked was, have you had any Englishmen around during the last month?"

"Why should I?"

It was hopeless. The only thing to do was to bring in the driver of the police-car, himself a sergeant, and that would probably start a row.

Then, Littlejohn suddenly became aware that the man with one eye was making signals to him. He couldn't wink, on account of his disability, but he was pulling his face hideously and jerking his head in the direction of the door. Littlejohn paid again and he and Cromwell left the place. Almost at once, the postman was at their elbow. They could hear his heavy breathing in the dark.

"He's drunk," said the man with one eye, and, judging from his own breath, he didn't need to go far to be that way himself, too.

"You'll get nothing out of him. His wife's run off with a local poultry-farmer. He thinks they've gone to Paris. He's taken to drink and he's always awkward when he gets one over the eight. Is there anything I can do? I heard you say you were police. Well, I'm a government official. We've got to hang together, haven't we?"

"I suppose we have. It's good of you to take this interest. I was just asking if there's been an Englishman...a little fattish fellow with a coat-of-arms on his breast pocket?"

"*Le blazer?*"

"That's right."

"Yes. I saw him. Didn't get a word with him, though. But he went in the *Chapon* and got the same treatment as you did. Incivility. He crossed over to the doctor's and I saw him going in. That's Dr. Matthieu. His surgery's just across the way there. See the light? Well, go along the path through the gate and ring. He'll be in. He's a bit past it now. Eccentric, you know, and a real caution. Still, half a doctor's better than none, isn't he? He'll talk to you. Matter of fact, he never stops talking. Good night.…."

Littlejohn had hardly seen what the monoculous postman looked like. He just knew he was medium built with one eye. It had been too dark in the inn to make him out in the shadows where he'd stood drinking. And outside, it was almost pitch black. Just a voice, and an alcoholic breath.

They crossed to the house over the way. An enamelled plaque on the gate. Cromwell shone his torch.

DR. MATTHIEU
CONSULTATIONS 10.0-12.0, TOUS LES MATINS.

They rang the bell. Shuffling feet, the door flew open, and there was the doctor. Carpet slippers, smoking cap, and he looked around eighty. A square-built, wiry, robust man, with a fine head, but completely bald, or totally shorn; they couldn't make out which. A clean-shaven face, with heavy folds of skin hanging from his cheek-bones. A huge Roman nose and a large sarcastic mouth. Probably a very clever man whose declining faculties had put him on the shelf.

"Come in…. Come in," said Docteur Matthieu after they had made themselves known. "I thought sooner or later either the French or the English police would be here. It's about Cheever, isn't it? I read it all in the papers. It's taking the police a long time, isn't it? And it'll take longer till they've found out who the second chap was. I mean the one who followed him. That was a murderer, if I ever knew one. A killer. But don't stand there in the dark. Excuse me keeping you there. Come in, come in. Marie-Louise! Marie-Louise! Bring the brandy and three glasses. We're in for a long session!"

Chapter XII
Pont De Veyle

"No, no, no. Not that local *marc*, good though it be. The Cognac, on the shelf at the far-end of the cellar.... These are special guests, Marie-Louise, and demand a special drink.... My sister: Superintendent Littlejohn and Sergeant Cromwell, of London...."

Marie-Louise, who always seemed in a hurry, was a small, thin, nervous spinster, who spent her time trotting here and there at her brother's behest. She had brought the wrong bottle. Corrected, she acknowledged the introduction by a smile and a slight nod executed whilst still on the trot, performed a right-wheel, trotted out and down to the cellar; then she trotted back again. Another exit; back again with a tray on which stood three goblets. Finale, still on the run.

"Marie-Louise and I were very attached when we were children. When I married, I'm sure she took an oath to remain single till my wife died, and then to return and keep house for me. It worked out as she wished and now she looks after me with great zest. This Cognac is the very best. My son is a wine-merchant and knows a fine brandy when he tastes one. Your very good health, gentlemen."

A pause whilst they went through the rites of trying the wine. It was excellent. Cromwell's eyes grew so round that the doctor burst into laughing.

"I see you approve, my friend. You don't get this kind of stuff in England, eh? Perhaps as well. You'd only pour it over your Christmas puddings and set fire to it."

A real Balzacian country doctor. The cosy room in which they were sitting was probably that in which he saw his patients. A large stove on the hearth, purring with the heat, and almost red-hot.

"I hope you don't find the room too warm. Nights here are damp most of the year. One needs a good fire to dry the place."

One side of the room covered in books, some of them with mould on the backs. An examination couch in one corner. An old desk. Two mahogany cases of instruments. Another case of medicines; bottles of all shapes and sizes. On a table, a large polished box, open, and displaying a fine old-fashioned cupping-set. You could imagine all kinds of things happening to the peasants who frequented the room. And when the modern wonder drugs didn't do the trick, the doctor resorted to blood-letting and perhaps herbal specifics.

"You are here for some time?"

Dr. Matthieu said it in a dry, professional voice, just as he might have done to a patient. And when one arrived, he probably carried-on in the same leisurely fashion, combining in his clinical enquiries a lot of personal talk to satisfy his own curiosity.

"We are sleeping in Mâcon to-night and returning by train to Arles first thing in the morning."

"Rather a hurried visit. A pity. I might have helped you a lot if you'd had time. Not much goes on in this neighbourhood that I don't know about. My practice is extensive and covers most of the country between here and Bourg-en-Bresse. Have you only just arrived?"

"Yes, doctor. We came straight here."

"Had any food?"

"A snack on the train."

The doctor was at the door of the room again, calling loudly.

"Marie-Louise! Marie-Louise! You might make it supper for three. These gentlemen haven't had any food since God knows when."

A little squeak in response and again the sound of busy feet.

"You needn't have troubled, sir…. And we have a police-driver from Mâcon outside in the car."

"Rubbish! My own supper's ready on a tray and I'm due to eat it. No trouble to add two more. And we'll attend to the driver. He can eat with the maid in the kitchen. It will be cold chicken. In these parts it's chicken, chicken, chicken, all day and every day. If a patient wants to express gratitude for a cure; chicken. Or thanks for the final death certificate of a parent who's taken a long time dying and holding up the inheritance; chicken. But good fat capons, always. No rubbish. I give them back the scraggy ones. You mentioned Arles. Interesting…"

"Are you the family physician of the Berluc-Vidals, sir?"

The doctor made diluting gestures as though deprecating the title.

"A touch of belly-ache, or a fit of the local ague, or perhaps one of the maids having a baby; yes. For the rest, anything serious sees the arrival of a consultant from Lyons or Grenoble. I may say, however, that as long as I have been in practice here, ten years, I've been in and out of the château

155

almost every week. It's two miles from here in the direction of Bourg."

"Ten years?"

"Of course. One doesn't spend one's life in a place like this. Unless, of course, like my brother, who had this practice before me from the day he graduated. He took it over from my father. A pair of come-day, go-day, God send Sunday doctors who loved the country and the peasants. I was a heart specialist in Grenoble myself and professor of the faculty there until my time came to retire. Then, my brother died, so I moved in to find myself something to do. I shall die in harness. But about the château and the family...?"

"We met the family at the Mas Vidal."

"I often spend a holiday there. A pleasant house at the right time of year. You are concerned with the death of an Englishman on the *domaine,* I hear."

"Yes."

"He came to Pont de Veyle before he left for the Midi and his death. He even called on me. The château was closed. The family usually go south for the summer and return in the autumn. There wasn't anybody left but me in the village who could talk intelligently to your man.... He spoke very queer French, you see. Cheever was his name, wasn't it?"

"That is so, doctor."

"Curious visitors usually enquire from Gastin at the inn. But his wife left him earlier in the year. Ran off with a poultry-keeper. A good-looking, wicked woman Gastin picked up in Lyons...off the streets presumably. Her departure upset the landlord. He took to drink and is still on the bottle. Next thing, I shall be putting him in a home for inebriates. He's impolite and most unaccommodating. Cheever found him so and crossed the road to see me. He said he'd got

156

toothache. A strange complaint for a man with false teeth! So I enquired the real purpose of his visit. He laughed and told me. He wanted to see Monsieur de Berluc-Vidal. He called him Monsieur Montvallon, but I put him right. The property passed with the last Montvallon, a female, when she married a Vidal. I told him where he might find Monsieur Denys in the Camargue. I asked him what it was all about. He then said he'd bought a small picture of one of the Montvallons and that a client who would buy it, wanted a history of the lady in the portrait. It was as simple as that. I then bade him good-bye, charged him for a consultation—for, after all, his toothache had vanished—and away he went."

"Did he show you the picture, the miniature, sir?"

"No. He said he'd left it with his luggage in the cloak-room of the railway station at Mâcon. I was disappointed."

Cromwell thrust his hand in his pocket, unwrapped his treasure once more, and passed it to the doctor.

"That's it, sir."

Littlejohn smiled. Cromwell's French was certainly coming along. The way he said: *Voilà, monsieur,* had quite an authentic ring with it.

The doctor held the little portrait under the shaded table-lamp and whistled.

"This is Clotilde de Montvallon. What was Cheever doing with this?"

"He bought it in an antique shop in Cannes."

"But how did it get there? Who could have sold it? It hung in the bedroom of Mlle Solange de Berluc-Vidal here at the château for as long as I can remember. You have met Mlle Solange?"

"Yes. She was at the *mas.*"

"A frequent patient of mine. The miniature of her great-aunt, many times removed, hung over the fireplace in her bedroom. It was there last year when I was called-in to see her. Very highly strung, Mlle Solange. A broken romance in her youth. I was sent for.... I still am ... when she has one of her nerve crises ... ."

Littlejohn nodded.

"Drink or drugs?"

The doctor chuckled.

"You are a shrewd man, Superintendent."

"You used the word *crise*, doctor. It has rather a finer shade of meaning in French than with us."

"It would be unprofessional of me to go into details of the case of Mlle Solange, sir. If I answer your question, will it be treated with caution? I may as well save you a lot of trouble by doing so. You could get the answer from any of the personal servants at the château."

"I can assure you of my discretion, doctor."

"She has outbreaks of drug-taking, then. They occur during periods when she seems to get at the end of her tether. When she realises how happy she might have been had she, like her great-aunt Clotilde, run away with the man of her choice, instead of allowing her father to lock her in her room and hound the man, her father's estate-agent, from the neighbourhood. Since when her neurotic and autocratic old mother has battened on her. The miniature, which Clotilde left behind in her haste, must often have reminded Solange of the matter. That, presumably, is why she kept it in a prominent place in her room."

"What happened to Mlle Clotilde de Montvallon, sir?"

"I never heard. Perhaps the pair of them went abroad. I never asked ... ."

Whereat, Marie-Louise arrived with the supper, which she laid with all speed on the table, trotting here and there in concentric circles, smiling, nodding pleasantly. She had all the features of youthful beauty, too, and had thrown the advantage of them away, and aged and lost them through devotion to her brother. The case seemed riddled with lovely, unhappy women. Marie-Louise kissed her brother on the forehead and he kissed her back.

"Good night, Théo.... Good night, gentlemen...."

She trotted off to bed as the clock struck eleven. Silence settled on the house. Not a sound outside. The doctor bade them draw up to the table.

A cold chicken, which the doctor dissected with all the skill of a surgeon instead of a physician. A most succulent salad. White bread and rich farm butter. Local cream cheese. And a bottle of white Mâcon. It all tasted fine.

Cromwell was thoughtful. He was bothered about his miniature. Now, the doctor said it was the property of Mlle Solange de Berluc-Vidal. Cheever, Madame Labourel, Devard, Rivaud.... They all had a different tale to tell about it. Who the hell did it belong to? And who had told the right tale about it? He felt somehow that he was now fighting for possession and maybe the decent rights and security of the woman in the picture. Twisters, shady dealers, liars, drug-addicts.... They'd all been concerned with the affair. And women, too, the victims of frustrated passions. *Passions dévastatrices,* the doctor has called them. He took a large swig of the excellent white Mâcon which seemed to circulate round his system like fire. He squared his shoulders. He'd be damned if he'd part with his miniature to anybody! It was going home to England with him, and there it was staying!

The doctor left them to bring in the coffee which was keeping hot in the kitchen. He returned with the pot, poured it out, produced more helpings of brandy, and then cigars. They drew together round the table like a trio of conspirators.

"You've only told us half your story, doctor. What about the other man you mentioned?"

"Ah! I kept the best until the end, deliberately. After a good meal and when the house is asleep is the best time for the sinister denouement. The man who followed Cheever.... The man who said he had the stomachache...."

He raised his glass of brandy and eyed its golden contents against the lamplight.

"Your very good health, both of you. And good luck with your murder case."

He drank, smacking his lips with relish.

"You will not find very much help in the course of your enquiries. The Camargue, of course, is a closed shop. You have to be one of the initiates, a local, to learn anything of what goes on there. However much one of the inhabitants is detested, against an outsider, especially a foreigner like Cheever, he is favoured. *Il est d'ici*, he's from here, they say, and gather round to protect him."

Littlejohn knew it all by heart, now, and agreed with the doctor. But why this little lecture? The next exciting sentence gave the reason.

"The man who followed Cheever, the man with the belly-ache, was from Provence. It would surprise me if he hadn't had roots in the Camargue at some time or other. His speech betrayed it. He may have been a *gardian*. In any case, his southern origins have made your investigations difficult. I just say that in passing. Now let me tell you about him. First, some more brandy...."

Both Littlejohn and Cromwell wouldn't for anything in the world have missed this intimate bit of French courtesy, but now they were slowly entering a fog of Mâcon and good brandy from which it was difficult to keep clear and listen carefully. The stove snored away and its comfortable warmth pervaded the room. The bouquet of fine Cognac had now chased away the more delicate scent of the gentle Mâcon. The chicken was a mere mass of bare bones, the salad and the cheese two lamentable remnants. In a quiet, civilised way—what a night!

"The man gave no name. Or rather, he hesitated when I asked for it, and then said Leblanc, which is like saying Smith in England. It conveyed anonymity. He said he was passing through on his way to Lyons in his van. He had a small commercial vehicle, such as travellers use for samples or itinerant market-men for their wares. He had eaten some fish at Dijon and it had disagreed with him. Could I help him? I asked him what brought him to Pont de Veyle so far from the main route...if he *were* going from Dijon to Lyons. He then had the audacity to say that a friend of his, whom he'd seen the day before, had recommended me...."

The doctor paused for effect, leaned back in his chair, and poured out more brandy. Then he rose and went and slowly opened the door of the room. A pause. A sound of giggles and titters from the inner parts of the house.

"Your driver and Mélanie seem to have settled down comfortably. They'll be filled with regrets when you decide it's time to go."

He sat down again.

"I examined him. Another faked case, I'm afraid. I gave him a good dose of purge. If he was really going to Lyons, he would need to desert his vehicle several times on the way and flee behind the hedges in the Dombes.... He tried to be casual. His friend's name was Cheever, an Englishman. He had business at the château de Montvallon. He thought he'd call there to see him. Where was the château?"

Another pause.

"Naturally, I had no idea that Cheever was going to meet his death. I simply told the second man that the family were not at home, but were in residence at their *domaine* in the Camargue. I even mentioned the nearby village of Méjanes. It wasn't until next day, when the post came, that I found out the real truth about the visit. He'd been enquiring at the *Chapon Gras* and Gastin had given him the customary short shrift. The postman had been in the inn at the time and met the man when he left. He'd said that Cheever had been in the village the day before and had called on me. Hence the second man's story about Cheever's recommending me to him. The postman had also told him about Cheever's enquiries for the way to the château and that the family were absent. So, that is the tale. I had my revenge by the amount of purge I gave him."

"Did you notice the van, sir?"

"It was parked over the road near the inn."

"The number of it? Did you manage to see the registration?"

"No. But I saw the name of the department. It was Seine-et-Oise."

"What type of man, sir?"

"Large, swarthy, heavy, with a flowing paunch and huge limbs. I wouldn't like to meet him in a fracas."

"Moustache?"

"Yes, large and dark. Thin black hair, bald at the front."

"Is Mantes in the department of Seine-et-Oise, doctor?"

"Yes."

"I think we know the man. A fellow called Valdeblore ... ."

"What did I tell you? Valdeblore is a southern name. There's a place called Valdeblore just above Nice."

This was a startling revelation indeed! An antidote to the soporific effects of brandy and the excellent supper!

"Would it be trespassing on your kindness if I asked to use your telephone, doctor?"

"No. It's in the hall. I'll come and fix it for you. At present, it is switched through to my sister's room. She insists on taking all the night-calls first. She screens them, you see, and will only waken me and send me out if they reply satisfactorily to her questions. As I said before, she coddles me."

They rang the Sûreté at Marseilles. Audibert was at home, they said. He had probably read his children another instalment of *Treasure Island* and gone to bed, thought Littlejohn. But there was only one thing for it. He asked for Audibert's home number.

The usual polite answer came over the wire. Yes, the Commissaire was in bed. He had retired early expecting to be called up later to one of his children who was sick. It looked like measles. *Rougeole.* Littlejohn hadn't come across the word before, but he later found it in Cromwell's little book, *Comment-ça-va?* He was relieved.

Littlejohn explained to Audibert what had happened and gave a brief account of his adventures in Pont de Veyle.

"I will ring up Mantes, Littlejohn, and tell them to keep an eye on Valdeblore. We have business at Arles to-morrow, but can, perhaps, get along to Mantes later in the day."

Pont de Veyle, Mantes.... From one end of France to the other, and back again. What a case!

"I'll ring the police at Mâcon later and ask them to let you know what Mantes have to say. They can telephone you at your hotel."

"Right. I don't know where we're staying, but the police have booked the rooms."

"Good night, *mon ami.*"

They felt they couldn't thank the doctor enough, not only for his help in the case, but also for the delights of the meal. He told them to come again and thanked them for honouring him as guests.

The police driver emerged from the kitchen glowing with good will, good wine and food, and whatever other secret pleasures he had enjoyed during his stay. In the room behind, peeping at the visitors, stood a handsome, buxom country girl, her eyes alight, her apple-cheeks aflame. She couldn't stop giggling, which made the policeman a bit sheepish and awkward. He made up for it later, however, by many more visits to Pont de Veyle, eventually leading Mélanie to the altar. Which was the only unpleasant thing arising for the doctor from a very happy evening. Good maids are hard to get!

Pont de Veyle was asleep when they left. Dead silence everywhere. The river quietly on its way, a light in an upper room of the inn, the sombre masses of the houses here and there. A shop or two, one with a sign just discernible. *Coopérative de Bresse*. Fields dotted with hen-runs, and the birds all sleeping ....

The police had found them comfortable rooms in a good hotel on the quay facing the Saône. The clocks were striking two as they said good night and turned in.

At four o'clock the telephone at Littlejohn's bedside rang. The police at Mâcon. They apologised profusely. There was nothing the Superintendent could do before morning. Everything was in hand. All police stations would be advised; close searches everywhere instituted. But they understood that the Commissaire Audibert had promised to let Littlejohn know at once.

The Mantes police had called at the *Butte Verte* to enquire about Valdeblore. He had not been there for three days. His wife didn't even know where he was. He had completely vanished.

CHAPTER XIII
A COWBOY'S CONFESSION

They were up and about early the next day. Littlejohn not only wished to see the hotel where Cheever had spent his last night alive, but had also taken a fancy to visiting Pont de Veyle in the daylight. The police, therefore, agreed to take him and Cromwell by road to Lyons, where they could catch the express for Arles at half-past ten.

The Hôtel des Tilleuls, where Cheever had stayed, was a seedy café among the side-streets at the back of the river-front. The ground floor consisted mainly of a bar with a long zinc counter at which a crowd of workmen were drinking before starting work for the day. A spiral staircase ended up just behind the bar and this led to the room Cheever had occupied. A cheap place which would obviously appeal to him. A tall, red-haired squinting man was serving drinks under the eye of a big fat woman in black. It was she who met the police as they entered. Somewhere in the streets outside, a hooter sounded, most of the customers drank up, left the place, and started sorting out their bicycles from a heap by the door. And then they rode away, chattering together.

"Here again! I thought it would have all been over by now. Haven't you landed your fish yet?"

The woman wasn't pleased to see them, held them where they stood near the door, and indicated by a flick of the thumb that the cross-eyed man would go and get his breakfast.

"These are two English detectives. Just tell them what they want to know and it'll soon be over."

The Inspector who was with them looked up from the country. Small, thick-set and strong, with a large brown moustache, he took his job seriously and was respected.

"I can't tell them any more than I've already told you. He came, went to bed, got up, ate his breakfast of bacon and eggs, and went. No fuss. Not even a lot of drink. He insisted on the bacon and eggs. What's the use of living in a poultry-yard if you can't get a fresh egg or two, he said."

"Did he ask you the way to any particular place?" said Littlejohn.

"Yes. Let me see. It was Pont de Veyle. I remember because I had an uncle lived there once. I told him to take the bus. He went off without another word."

"What made him come here? It's a bit out of the way and ...."

"He said a pal had recommended it. Clean, good, and cheap. That's what he said, and he was right."

"And his room has been occupied quite a lot, since?"

"What do you think? We don't keep this place for love. We *let* the rooms, not leave them empty."

"Here, here, here. Just mind your manners."

The local officer said it in a reproachful voice like a bassoon.

"Well. You people think we're made of money. We've three rooms to let, and they're always in use. Why, since the Englishman was here, about a dozen ... nay more, have slept in that room. Sometimes three in the bed. And it's always turned-out after."

"Did he leave anything behind in the room?"

"No. A cigarette packet and a lot of spent matches and fag ends. But they all do that. He was no trouble."

"Did he say who recommended the hotel?"

"I've forgotten. Somebody in the north where he'd been."

"Is that all?"

"Why? Should there be more? He talked quite a lot, but I couldn't understand half he said. Now and then, I'd get what he wanted, after a struggle. But his French was queer. He thought he was speaking it like a native, but he wasn't. Not by a long way. It made one or two of the customers laugh. He'd spill a mouthful of things and then he'd say *Savvy?* or *Compree?* And to make him feel at home, they'd say *Oui,* and he'd look pleased…. That's all I can tell you."

Pont de Veyle looked clean and very different in the daylight. The crossroads, the river, and the main highways sprawling away in different directions. A few villagers lounging outside what looked like the *mairie,* judging from the flagpole. Women in black coming and going at the village shop. A car in front of the doctor's house, which was trim and pretty in the sunshine. Gastin lounging at the door of his inn, carpet slippers on his feet, and dressed in his shirt and trousers with the braces dangling. His paunch hung heavily almost between his knees and he scowled to right and left as though expecting his wife and her lover to return any minute.

The Château de Montvallon lay two miles along the Bourg highroad. Flat fields on each side, subject to constant floods from the Saône. Poultry everywhere. Cromwell, always eager to learn, talked to the driver and made a note or two in his black book among items of crime. *Bourg* hens: grey, with black and white feathers. *Beny-Marboz* hens: pure white and bigger. And *Louhans,* which, the chauffeur informed him, laid an egg a day, all the year round, without any trouble or special diet. The soil looked wet, cold and full of clay. Cromwell tried to quiz the driver on the wines of the locality, too, but drew a blank. He liked cheap Mâcon red, but all he knew was how to drink it. Now, poultry...Well, he reared a few himself. *Beny-Marboz,* for eating; *Louhans* for eggs. He promised to send Cromwell a *Beny-Marboz* at a cut rate, which the sergeant paid. It arrived eventually, with all the paper off, a mere mass of string and labels, smelling weeks old. The dog disposed of it, *en casserole.*

The château itself was approached through a small forest of mixed trees, which opened on to a well-kept lawn broken by a drive leading to the house itself. A fine old stone building, with tall oblong windows, a terrace approached by twin staircases ending on a platform before a large artistic door. The windows were all shuttered and the place looked dead. Rooks cawed in the trees and a flock of starlings rose from the lawn and sped away into the distance. Someone was playing a piano somewhere and doing it well. The gendarme who drove the car approached an old gardener, who was digging in the heavy soil of a large rosebed.

"Anybody at home?"

"No. The place is shut up except for the caretaker."

He took no interest in the visitors and returned to his digging.

"Who's that playing the piano, then?"

"The village schoolmaster. You can't stop him or touch him. He's got permission from Monsieur. He hasn't a piano of his own, and there's only a little organ in the church. So..."

He went on among the roses.

They'd seen the château and that was all. They couldn't start prowling through the rooms, so they had to go. Littlejohn gave the gardener a couple of coins. He obviously ought to have done that first, for the old man then showed himself inclined for a gossip.

"What brings you here, monsieur, and with the police? Don't say it's collecting a debt, because Monsieur is known for paying his accounts on the nail. Second Tuesday every month at eleven in the morning. That's what it is to have money. Not made from the land. It don't come that way now. Mills ... Mills, that's what it is. He's mills at Grenoble that's goldmines...."

"I see. I'm from England. Just looking around. The policeman's a friend driving us."

"English, eh? Fought side by side with them on the Marne against the *boche*. One here a month or six weeks since. Asking if he could see in the château. Pictures, he wanted to see. Asked for the master. Told him to be off. I didn't fancy his sort. He asked where they was if they wasn't at home. Told him on the Camargue. Never been there myself. Never wanted to go, even when I was asked. My old girl doesn't like foreign parts."

"So, he went?"

"Oh, yes, he went. Matter of fact, another fellow came next day. Wanted to know if the first chap had been here."

"Big, husky, with a large black moustache?"

"That's him. I'll bet he was chasing him round for some dirty trick the first one had played on him. I told him I'd sent him to the Camargue...."

The old man cackled and showed his toothless shrunken gums. He was true to type. The years pass, the roads get busy, transport brings the world to them and takes them to the world.... Radio, television, cinemas, even wars.... They remain the same. They left him still talking to himself like an old gramophone, even when they were far out of earshot.

Arles seemed like a new world when they got there. After a run through the Dombes—where Cromwell hung almost half-way out of the window counting the innumerable lakes and watching the professional catchers draining them and shovelling solid masses of fish into tanks for transport, live, far and wide—they struck Lyons and joined the train. Littlejohn snoozed most of the way and awoke under the hot searing sun of Provence again. Vivid colours, vivid people, lethargy of the heat, easy-going surface with passion ready to boil up from beneath. Audibert met them and began to talk about food right away. He looked as fresh as a daisy again, dressed in his immaculate dark suit, his shoes sparkling, his linen cool and white.

"Back again."

"Yes, here again. I'll tell you what's been happening whilst you've been away. But not before you've had some food."

"Could I telephone first? A call to Francaster, England?"

"Of course. We'll go to the police station. Marion is out at the Mas Vidal, clearing up one or two things. It is also the funeral of Davso to-day. The medico-legal department have finished with the body and the *juge d'instruction* said he might as well be interred."

The little police car flashed down the narrow streets, hooting the crowds away. The town was full of people. Women in the ancient traditional dress of the Arlésiennes. There was to be a *corrida* in the arena that afternoon. People were gathering for the arrival of the bulls, the *abrivado;* at the "bullfight", young hopefuls would compete and try to snatch the trophies from between the horns of the bulls with their *rasets,* their iron combs. Then the departure of

the bulls, the *bandide*. Some of the competitors were strutting about in their white shirts and already a band was playing excerpts from Bizet's *Carmen*.

"Get me Francaster, England, 1212. Yes, 1212. I don't
care if it *is* engaged. Clear it. Urgent...."

Audibert brushed all difficulties aside.

"Have the call put through to the *Hôtel Nord-Pinus* when
it comes. We're going there for lunch. Keep the telephone
people on their toes, too. This is urgent."

"Yes, sir. Certainly, Monsieur le Commissaire."

They left the police station and began a late meal. As
they ate, Audibert told them the news.

"Féraud, head man at the Mas Vidal, has confessed to
killing Davso. He said it was in self-defence. It occurred
whilst you were all at the *mas* after interviewing Davso. He
stated he left the room whilst you were occupied having a
drink, and went back to Davso's cabin. He was sure Davso
knew more than he said he did and thought that perhaps
he, Féraud, being a local man and used to the *gardians*, could
make him talk. Instead, Davso, who was drunk by then, grew
truculent, then violent, and went for Féraud with his trident. Féraud defended himself, merely trying to fend Davso
off. Instead, the blow caught the old man on the head and
he fell unconscious. When Féraud examined him, he found
him dead. He hurried back and didn't say a word."

"Why the sudden confession?"

Audibert sipped his brandy carefully, then shrugged.

"He said it was on his conscience and he thought he'd
better make a clean breast of it before anyone else became
involved. He has told some lies. For example, the autopsy
revealed that Davso died from a broken skull, but he wasn't
drunk. There was, in fact, no alcohol of any importance in

the stomach. There was a lot of patent medicine, cinchona bark for the ague, but little else."

The landlord hurried in.

"England on the telephone...."

Sadd couldn't get over the idea of Littlejohn speaking from Arles.

"Why, you sound to be just across the street, sir!"

First, Sadd was to go to Mrs. Cheever and ask her if her husband had, when he opened the miniature, found anything strange hidden in the back. In any case, was there a local analyst whom Cheever might have consulted? If so, had he had a packet of drugs examined lately, and with what result? Mrs. Cheever was also to be asked where her husband was in the habit of hiding valuables which he carried on his person. Were they all in his wallet, or in some secret pocket or other?

"Got that, Sadd? Please hurry, then. Ring me back here, at the police station, Arles 808-32...."

More arrangements to get the message through to Littlejohn and then they started out to the Mas Vidal.

"You won't want to see Féraud, Littlejohn? He's in gaol here. Marion and the judge were up half the night with him trying to get a proper tale out of him, but he stuck to his first statement like glue. Now about your trip to Pont de Veyle... Did you get to know anything?"

On the way Littlejohn told Audibert all about it.

"I've filled in many gaps. First of all, Cheever bought the miniature in Cannes."

"Excuse me, but we are at present holding Casimir Labourel, the nephew of the woman in the shop, on a charge of illicit drug trafficking. So far, he has denied all knowledge of the miniature. He will talk in time. You were saying?"

"Cheever bought the miniature. I think it was sold by mistake. Presumably Madame Labourel knew nothing about the reason for its being in the shop, except she thought it was for sale. In actual fact, it had probably been sent by Mlle Solange de Berluc-Vidal. She is a drug addict, is carefully watched by the family to prevent her obtaining supplies and breaking-out again, and therefore must have conceived the idea of getting drugs hidden in little antiques of one kind and another, from the shop, which, with Casimir's connection, was very easy. There was a mistake, and Cheever got away with one such package, in the miniature."

"And when he discovered the packet in the back and found out what it contained, he was too curious to keep quiet?"

"That is right. I think he could have genuinely sold the picture at a considerably enhanced price once he knew the complete history of it. So he killed two birds with one stone. He went from London to Pont de Veyle, staying the night at Mantes with his friend, Valdeblore, on the way. From Pont de Veyle he went to Cannes to pursue enquiries about the contents of the back of the miniature. The Labourels *must* have received a shock. They presumably hatched out the cock-and-bull story for Devard to tell Cheever. Having sent him to Devard, they thought they were rid of him. Cheever, however, floundering, as *we* did, in a surfeit of lies, went off to Mas Vidal to investigate there. He had been told by the doctor at Pont de Veyle that the Montvallon family were there for the summer. I don't know what happened, but Cheever met his death as a result."

They had, by now, left the rice fields and vineyards of the Camargue behind and were driving through the wilderness of pools, salt-grass, rush-roofed cabins and arid pastures again. It was past four o'clock and the sun was slanting towards the west, casting shadows from the twisted trees and bushes and touching the tips of the waves on the *étangs* with silver and gold.

As they neared Méjanes, there was an atmosphere of holiday, of fête about the place. Groups of cowboys sat on the terraces of wayside cafés, *chopines* of wine and glasses in front of them. A dozen or more *gardians,* shaved, wearing black jackets, black hats and ties, and carrying their tridents aloft, passed on their white horses. Then a vehicle, a light cart, drawn by a white Camargue horse covered by a black cloth, trotted by. It was the funeral car of Davso, to whose burial all these had been. He had been a lonely, self-contained man, but he was a *gardian,* and his fellow cowboys had been to pay him their last respects. The wild looking horses, the expert riders astride them with such dignity, the gallop raising the dust; all a fine sight. Now and then, a cowboy with his girl sitting in the saddle behind him, or a girl riding alone. Davso, the beggar, had been given a dignified and impressive finish.

Littlejohn was ending his tale.

"But something happened early on Cheever's travels. At Mantes. The result was that Valdeblore followed Cheever to Mâcon, Pont de Veyle and, I'm sure, Cannes and the Mas Vidal. Why he did so, I don't know. It might have been that he was after Cheever's money. I hardly think so. It had something to do with his daughter, who, by the way, is the mother of a child by Cheever. From what the doctor at Pont de Veyle tells me, Valdeblore wasn't following Cheever out of curiosity. He was angry, murderous. It may easily be that he caught up with him at the *mas* and killed him there."

The car ran into the courtyard of Mas Vidal. A number of *gardians,* dressed in their best, some of them with their wives and girls, were festooned on wooden seats outside their own dining quarters drinking wine. Indoors, they found Marion with Denys de Berluc-Vidal. They had both been to the funeral.

Marion looked out of temper. He had, in the heat, been trying to get more information about the crime to which Féraud had confessed.

"I have spent a wasted day, Monsieur le Commissaire. A wasted day."

Berluc-Vidal made an impatient noise.

"What else do you expect to find out? Féraud told a perfectly reasonable story. He is in prison for it. Presumably, he will be there for some time until he's paid the price of his folly. There's nothing more ... ."

"May we sit down and talk a little, monsieur?"

Audibert said it calmly, but there was an ominous note in his voice.

"You may sit, of course, and I'll ring for some wine. But I don't see the use. We've talked all day and got nowhere."

They were in the same room as before, with a wide outoutlook across the west and the lonely *étang* behind, over which water fowl seemed to be in a continual state of agitation. As Littlejohn looked out, a flock of wild geese slowly flew above the water in formation, a beautiful, almost touching sight, so remote from the sordid affairs now in hand.

"And now, monsieur, my friend Superintendent Littlejohn would like to ask you one or two questions. Please treat them as official. Although he is of the English police, he is my colleague, and I am behind him. It is as though, let us say, I myself am speaking with his voice."

Berluc-Vidal reared and his nostrils dilated.

"What is the point of it all? This is stupid waste of time. It has got to cease, for it is doing no good. Let me tell you, my brother is a Senator and unless we are left in peace, I shall complain."

A sad little smile from Audibert.

"I am sorry, monsieur, but I don't care if he is the President of the Republic. You will either answer my friend's questions, or we will all go to Arles and there you will stay until you do. Well?"

The wine had arrived and Berluc-Vidal remembered he was their host. He shrugged.

"You are very impertinent, commissaire, but Monsieur Littlejohn is our guest. What does he want to know?"

Littlejohn took a sip of his wine; the excellent white of Mâcon again. The first and best question seemed to be the one which was still being asked by Fred Uncles, M.P.

"What happened to Cheever?" he said in French.

And Denys de Berluc-Vidal's glass slipped through his fingers to the floor.

There was a diversion whilst they mopped up the mess and broken glass.

"Cheever?"

Monsieur de Berluc-Vidal didn't look very comfortable.

"The Englishman whose body was found in the Vaccarès, sir. He came here from Cannes to enquire about the miniature of your relative. He asked for you. What did you tell him?"

Berluc-Vidal was at a loss. Now, he didn't know how much the police knew. He tried to pass it off lightly.

"I showed him the door. He was an impudent little nuisance."

"What time did he call, sir?"

"About sunset, as far as I remember. Why?"

"How did he get here? By private car, or bus?"

"I later learned he came by train and walked from Albaron station. Nothing is missed in these parts, especially strangers. Some of our *gardians* heard he arrived by the 2.15 out of Arles. He must have walked from Albaron. He was here after five o'clock, I believe, and would certainly miss the last train back. It leaves Les Saintes at 5.25."

"So, he was stranded, short of taking a hired car?"

"Obviously."

"Perhaps he stayed the night."

Berluc-Vidal started.

"What do you mean?"

"There is an inn somewhere about, I presume."

"There is a small one in the village."

"Or else, being a careful man, he might have put up for the night...shall we say in one of your outbuildings among the hay?"

The result was electric. Berluc-Vidal jumped to his feet, his face red with rage beneath the tan.

"How much more?"

The quiet voice of Audibert intervened.

"Now that we know Cheever came here and was seen, apparently stranded, his train gone, we shall want to know what happened to him then. *What did,* monsieur? If you know, speak. If not, we shall question every man on the Camargue. We will start on your own *gardians, now.* And there will be no more lying or secrecy. Woe betide anyone who tries to deceive the police!

And the way he said it, it sounded like a death knell!

Berluc-Vidal shrugged. He had recovered himself.

"I had better tell you. I must confess I didn't care to be mixed up in this. I only wanted peace and quiet here. I have tried to avoid a hurricane of police investigations, but now

I find I am to suffer them whether or not. Cheever stayed here the night."

"With the *gardians*?"

"No. In the hay in one of the sheds. Or presumably he did. He was found there next morning. He had been strangled."

Marion jumped to his feet, but the hand of Audibert gently restrained him. The man from Marseilles was as calm as ever.

"But why, my friend, have you not said so before? All this work, all this time wasted trying to trace the man's movements. And now, you say, he was killed in your own barn. Who did it?"

"I don't know. It wasn't one of my men. I investigated that. I had them in, together and one by one. They would not lie to me. They were all indoors, and vouched for one another. In any event, who would *kill* an intruder like that? Kick him in the pants and send him on his way, perhaps, but more likely give him a bunk in the men's quarters, a breakfast in the morning, and then off to the train on the back of a *gardian's* saddle."

"Why did you not let the police know?"

"I didn't want a fuss on my *domaine*. Nobody of mine had killed the man. Why should they? He had, perhaps, found someone else in the hay before him and they had fought. In any event, the easiest way seemed to be to move him from my estate and put him where he would be found. That seemed to me to be a good solution. I told Féraud to see to it. Then, the body was discovered in the Vaccarès. I asked Féraud why the hell he'd put it there. He said the man had no papers in his pocket; his pockets had been emptied. He was a foreigner. An unknown. He therefore thought it wise to make the body vanish and be sure of no more trouble. Instead, we might just as well have put the body in the courtyard and sent for the police. That is the truth and I am conveying it to you because I don't want my *gardians* bothering. They are my boys and I am responsible for them. I am telling you this to avoid trouble for them, as you propose, you say, to harass and question them until they don't know whether they're on their heads or their heels."

Marion put his head in his hands.

"That means going through it all again. There are about forty *gardians* concerned. It will take years."

Audibert patted Marion on the arm.

"We know the murderer, *mon ami*. Now that Monsieur de Berluc-Vidal has been so gracious as to take us into his confidence, the whole matter clears. Do you know a man called Valdeblore, Monsieur de Berluc-Vidal?"

"Valdeblore? No. Nobody of that name has ever been connected with me or my affairs."

"Are any of your men likely to know him?"

"You can ask, but I don't think so. I usually know most things in these parts. Why?"

Audibert turned to Littlejohn.

"My friend here has found the murderer. His name is Valdeblore. He has vanished. I wonder if he's hiding in the Camargue. It will be like hunting for a needle in a haystack."

"No, it won't. If he's here, my boys will find him."

"Tell them, then, to scour the place for a tall, fat, heavy man, dark, and with a spreading black moustache. If they don't see him, they must also ask everyone they meet if they know a Valdeblore or ever knew one. It is a southern name and someone might chance to know the man. And now about Féraud..."

"What about him? He's confessed, hasn't he?"

"Yes."

The maidservant entered and whispered to her master.

"A telephone call from Arles police for you, M. le Commissaire. Take it in the hall, if you wish."

Audibert left at his same easy, leisurely speed.

"Another glass of wine, gentlemen?"

Berluc-Vidal did the honours as though his failure to inform the police about what happened to Cheever was fully forgiven.

Audibert was back.

"The news from Francaster, my friend. Cheever visited a local chemist... wait...."

He referred to a neat piece of paper in his hand, covered in his own equally neat notes.

"I will read what the police took down from your colleagues in England. 'Cheever visited a local chemist, who is also an expert analyst. His name is Frank Hazlitt. Hazlitt said the contents of the packet were known as *snow*, otherwise powdered cocaine. That was number one. Number two, Cheever carried his passport and papers in the inside pocket of his jacket. His stock of money was in a secret oilskin pocket stitched in the lining of his trousers.' That is all."

"Thank you, Audibert. Whoever disposed of the body and Cheever's identity papers missed finding the money hidden in the secret pocket. Davso found the trousers either on the body or off it, and took the money we came upon in his treasure-chest. May I carry on now?"

"Of course."

"May I ask, Monsieur de Berluc-Vidal, if after the matter of the miniature had been discussed, and my friend Cromwell had shown it to you, anything more was said about it in your family that day?"

"I think it was casually mentioned."

"Was your sister, Mlle Solange, present?"

"No. But I don't see what this has to do with ..."

"Please bear with me. Did she know that my friend had it?"

"It may have been talked about the day after, but my mother wasn't well when you were here and my sister was very much occupied with her. Now, may I know what all this is about?"

"So, she may have thought Cheever had the miniature with him when he came here? Did he mention it when he called to see you?"

"Of course. That was the purpose of his visit. He said he wished to see me about it; that it was in his possession."

"But he didn't produce it for you to see?"

"No."

"Where did your conversation with Cheever take place?"

"In the courtyard by the side-door of the house."

"What rooms are near it?"

"My mother's and then my sister's."

"Your sister would overhear the conversation?"

"Certainly, if she wished. The fellow spoke atrocious French, and seemed to think that by shouting it to high heaven, it would be better understood."

"Your sister is a good horsewoman?"

A pause. Berluc-Vidal looked bewildered and very irritated.

"She is excellent. Better than any man on the *mas*. But why all this? And haven't we discussed my sister quite enough?"

Littlejohn didn't appear to hear the questions.

"Is Mlle Solange at home?"

"Yes. She is in her room. The arrest of Féraud had greatly upset her."

"They are in love?"

This was too much.

"How dare you! What has that to do with the case? Besides, the man's a ranch-foreman. My sister...."

He seemed about to say 'my sister is my sister', and then halted, short of words and patience.

"All the same, Féraud loves your sister. So much so, that, I think, to shield her, he confessed to a crime he did not commit."

"Are you going mad? Audibert, I beg of you, put an end to this crazy interrogation at once...."

Audibert smiled, shrugged, and lit one of his elegant little cigarettes.

"I suggest that Mlle Solange overheard your conversation with Cheever about the miniature and thought he had it in his pocket. He was murdered afterwards and the body vanished. *She had to have that miniature.* When she heard the remains, minus flesh and clothes, had been found, she thought the miniature had gone, too, for good. But when Féraud returned and perhaps suggested that Davso had found the corpse first and maybe rifled it, her craving awoke all over again."

"Craving? What craving?"

"Drugs. She thought they were hidden behind the picture."

Berluc-Vidal was standing and behaved just as though someone had shot him through a vital part. He crumpled up, sat down, and put his head in his shaking hands.

"How did you find out?"

"The antique shop in Cannes is an undercover source of supply. Mlle Solange sent the miniature there, ostensibly to be cleaned or valued, but actually to bear back a packet of 'snow', *chnouf,* as you call it."

"I might have guessed. I thought at first that she was cured. Then she showed all the signs of a relapse. I couldn't tell where she got it."

"When she heard Davso had perhaps stolen the contents of Cheever's pockets, she couldn't wait. She left the family here—I was with you, remember?—and rode to Davso's cabin. It was empty. She started to search the place. Davso returned. She struck him down with a trident. I've no doubt with some justification. He was a nasty piece of work. I would put nothing past him. Féraud, who loves her, guessed what had happened. He took the blame. He was out of the room when she left to go to Davso's *cabane*. Maybe he saw her go...."

Littlejohn did not get any farther. The door to the hall was half-closed and suddenly opened wide. There, tottering and wild-eyed, stood Mlle Solange. She tried to walk a pace, halted, and then pitched into the room and fell unconscious.

CHAPTER XIV
CLEANING UP IN CANNES

"**B**y gum, my dear," said Mr. Fred Uncles, M.P. for Francaster, as he opened his morning paper. It was in French and came by post every day during the Cheever sensation. Mr. Uncles was an amiable and very efficient M.P., anxious always to do his best for his constituents and keep his seat. He had excelled himself this time. He translated the headlines for his wife.

CHEVVER AFFAIR

GALAXY OF FAMOUS DETECTIVES ON THE CASE SCOTLAND YARD AND FRENCH SÛRETÉ CO-OPERATE ARREST IMMINENT

"I wish to God they'd spell things properly, though. The fellow's name was Cheever, not Chevver!"

Had he seen the galaxy two hours after reading the news, he might have ceased his smiling. They were lolling in the sun on a terrace of the Croisette, at Cannes, drinks spread about them, waiting for lunch. Littlejohn, Dorange, Audibert, Cromwell and Pignon.

They had left Arles that morning—all except Dorange, who had turned up at Cannes from Nice—just as Dr. Matthieu arrived from Pont de Veyle. Berluc-Vidal had sent for him to deal quietly with the case of Mlle Solange. She was a complete nervous wreck. She had taken to drugs to relieve her nerves shattered by a domineering and possessive mother, who developed a fresh ailment every time she saw her daughter beginning to enjoy life. She had driven away any number of suitors.

Solange had confessed to defending herself against Davso. He had entered, to find her in his cabin, for the purpose guessed by Littlejohn. He had grown offensive and odious and then tried to embrace her. He had chased her as she fled from the cabin and, seizing his trident, she had thrust the prongs in his chest to ward him off.

As he staggered back, she had hit him savagely on the head with the shaft of the trident.... As soon as police formalities had been disposed of, Matthieu would take her home to Pont de Veyle and he and his sister would look after her. The examining magistrate was sympathetic and believed her story, and her uncle, the Senator, was on his way to help him make a favourable decision. Féraud had been released, was going with the party to Pont de Veyle, and hoped for happiness one day when Mlle Solange recovered.

Thus another dark secret was thrust into the Montvallon family closet.

The *corps* of detectives was a mixed one. Physically, Littlejohn towered massively above them all, calm, courteous, imperturbable and humorous. Every time he came to Cannes, it was the same. The holiday feeling took hold of him, work became a bore, and he wanted simply to sit there and watch the crowds go by, trying to sum up the queer individuals who composed it. There was a film festival in progress and a mass of stars, producers and directors, to say nothing of a flock of critics, jostled one another for the limelight, strutting about, dispensing autographs, the women trying to outdo each other in *risqué* attire, the men trying to look tough or amorous according to the rôles they usually played.

Dorange seemed lost in thought. Wearing his famous off-white suit, his snake shoes and belt, a red carnation in his buttonhole, he smoked his cheroot placidly. Now and then, a passer-by, recognising him, recoiled or else turned pale, and tried to get past as quickly as he could.

And Audibert, smart in his dark suit and spotless linen, was busy ordering the lunch.

Cromwell had just written home to his wife and to the eldest of his daughters, with whom he regularly corresponded—a letter every day—when away. He was now occupied in gathering copy for his next epistle. That morning he had bought a small album from a chain-store in Cannes. "I might get a chance to obtain an autograph or two from the film-stars," he had told Littlejohn, in his modest, homely way. "If my eldest girl, who's at boarding-school, could show it to her friends there, it would create a sensation." "What's that?" Dorange had asked him, seeing the album protruding from Cromwell's pocket. He never missed a thing! Cromwell had explained. "Leave it with me...." And he had taken the book and put it in his own pocket. Next morning he returned it, full from cover to cover. Film stars, directors, critics, reporters, poets, novelists, oil tycoons, gamblers, foreign potentates and princes, sportsmen, courtesans, soldiers, sailors, diplomats, camp-followers, crooks, scientists.... Cromwell began to wonder if Dorange had signed them all himself! However, there they were, collected by detectives, policemen, door-keepers, hall-porters, newshawks, dope-pedlars, toadies, blackmailers, and a score of other honest people who admired Dorange and would do anything for him.

Mushroom caps stuffed with beef; mutton chops; Soufflé au Marasquin; ewes' milk cheese…. They all came and went. And over coffee and Cognac, they began to discuss the case again.

"This afternoon we shall clear up the Cannes end of the case. Then, there is the matter of laying our hands on Valdeblore. It may be like hunting for a needle in a haystack. He served in the underground during the occupation. He might, therefore, have gone to earth in some impregnable secret hideout. We shall see… ."

Audibert seemed confident enough. Many of the French police had been underground men, as well, and knew the "retreats" like the backs of their hands.

At the Town Hall in Cannes, the police were waiting for the visiting detectives. A large room with clean white walls on which were a number of administrative notices stuck by the corners with transparent tape. A red-tiled floor, leather-seated chairs, a polished table, and a bust of Marianne on a stand draped with a tricolor. A padded door led into another office. It looked as though they were going to conduct a solemn and ceremonial inquest into the affairs of Madame Labourel and her nephew.

They all sat down and Casimir Labourel was brought in by a local inspector. Littlejohn had not seen him before, but could guess what he was like at his best; a visiting, yachting aristocrat who had put in at Cannes for a day or two's change. Now, Casimir looked nothing of the kind. He had been tall, willowy, prosperous-looking. A long face, large dark eyes, firm chin, proud hooked nose, small dapper moustache. Long-legged, and self-assured when all went well. Now, it wasn't going well. He hadn't had a shave, his hair was tousled, and he walked with difficulty, for he had been in a cell overnight and they had removed the laces from his elegant shoes and the belt from his expensive flannel trousers, as well as the tasteful tie from his silk shirt, just in case he tried to escape or hang himself. In the course of his stay there, he seemed to have gone thinner, for the skin hung on his face in folds, like those of a suit which is too big.

"Sit down."

"I want my lawyer. I've a right to see my lawyer."

"You can see him when you meet the *juge d'instruction*. We just have to ask you a few questions."

"I won't answer them without my lawyer."

Audibert waved his hand in dismissal.

"Very well. Take him back to his cell. We thought he might tell us enough to merit our releasing him. We'd better wait a day or two until the examining magistrate is ready."

Casimir had been in process of rising to try to make a dignified exit. Now he sat down again.

"Better ask away, then. If I can go, the sooner the better. I've business to do and it can't wait. Can I have a drink?"

"Give him some beer."

Audibert passed him one of his elegant little cigarettes. Casimir looked at it in disgust, noticed the brand in gold letters on the paper, changed his mind, and accepted a light.

"My colleague Littlejohn will ask you some questions. You will answer them properly as though the local police were putting them to you. Understood?"

"Yes."

"All right; give him his beer."

Casimir drank thirstily, hunted in his pocket for his handkerchief, found they'd confiscated that as well, so dried his lips with his fingers.

"Please tell us how you came by the miniature which has figured so much in this case."

"I don't know what you mean. My aunt deals with the antique side of the business. That is, as far as the shop is concerned. I'm out doing the buying of big stuff at sales and such like."

"Don't evade the issue. You make a business of selling drugs...."

"I deny it! I..."

Audibert intervened.

"Your boat and flat have both been searched. I've no doubt you have quite a good hiding-place for the bulk of your stock, but we've found enough to get you imprisonment for life if we proceed against you. Behave yourself, help the police on a much bigger case than your petty smuggling, and put a better light altogether on your own misdoings."

"O.K., then. But I shall deny the smuggling and selling of drugs. I do a pharmaceutical business. Any of the local chemists will tell you."

"All right, all right. You can plead that later. Now answer my friend's questions."

Littlejohn took over again.

"You supplied drugs to Mlle Solange de Berluc-Vidal...."

"She took them under doctor's orders. The doctor was too far away for her to get a prescription quickly, so I let her have a small supply to tide her over."

"I know you did. She was watched and had to get them by stealth. In this case, she sent you a miniature of a relative and you arranged to put a packet behind the picture, between the back and the ivory. Am I right?"

"Yes. She telephoned, sent the picture, and I was to return it by post to the Camargue. She said it was one of a great-aunt who eloped with the man who painted it."

"As a matter of interest, how often did this happen?"

A pause.

"Only that once."

Audibert made a gentle clicking noise with his mouth.

"Come, come, my friend."

"Well, once before. It was in a hollow ring she sent to be cleaned. There was a cavity under the setting. I don't know why she kicked up such a fuss. Melodramatic, I called it. She said it wouldn't arouse suspicion. I believe drug takers get that way. A bit balmy and odd. Crafty...."

"I'm sure you know all the little oddities. How did the miniature find its way to the shop, then?"

"I had it in the room behind—my office—and it some-how got in the shop. As ill-luck would have it, there was, at the time, an English dealer buying things from my aunt. He was poking around among the pieces for sale and came upon the miniature. He made an offer for it and my aunt sold it. When I found it was missing, I asked her about it, and she said the man Cheever had just gone out with it. I tried to find him, because the thing wasn't mine. But he was nowhere to be seen."

"How did it get out of your office? Do you know?"

"All I can think of is that my aunt took it. She'd been in just before Cheever called. I give her commission on what she sells. She must have sneaked it out for something else to earn a few francs on. It was attractive and sure to go at a decent price."

"I've met your aunt a time or two. She seems hardly the kind to do dirty tricks."

The local inspector added his word.

"We've questioned her. She said she thought Casimir Labourel had put it in the shop along with other things for sale. She says she certainly didn't take it from his office. I know Madame Labourel well. She's always struck me as honest and truthful. In fact, she's helped us a lot at times with stolen goods and the like."

Dorange removed his cheroot.

"Have you thought about the monkey?"

He grinned and almost looked like a monkey himself.

Casimir's face fell, and then rage seized him.

"I never thought of it! Blast and damn the creature to hell! That's it. She keeps him on a chain when the shop's open, but when it's empty she lets him free and he's all over the place, chucking stuff about and making a mess. I've told her he'll have to go, but she says if he goes, she'll go, and I can't very well give her the sack. After all, she's my only relative."

"Your consideration is very touching."

"You needn't be so sarcastic, Monsieur Audibert. That monkey's cost me a pretty penny in his time. For ten years he's stolen and hidden jewellery of all kinds, torn up old maps, fouled priceless tapestries, and two years ago, he threw a box of duelling pistols through the window. And now.... Well, I shall tell my aunt, if he doesn't go, *I'll* go. And that'll mean shutting-up the shop. She says the monkey is the only friend she's got. She seems to forget me...."

"Does she? Deplorable. Let Superintendent Littlejohn proceed."

"What happened when you couldn't trace Cheever?"

"I got scared in case he opened the back and found the powder, didn't know what it was, and took some. He might have poisoned himself."

"He might, easily. But he wasn't the sort who would swallow a packet of powder from the back of an old miniature. He might have had it investigated, though. And then he might have gone to the police. And the police might have come to the shop where he bought the picture. You wished to be in a position to deny there ever were any drugs in the back. So you concocted an elaborate tale about a document in the back giving a history of the woman in the picture."

"...I couldn't very well admit it. sir. It would have involved Mlle de Berluc-Vidal."

"So, to protect her, you arranged some elaborate precautions?"

"To protect her and my aunt, yes."

"To protect yourself, you mean. Drugs coming from the shop would have involved *you*. So you were prepared to give Cheever the lie, say he was trying to blackmail you, and bring your aunt and Devard into it to bear out your story."

"Don't be so hard, Monsieur Audibert. You keep picking on me and all the time I'm only trying to help."

"Don't take the police for fools, then. Please go on, Littlejohn."

"Did your aunt open the back of the miniature?"

"No. She hadn't the chance. The damned monkey had no sooner taken the picture and dropped it in the shop than Cheever was in and bought it."

"So you made up the tale about the elopement and the cholera and persuaded your aunt to tell it to Cheever?"

"Yes."

"Good. That lets her out, then."

"Does it let me out, too?"

"Let me ask the questions, please. Your aunt knew there was some kind of enclosure—a letter or something—in the back of the picture?"

"When I asked her what she meant by selling it, we had a real row. I told her she'd let it go for a song. I couldn't very well tell her about Mlle Solange and her cocaine, could I? I said it was a precious family thing and worth a lot. She then replied that, in handling it when bargaining with the Englishman, she'd felt a bulge of something through the paper on the back. Then, it suddenly dawned on me that I could make out it was that document which made the miniature valuable and, at the same time, give her a tale to tell anybody who might come enquiring later about the picture."

"Meaning the police?"

"Certainly not. No. I thought Cheever might come back asking about it. And he did. She told him the story. She believed it, you see, and was convincing. I'd had to make it a long one. She's as cunning as her monkey, you know, and she said the paper behind must have been a large one, it bulged a lot. So, I had to give her a good tale to match."

"Cheever didn't believe her, did he? She had to send him to Devard to get it confirmed. Who *was* Devard?"

"A friend of mine. He did odd jobs for me now and then."

"A born liar, whose real name was Brassard. A smuggler."

"I wish you wouldn't keep thinking so badly of me, Monsieur Audibert...."

"Devard ran off after his visit to the police. He was so scared of you, Labourel, that he concocted an enthusiastic lie about faking the miniature himself. His fear gave wings to his imagination. He's disappeared now, and if the concierge, to whom he owes the rent, could lay her hands on him, there would be another murder."

Littlejohn removed his pipe and finished his questioning.

"You told your aunt you'd bought it from Devard?"

"I said I'd got it out of a wardrobe there which I bought. To make it look real, and to make out she did the dealing and buying in the shop, she told Cheever that *she*'d bought it and how she found it. No harm in that, is there?"

"No. Devard led Cheever and the police up the garden path for quite a time. I suppose Cheever couldn't get a proper tale about the drugs. I think he might have smelled a little profit out of it by blackmailing, but your aunt and

Devard confused him so much that he couldn't pin the blame on anybody. You were successful, there, Labourel. So, Cheever went off on his main business, to find out more about his miniature. I've no doubt he switched his curiosity from Cannes to the Mas Vidal, not only because a true history would add value to his picture, but in the hope that more about the drug packet might be forthcoming from the family. However, that clears up the sorry confusion in the case caused by your dope-dealing and lying."

"Look here…. You said…"

"Never mind what he said. The examining magistrate will be here later this afternoon and he will decide whether or not to deal with you as you deserve. It will be mentioned that you have answered questions properly."

"You're not going to keep me here any longer?"

"That is for the judge to decide."

"Well, I'll be damned! You've cheated me…. At any rate, you might let me have my tie and my belt and shoelaces. It's a scandal. I'm being treated like a crook or a murderer."

They led him off still shouting protests and threats.

Outside, everything was going on as usual. There might have been no crime at all. Boatmen at the harbour busy touting for business. Fishermen laying out their nets to dry in the sun. The women in the flower-market watering their blooms to keep them fresh. Crowds walking along the Croisette and the old port enjoying the view and the sunshine. Sailors repairing and tinkering with the expensive yachts tied up in the harbour.

A tall man in a yachting suit and white cap passed with a girl on either arm.

"That's Lord Gargoyle," said Dorange.

Littlejohn jumped! He'd never heard of him and, in any case, the name sounded comic and phoney.

"...We've got an eye on him. He's doing a currency fiddle...."

It was time for the party to break up. Dorange was due back in Nice, and Audibert and Pignon were returning to Marseilles. To-morrow, Littlejohn and Cromwell were off to Mantes to make some enquiries about Valdeblore from Madame Valdeblore and to confer with the police there.

A gendarme came hurrying across from the police station. He had a message for Audibert. Marion was on from Arles. Dorange said *au revoir* and the rest returned with Audibert.

It was news from Denys de Berluc-Vidal which Marion passed on. Vidal's men had been enquiring from neighbours and friends on the Camargue about anyone named Valdeblore.

"One of our *gardians* asked an old mate, an elderly man, from the Mas Gabriel, near Salon. He recollects a head shepherd called Valdeblore when he was a young man. They both worked at the Mas des Grives in the Crau. Valdeblore must have been dead for years. He had two sons, however, and he's sure one was called Henri. He knew him as a boy and he was often about the *mas* helping his father with the sheep. That is all. Not very useful, but it's the only case where the name occurs."

Audibert returned to his colleagues, caressing his chin thoughtfully.

"We really ought to go to the Crau and make enquiries at the Mas des Grives. Ever been to the Crau, Littlejohn?"

"No. Is it worth while?"

"No. It's a desert of stones, lakes and moors. Worse than the wilderness of the Camargue. The stones seem cemented together and make most of it impossible to cultivate. There are a few farms where canals have been run or pumps made to cultivate them. The Mas des Grives is one of these. The chief occupation there is sheep-breeding and rearing. In winter they feed on the sparse fields and in summer they are driven away to the alpine pastures of the north when the sun has dried away every blade of grass in the Crau. In winter, too, the alpine cattle are sometimes driven down to the Crau for pasturage. A desolation to which I wouldn't care to take you for pleasure."

"Where is it situated?"

"To the west of Marseilles between the town of Salon and the sea. Pignon shall make a little trip there when we get back to Marseilles."

Pignon smiled at Cromwell, who was looking very anxious.

"I see my friend Cromwell is curious."

Littlejohn thought for a minute.

"Go, then, old chap. You may see some more birds for your collection. I'll fly from Nice to Paris, take the train to Mantes, and then return here if I'm wanted. You can go around the Crau, with Pignon."

They hadn't said good-bye to Dorange, but that didn't matter. Littlejohn had made up his mind to return to Cannes for another spell of the holiday feeling. He felt that all this shuttling to and fro in France had earned a few days' rest and, wherever the trail led later, it was going to finish by the blue sea and hot sun of the Mediterranean.

CHAPTER XV

THE PHILANDERER

Littlejohn pushed open the door of the *Butte Verte*. There was nobody in the place, although it was noon and time for lunch. The bar was deserted and forlorn and the dining-tables bore the stains of last night's slops...or were they those of many nights ago?

It was as though, with the departure of Henri Valdeblore, all the spirit and all the customers had gone as well.

There was no sign of life and Littlejohn had to beat on the zinc counter to attract attention. Eventually Madame Valdeblore, the old woman, as Littlejohn had got to thinking of her, appeared from behind the glass-panelled door at the back. First she drew aside the muslin curtain which covered it, peeped through, and then she materialised.

"Oh, it's you. I thought we'd be seeing you again."

It was said in a dull, flat voice. She had looked old and worn when last he was there; now she seemed even worse. Her shoulders stooped, her hair was anyhow, and the old look of ennui had given place to one of bitter despair.

Littlejohn followed her to the rear of the premises and through to the private quarters. He was surprised to find that there was a step down behind the door, which gave on to a narrow passage from which a flight of stairs rose, and then another door leading to a room on the left. In the dim light from the window, which seemed to overlook a back alley, he could see another woman sitting at a table. It was Rosalie, the mother of Sam Cheever's boy.

Rosalie was eating with her elbows on the table. It looked like the old mess of sausages and sauerkraut again, but the light was too poor to show anything clearly.

Madame Valdeblore was fussing about the room and Littlejohn found out that she was clearing some papers and rubbish from a chair for him to sit on. She pushed it forward.

"You might as well sit down. We thought you'd be here again sooner or later."

"Why?"

"We had the police from Mantes all over the place, trying to discover where Valdeblore was hiding. As if he'd try to hide here, although I must admit it's a bit of a rabbit-warren. If he had been here, I'd have told them where he was. Both of us would, wouldn't we, Rosalie?"

Rosalie sniffed and made no reply.

Something had happened to the old woman since Littlejohn had seen her last. She had grown more talkative and sarcastic, as though someone, probably Valdeblore, had done her a dirty trick.

Suddenly she switched the light on. A bare, large bulb, without a shade. By its naked glare everything in the room stood out harsh and stark, including the girl at the table. She screwed her eyes up as the light hurt them and then went on with her eating. She, too, looked a picture of despair.

The old woman eyed Rosalie with disfavour.

"I told you somebody would be coming. The police are never away. You ought to have got properly dressed instead of hanging round like a slut in your underwear half the day…."

Rosalie was wearing a shabby dressing-gown over very little else. Her scanty underclothes were plainly visible, but she didn't seem to care.

"Do you hear me? Get off with you and put something decent on."

Without a word, Rosalie left the room, shuffled along the corridor, and they could hear her going slowly upstairs.

"She's taken it bad."

The old woman said it sadly, as though her daughter was the suffering one instead of herself.

"What has she taken badly?"

"The whole business. It's made us the laughing-stock of the town."

Littlejohn had already called on the police at Mantes with an introduction from Audibert. They had been very helpful, but when they'd offered to accompany him to the *Butte Verte,* he'd asked if he could go alone. They had been more than a bit surprised, but he'd explained that perhaps Madame Valdeblore would talk more freely if he went unaccompanied. It would be informal and unofficial.

"She'll talk to you, right enough. Once, she was one of the women in Mantes who said least. You just couldn't get a word out of her. Now, since Henri's bolted, she hasn't stopped talking. It's as though when he was there, he made her shut-up, and now that he's gone, the lid's off," said the local inspector.

But they had told him one surprising thing. The Mantes police wanted Valdeblore, too, and on another matter than Cheever's death. The body of Lola Petitfils had been found in the Seine, not far from Mantes. She'd been strangled. A good-looking girl, was Lola, who'd worked behind the bar at the *Butte Verte* when they were busy. Before her disappearance she had talked of going off to Paris, so nobody had bothered much. She'd lived alone with her mother, a well-known tippler, and the old woman hadn't troubled when her daughter didn't write. But a few days ago, the body had been found in the river. It had been there for some time....

"How was Valdeblore connected with her, except as her casual employer?"

The Inspector smiled.

"He was more than her employer. We knew that in the police, although his wife doesn't appear to have suspected it. When we told her, she went off the deep end. It seems she's always trusted him and thought him faithful to her. Funny thing, isn't it? A big, full-blooded fellow like Valdeblore with his silent slut of a wife, an old woman before her time. And she thinks he's true to her. He and Lola used to use an hotel on the other side of the town. Our men knew it had been happening for years. When we told the old woman it seemed to drive her off her head. She said she hoped he was found and when he was, she'd use a carving-knife on him. Any news about him?"

"No.... He's found a good hideout, I'm sure. So, you think he's killed Lola as well as Cheever?"

"I'm sure of it. Both cases are connected. We've been making enquiries, of course, since Lola's body came to light the day before yesterday. It seems she was seen with another man just before she disappeared. An Englishman, dressed in a blazer!"

"Is that so? Who saw them?"

"They went to the hotel Valdeblore used to take her to. That's one of the first places we visited. It's a scruffy sort of dump. The landlady wasn't helpful at first, but we have our ways of making people talk. I said we'd shut her place up. She was only too glad to talk then. The girl took Cheever there twice. Then, Valdeblore went asking if they'd seen

Lola about. Of course, the landlady said no. She didn't want any bother. But that was enough for us."

So Littlejohn understood what Madame Valdeblore meant about her being the laughing-stock of the town.

She sat down on the chair Rosalie had left. There was another empty plate on the table, as clean as though it had been washed-up. The old woman had obviously mopped it up with bread after eating her meal. Valdeblore's misdoings hadn't spoiled her appetite!

"I was saying, it's hard for Rosalie."

"Why for Rosalie? Isn't it hard for you, too?"

"She's young and expected things. I've had my life and my fun and I don't expect anything more. Sammy had promised to marry her one day. He'd said as soon as he could put his affairs in order and get his money over here, he'd leave his wife and come and open a shop for Rosalie and then he and her and the boy could live together. It was the boy Rosalie cared about. He's a nice kid."

"Where is he now?"

"Gone to my sister's at Caudebec. We didn't want him here with all this going on. And now it turns out that Sammy was simply making fun of Rosalie, deceiving her, after all. It wasn't fair of him. It's taken all the heart out of her. It's a good job he's dead. She's as good as a widow a second time now. It seems more decent, although she won't see it that way."

"But what about you, Madame Valdeblore?"

He couldn't understand her attitude and couldn't help asking the question. In spite of what the local police had told him, she didn't seem very much cut-up about the absence of her husband.

"Me? H'mph. As I said, I've had my bit of fun. I knew he wasn't faithful to me. Women know, you know. But I didn't know he was going off to dirty little hotels with a slut of a barmaid like Lola Petitfils. That's what makes me mad. He might have chosen somebody of his own class, or better. After all, he was a business man and was respected in Mantes. Well, never mind. He's paid for his folly."

"He hasn't paid yet. He's nowhere to be found."

"He will be. Mark my word, he will be. I wouldn't be surprised if you had a good idea where he is now."

"I can't say I have. Do you know?"

"If I did, I wouldn't tell you. When my time comes, I'm going off to find him and I'll just tell him what I think about him and his fine street-walker. Lola Petitfils, indeed!"

"Have you had your lunch?"

It came out suddenly. The woman was quick enough to notice that Littlejohn was eyeing the food. Under the light it was revealed as a small roll of beef and not sausages. It looked very appetising and made Littlejohn remember that he'd not eaten since breakfast at Cannes, very early in the morning.

"No, thank you, Madame Valdeblore. I must be getting along. I called to ask if you'd any idea where your husband might be."

She smiled faintly.

"And you expected me to tell you?"

"No. Not now we know one another better. What were you before you married Valdeblore?"

He couldn't think why he asked it, but he was interested in people, and now that she talked freely and had revealed a bit of her character, he felt he would like to learn more about her.

"I came from Vence, a pretty little hill-town above Nice. My father had a pottery shop there. He was highly respected in the district."

She paused and sighed, as though things were returning to memory.

"And Valdeblore? How did you come across him?"

"He worked for a time on one of the hill farms. He'd been born not far away and his father had moved to the Crau and become a shepherd there. His mother died when he was young and his father couldn't bear the life of Nice without her, he said. Henri helped his father with the sheep until he was sixteen and then found work on a farm near St. Jeannet, not far from Vence. He used to come to town on Saturdays and kept visiting the shop, pretending to want to buy things, but he was really calling to see me."

It was like a dream, or a film at the cinema. Littlejohn could imagine a flashback of Madame Valdeblore, young and pretty, among the pottery which they sold to the trippers at Vence. And Henri Valdeblore turning up and winning her among the pots and souvenir-hunters. He looked at her quietly. Fat, shabby, hair all anyhow, eyes from which the light had died, hands rough and inflamed with hard work and perhaps dropsy, which her swollen ankles indicated.

"...My father wouldn't hear of him taking me out. He hated the sight of Henri. There was nothing for us to do but run away. At first, we went to Nice. We were married there and Henri helped in the markets. Rosalie was born, we saved a bit, and then my sister, who's always been good to me, married a sailor on a yacht that put in once at Nice, and came up here to live at Caudebec. She wanted me to come near her and said there were good chances up north. We came to Mantes and set up this café. There have been wars and troubles, but we've stuck it. Now it's over."

She seemed too full of apathy even to weep. Instead, she cut off a slice of the beef roll and started to chew it.

"Of course, the police told me what had happened. Henri had either introduced Cheever to Lola, or else Cheever had come across her somewhere. That's quite likely. When Henri found Cheever had cut him out, he must have gone mad. I'm not saying he killed Lola. But I know he had it in for Cheever. It was on account of Rosalie, you see. When the boy was born, Cheever promised Henri he'd put it right as soon as he could and we both believed him. Henri was madly fond of Rosalie. She was all he had. She never worked. He said he'd work for both of us, and when she married a decent lad of the town, we were both delighted. He was killed in the war, of course. She'd always been fond of Cheever some way. I don't know why. He had a way with him, even when she was a little girl. Always bringing her toys and when he spoke in his queer French, she understood every word. No, it was Cheever betraying Rosalie made Henri see red. He went off after him as soon as he found out. Somebody mentioned to him in the street that he'd better watch his pal, the Englishman. He couldn't believe it and made some enquiries in the town. When he was sure it was true, he went away. He didn't say where he was going, but he went. I didn't know at the time what it was all about. The police told me after Lola's body was found, by which time Henri had been vanished for some time. But I do know he went off for a few days in an old van he has, saying he'd business. Cheever had told him where he was going, so he'd soon find him. When he came back home, Henri was changed. He just sat and brooded, until one day, he went off without telling either of us. He left this place in Rosalie's name, we discovered, too, and only took a few thousand francs with him. The rest he left behind, as though he was never coming back."

So that was it, and it was the motive for the murder of Cheever. Not so much that Cheever had stolen Henri's mistress, but that he'd betrayed the apple of Henri's eye, his Rosalie.

The sun was shining down the alley at the back, but the window was so small and dirty that it stole all the light before it could enter the room.

The old woman was getting anxious about Rosalie and went to the bottom of the stairs and shouted up.

"Come down! It's rude of you sticking up there when we've a visitor."

She returned.

"You must excuse her. She's had a bad shock."

The Inspector at Mantes police station had said Madame Valdeblore had gone off her head about Henri. It might have been true to the extent that she had thrust her own troubles far back in her mind and was concentrating on those of her daughter, which were actually far less than her own.

Rosalie was back. She just stood there looking at Littlejohn with her large dark liquid eyes, as though expecting him to tell her some good news.

"Well, don't stand there saying nothing. If you've nothing better to do, go and tidy up the café; it needs it."

The old woman turned to Littlejohn again.

"Sit down. I expect you've more questions to ask...."

There weren't any more, except the one she wouldn't answer. Where was Valdeblore? But Littlejohn felt he couldn't just say good-bye and walk out. The job didn't seem finished. It crossed the Superintendent's mind that Valdeblore might no longer be alive. The local police had said how Madame Valdeblore had taken-on when she heard of his infidelity. She'd gone crazy, the Inspector had said. Suppose she'd thrust a knife in her husband's back and hidden the body.

Rosalie suddenly appeared from the bar again. Even now she wasn't properly dressed. She had no stockings on

and her bare feet were in carpet slippers. And she hadn't
had a wash. Dark rings under her large eyes and her hair
combed roughly back and held in place by an old piece of
ribbon from a chocolate-box. Her mother looked surprised
to see her again.

"Well? What are you back for?"

"There's nobody in the bar. I might as well be here as
lolling round in front."

"The place needs cleaning."

"It can wait. Nobody's likely to call since dad went. You
know as well as I do that all the business has gone."

"Don't stand grumbling there. Get the gentleman a
glass and bring the Calvados bottle."

Littlejohn didn't want any Calvados, but he said nothing. He had an impression that something was going to boil
up soon, so he'd better sit and wait.

Rosalie returned with the bottle and three glasses. Her
face wore a sulky expression and her mouth drooped at the
corners. The old woman snatched the bottle, poured out
two glasses, and passed one to Littlejohn.

"What about me? Don't I get any?"

Madame Valdeblore slowly raised her head in astonishment. Rosalie was the quiet, inoffensive sort who allowed
herself to be imposed on. It was something fresh for her to
speak for herself.

"Here you are. Nobody's stopping you."

Madame Valdeblore passed over the bottle and a glass
and Rosalie helped herself liberally.

"Here, you. You're going to make yourself drunk. Go
easy on the *Calva.*"

"I've gone easy long enough. It's time I started to look
after myself a bit. You think I don't know what's been going

on. Well, I do. And I've just been waiting for Sam's friend to come back so that I can tell him."

Sam's friend! That was a new one. It seemed that Rosalie thought that anybody from England was a buddy of Sammy Cheever.

The old woman was uneasy. She now seemed anxious to be getting rid of Rosalie and rose to her feet to try and make her leave. She shuffled across the room and took her by the arms and tried to turn her round and push her through the door.

"Now go up to your room, Rosalie, and don't keep getting so upset."

She turned to Littlejohn.

"You'll have to excuse her. She's had a bad shock. She was very fond of Sammy."

For the first time the younger woman showed signs of spirit. Her cheeks flushed and she shook her mother off.

"Get away! You've excused me long enough. First it was my husband getting killed by the *boche*. She's had a shock. You'll have to excuse her. And then me being mauled by the gestapo. Another shock and more excuseme's. Then it was Sammy Cheever's kid. She's not herself. Don't take any notice.... And now, Sammy Cheever's dead and my dad's run away, and I'm to be excused again. Well, I've had enough."

"You keep a civil tongue in your head, my girl, and remember there's visitors here. He doesn't want one of your tantrums. You'd better go and clean the bar."

"I'm staying here and I'm going to have my say. And that's flat."

She sat down at the table, poured out some more Calvados, and drank it off.

For a moment there was dead silence except for the old woman's asthmatic breathing and the ticking of an old alarm clock on the rough sideboard along the far wall. Somebody in the alley beyond the window suddenly opened a door, threw out a lot of garbage, and then there was quiet again.

"Well…. Who's going to speak first?"

Rosalie, in her new aggressive rôle folded her arms and faced the other two.

Littlejohn began to fill his pipe.

"Suppose you speak first, Rosalie…."

Littlejohn addressed her by her Christian name. He couldn't think of any other.

"I've not much to say. It's only this. I've been the mug here long enough. Now we're going to have a change."

The old woman got to her feet and swayed on her dropsical legs.

"What do you mean… mug? You've always had a good home. Well… haven't you? And we've kept little Sammy, too, and seen him grow up and short of nothing, haven't we?"

"I've worked for it. You can't say I haven't. But now, Sammy's dead, dad's gone for good, and I look like being left with a café nobody wants and nobody will come to again. You know it was dad kept the place together; without him it'll *go* to the wall."

"We'll have to work it up again."

"*We*, did you say? You mean *me*. Well, I'm not having any. Not without some of the cash dad left behind. You're not taking that with you."

"Hold your tongue, you…. You must really excuse her, sir. She's not herself and imagines things."

The younger woman rose to her feet and the pair of them faced one another glaring and their breasts heaving. And then the old woman suddenly slapped Rosalie's face.

"And now you can go to your room and behave yourself."

Littlejohn rose, too. He'd no wish to be involved in a fight between two women, but the situation was critical and it looked as if there was going to be an interesting turn of events very soon. It came, and very quickly. Rosalie pushed her mother away so hard that the old woman would have fallen flat on her back if there hadn't been a chair just behind her. As it was, she only just rescued herself from a somersault.

"Now, you listen to me. You needn't think I don't know what's been going on. You and your play-acting. Pretending you hate dad and you'd kill him yourself if you could find him. Don't make me laugh. Find him.... You could lay your hands on him any minute."

"Don't heed her. She's not herself...."

Littlejohn stood between the pair of them.

"Now, Rosalie, what is all this?"

"As long as they treated me decently, I was on their side. But now, she's planning to run off and join dad, and leave me and Sammy here on our own. How are we going to live? Not on the streets, I can tell you. She's never liked me. I was my father's girl, and we were as thick as thieves the two of us. No wonder he preferred me. Her with her complaining and her idle ways. She never raised a hand to help in the bar. She always thought she married beneath her and dad wasn't good enough. Well.... Now dad's on the run and he's got away safe. I'm not having her going and finding him and leading half the police of France to where he is. If she'll leave him alone, he'll be all right. But if she goes to him and hangs round his neck, as she's always done, he'll soon be behind bars. That's all. I'm telling you so that you'll know and she'll have to stay here where she belongs. Now you know, she won't dare leave. Dad would kill her if she led the police to him."

The old woman sat where she'd fallen, her eyes glassy, her head lolling.

"You've done for us both, my girl. You've done it now. We'll never see your dad again."

Tears began to trickle down the old woman's cheeks and she let them run to her chin and fall on her woollen jumper and dry in.

"So you know where your husband's hiding, Madame Valdeblore?"

She nodded.

"I've a good idea. He was there in the war and he always said he'd go back. But I won't say a word and now that you know, I can't go and find him. So, I might as well be dead. I'd forgiven him for the other women. What could you expect? I'm ten years older than he is. We might have started again somewhere when things had blown over."

Another silence, with Rosalie helping herself unsteadily to another drink.

"You'll have to stay here now, mother, and we'll all live together."

"I never want to see you again. I've finished with you."

"We'll see. You wouldn't be told. You insisted on going to try and find dad. Well, I made up my mind you weren't going to spoil it all."

Madame Valdeblore started to weep properly. Her floppy frame shook and she wailed aloud. Rosalie gulped down the brandy.

"It won't be so bad. We'll get along...."

There was nothing more to be said. Wild horses wouldn't drag any more information about Valdeblore from the two he'd left behind. The girl whom her mother described as a bit soft and on whose account Cheever had been killed; and the old woman who'd planned to bolt and join his murderer and had been prevented.

Littlejohn bade them good-day and they made no reply. He left them there; Madame Valdeblore still howling and Rosalie sitting drinking Calvados and half smiling to herself.

As he let himself out, he found there was a customer in the bar. A half-drunken man with a thick straggling moustache and wearing an old peaked cap. He was thumping the zinc counter limply.

"Is there nobody in...? Where the 'ell's anybody?"

Littlejohn turned back to the inner door.

"Shop!" he called loudly, and then he left them to it.

CHAPTER XVI
SHEEP AND GOATS

There was a message waiting for Littlejohn when he called back at the Mantes police headquarters. It was from Audibert.

Important lead. Meet you Cannes to-morrow early.

He told the Inspector at Mantes what had gone on at the *Butte Verte*.

"We thought there might be something of the kind. She overdid the act. We had our eye on her. Now, after what Rosalie said, the old woman won't move. And we're wasting our time if we try to make her talk. She's like a clam when she wants to be. Had we better arrest her?"

"No. If I were you, I'd leave her for the time being. Just keep an eye on her and see she doesn't make a bolt in spite of it all. We may have more news for you in a day or two."

Littlejohn just had time to eat a meal at the station, get the train for Paris, and catch the late 'plane from Orly to Nice. Cromwell was waiting for him at the airport with Dorange, and the three of them went off for dinner. Cromwell was full of his adventure of that morning.

"We went to the Crau. God-forsaken spot. A complete desert, a stony wilderness."

He consulted his large black notebook, in which he'd written down his itinerary.

"We went from Marseilles to a town called Salon. There's a road there straight as an arrow all the way to Arles. Hardly a village or a soul in sight. Just barren stony fields, with here and there a bit of a shack, some cypresses, and a few acres with odds and ends growing."

He looked at his book, and frowned. There was a cryptic entry. *Nostradamus-Salon.* At Salon, Pignon's English and Cromwell's French had suddenly given out. The Frenchman had tried to tell his colleague that the famous astrologer was buried in the church there. *Nostradamus* was the name of a horse Cromwell had once backed and had brought him the only money he'd ever won in his life. Twenty-five bob.... At twenty-five to one. He couldn't sort it out.

"We went along the road to Arles for a bit, and turned left past an air-force depôt, and then the Crau got wilder than ever. We passed a lake...."

He took another peck at his book.

"The Etang d'Entressen. A little moth-eaten village of the same name, where we turned again for a few miles, and there was the Mas des Grives. It was a bit ramshackle, but they were decent folk. It stood in the middle of a real dried-up desert. They had a few odd sheep, but they said the rest had gone to the Alps to a place called...."

Another reference.

"Vercors. And now, this is interesting."

Littlejohn smiled gently. Cromwell possessed the great grace of wonder at all things new and strange. He was ready to deliver a little lecture on his tour to his girls when he arrived home.

"*Transhumance*... that's what they call it. When the grass of the Crau dries up in the spring sunshine and they've nothing more for the sheep to live on, the shepherds set out and drive them along age-old sheep tracks, called *drailles,* for hundreds of miles to the mountains north of Provence. And then in the autumn, they bring them all back again to the Crau. It's wonderful. Just imagine it!"

Cromwell sat back, his eyes far away, beyond the blue sea and the mountains of the Riviera to the uplands of the Alps where thousands of sheep were feeding.

"And how does that affect Henri Valdeblore, old man?"

Cromwell came back to earth, still enthusiastic.

"All the young men were away from the Mas des Grives. They'd gone with the sheep. The sheep-owner's wife and four kids were there and an old grandad, who kept telling us he was eighty-four next birthday. His memory's failing, but not for things in the past. He remembered when old Valdeblore was head shepherd there. Grandad wasn't there then. He worked as head shepherd himself on the next farm. He remembered little Henri, as he was then, too. Even when Henri was a lad he used to go with the sheep to the mountains along with his father."

"Ah, I see."

"Yes, and this is the point. The Vercors is a great place of refuge. There were large armies of the underground there in the war and there were big battles there. The *boche* burned down whole villages in reprisal. That's why the Commissaire Audibert suggested we went to the Crau. He said it was a thin lead, but the best we've got. The pastures leased by the Mas des Grives are above a village called La Balme-St. Martin."

"About thirty kilos from Villard-de-Lans," added Dorange.

"When Pignon and I got back from the Crau with the news, the Commissaire rang up Villard-de-Lans. They rang up La Balme.... News came back in quick time. There's no police post at La Balme, only a village bobby... a *garde champêtre*...."

Cromwell smacked his lips over the latest addition to his vocabulary.

"The *garde* seems to know all that goes on there. I guess it's like our own village bobbies. They miss nothing.... He said there were five men with the Grives sheep and that a sixth man joined them a few days ago. We asked for a description. I'm prepared to bet from what we got, that it's Valdeblore!"

"So, now we've another trip. To the Vercors, this time."

"The Villard police promised to investigate, but the Commissaire Audibert said he'd come himself and we could join him. Meanwhile, the *garde champêtre* has to keep an eye on all comings and goings at the pastures. There's only one real way up; the rest means a lot of vigorous mountaineering and, provided we don't startle our man, we might get him easily.... We're due to start first thing in the morning. Nine o'clock from Nice by road."

"And to-night, you are both staying with me," added Dorange. So Cromwell had yet another adventure. This time it was at the rose-farm of the Dorange family behind Nice, where the Inspector's father and mother lived in a villa. There, with great courage, they were re-planting the whole *domaine* with new rose bushes to replace those destroyed wholesale in the great frost of the previous winter.

Audibert arrived at Nice dead on time, with Pignon driving the large police car. The five of them were on the way just after nine. The route lay through the mountains behind Nice and climbed gradually through gardens, orange groves, and rose nurseries to the wilder lands of High Provence, where the main roads converged at Digne. They halted there for a drink at eleven-thirty. They had been serious about the business before them and the chances of their guess proving right and their running their quarry to earth. The sad, grim little town of Digne did not improve their mood. They were quick to leave it and continue through the lavender country and the desolate and forsaken perched villages, and then through the gorge of the lively Durance at Sisterton. In the distance, the first heights of the Vercors appeared.

The left fork at Sisterton led through Aspres to the pass of Col-de-la-Croix-Haute, where the Mediterranean is said to end and the north begin. At Die, they were in the Vercors itself. A police car was waiting, as arranged, at a side-road between Die and Villard-de-Lans. Here the narrow road led to the small village of Balme-St. Martin. The village constable, his bicycle beside him, was with the two officers from Villard.

It was just after one and the sun beat down mercilessly on them. All the same, it had none of the relentless persistence of the Mediterranean heat. Now and then, a cool little breeze, soft from the mountains, arose and kept them fresh.

Audibert, ever thoughtful, now opened the boot of the car and produced a hamper of provisions. Two chickens, rolls, butter, cheese and wine, followed by dessert. "One must not be caught out in these parts," he said, and they all fell-to.

They were in a tall, narrow gorge, with a river flowing far below the road. On either side precipitous cliffs of limestone, on which vegetation and trees clung precariously but obviously thrived from the damp soil. After lunch, they left the asphalt highway and took the by-road to La Balme. The country here opened out into a small amphitheatre of well-cultivated land with a bastion of rocky slopes leading to the mountains at the far end. It was at this terminal that Balme-St. Martin was situated. A few houses with shingled roofs, a small church, a farm or two, and a little stores, in front of which were spread a couple of iron tables and some chairs, for it was the village inn as well. The *mairie* was a cottage a little larger than the rest, with an annexe serving as a village hall. The tricolor was flying from the flagstaff. The mayor, a farmer, was busy in his fields, but Granon, the constable, who did his rounds on his bike, had raised the flag in honour of his visitors. Official notices posted at the door, some of them printed, some of them written in a large round hand and bearing the stamp of the *mairie*.

"Bring your rifle, Granon," said Audibert, and the *garde* looked startled. He was a tall thin man, built almost like a mountain goat, with a long, narrow, weatherlined face and an innocent, almost startled look. He was a bit put-out by this sudden invasion of distinguished visitors, especially as he didn't quite know what it was all about. His superiors from Villard hadn't told him much.

"I haven't carried it officially for at least five years, Monsieur le Commissaire. It was when a prisoner escaped from Gap and stole a shot-gun. He fled into the hills, but he surrendered on sight...."

"You'll perhaps need it to-day, my good Granon."

There was a halt whilst the *garde* armed himself and hunted for his cartridges. And then they were ready.

"It is an hour's climb to the Grives pastures. They come down once a fortnight with the donkeys for supplies of flour, rock-salt, oil and such like. Of course, if the gentlemen don't care for the trip on foot, there are mules or donkeys to be had."

Littlejohn smiled. He could picture himself and Cromwell mounted on a couple of asses pursuing a criminal to the bitter end. What a scoop for the newspapers at home, and especially accompanied by a photograph for their friends at Scotland Yard!

"We'll walk, thanks."

'Climb' was the right word! There was a well-worn track made by the sheep right to the pastures, but the shoes they were wearing were quite inadequate. Only Dorange of the visitors seemed at his ease as he padded along in his snake-skins like an Indian tracker. The rest stumbled uphill, sliding about as small mountain streams poured across the way, converting it into a swamp in places, or else reeling over the stones from some river bed or other, with which parts of the track were paved. First through a small pine-wood, across a meadow, and then a sharp rise.

The road began to run like an undulating thread, a shelf on the face of a great limestone spur. Up and down, up and down. Now panting upwards, then almost galloping down. On the top, precipitously above them, Granon explained, was a plateau of excellent pasture and some distance along this was the Grives flock, almost three thousand strong.

"They have been coming here for almost a century. Last year they left too late and lost a lot of sheep in the storms. Better luck next time!"

The two men from Villard were excellent company. One was a local man; the other, of all things, a Breton. Both of them tall, strong and well-built, and of military appearance, they took the climb in their stride. One of them, the jolly native of the Vercors, tangled with Cromwell most of the way in French. Cromwell, making up for lack of vocabulary by gesticulation, in which he was becoming more and more adept, explained the features of the case, giving the murdered man his now gallicised name, Chevver. Littlejohn then heard the man from the Vercors enlightening his Breton colleague with details supplied by Cromwell, and with great difficulty kept a straight face. According to the French officer, Chevver was an English M.P., who had fallen in love with a woman in a miniature he had bought, and who had been lured to the Vaccarès, and there murdered by his jealous rival, Valdeblore, who had then fled to the hills. In a sense, the tale would do. It was a bit more romantic than the true one and put Cheever in a more favourable light.

Here and there appeared a ruined cabin and then a large limestone building, occupied, the *garde* told them, by German troops during the war. On the way they passed three stone columns, memorials to the martyrs of the Resistance, who had suffered fearfully at the hands of the enemy, relentless and vindictive against their patriotism and bravery.

"There are more in the high hills and snows. I myself could tell you a tale or two."

Granon's jaws set like a trap and he whistled softly to himself one of the old songs they sang to while away the time as they hid in the mountains above, waiting for marching orders.

After an hour, they paused, hot and breathless, about half way there. Time in those parts is measured by the steady course of the sun and an hour's journey might mean two, or again three. It seemed strange to see Dorange without his eternal cheroot, but he, too, was beginning to flag as they reached the end of the climb. Then the road turned, and before them were the pastures.

The sight took away the breath of the visitors. A gentle slope of green well-knit turf which seemed to stretch for miles, and feeding upon it, hundreds of sheep. The air was clear and like wine, exhilarating and cool, and when the police had recovered from the uphill trek, they drew it in like draughts of some tonic. On the breeze came the faint oily smell of wool mingled with the rancid stench of goats. There were dogs, donkeys, a horse, and goats, as well as the sheep. They had walked all the way from the Crau. Sometimes the railway or motor transport was used for such journeys, but by foot was considered best. It gradually acclimatised the sheep from the hot Mediterranean to the chill of the mountain heights. The goats provided milk for the shepherds and for the orphan lambs.

The air was full of the symphony of bells. Sheep, goats, donkeys, even the horse, had bells round their necks. Some large, some small, all of them producing a strange nostalgic note which sounded for miles.

A man was sitting at the door of a large cabin on the fringe of the grassland. From thence spread the vast panorama of pastures rising to the snowline, dotted with boulders, and covered with the animals he and his mates had led there. To the left, in the far distance, the Mont Blanc range, with Mont Blanc towering above the rest.

The shepherd was performing a veterinary job on an ewe who had broken her leg. The splintered pieces of bone projected from the limb and he was carefully arranging them and setting and binding the fracture. The ewe suffered the pain without a sound or a protest. Finally, he took her in the hut, her legs tied to prevent too much movement, and came to meet the newcomers.

This was the head-man of the group, addressed as 'Sir' by those who knew him, and *Moun Mestré*, Provençal for *Monsieur*, by his mates and subordinates. He was stocky, stout and wore the heavy black beard he wouldn't shave off until he and his charges set forth again on the way home. He had the face of a Roman soldier and might have been descended from some legionary or other once stationed in Provence. His grey eyes were far-seeing and set in wrinkles like those of a sailor, and his knowledge of animals was vast, compassionate and accurate.

Granon and the shepherd shook hands.

"Greetings, *monsieur.*"

"Greetings, *garde.*"

There were introductions all round. Monsieur Head-Shepherd Alquier received them all with dignity. He passed round a bottle of diluted *pastis,* a crude but stimulating drink, and they all refreshed themselves. Then Granon explained the purpose of their visit. Outside, sheep gathered round the door licking the block-salt lying around, and a small ass-colt looked in inquisitively. There was a stove in the cabin, crude feeding and cooking utensils, piles of hay where the men slept, herbs hanging from the roof, ornamental collars and bells on leather straps for the animals.

Alquier rubbed his beard.

"Valdeblore is here. He and I were boys together on the Crau. I hadn't seen him for thirty years, but when he arrived we gave him hospitality. He said he had been ill and longed for the air of the pastures again. I could tell he was lying and insisted on the truth. He said the police were wanting him. He had done badly in business and in desperation he had stolen money. I believed him, then. It sounded more reasonable. I had no idea of giving him up or telling the police. It was no affair of mine. An old friend needed my help and hospitality, and I gave both. It is murder, you say?"

"Yes. And particularly cold-blooded, too. An affair of passion, which might well have been better settled."

The shepherd nodded. His was not the kind of mind which needed a lot of making up. He saw the truth at once and stuck to it.

"You had better go and take him, then. Or, do you prefer that I do it? After all, I am in charge up here and it is my responsibility. He is in the hut at the edge of the slope, there. He came down from the hills an hour ago and went inside. I must warn you, he is armed. He took my rifle out this morning and has it still. The foxes have been noisy in the night and he said he would try to find one or two. It is mating-time and the dog-foxes are on the prowl....."

Audibert nodded.

"You'd better leave him to us, *Moun Mestré.* Your responsibility for him has ended .... We will go to the cabin and call to him to surrender and come with us."

They were too late, however. Valdeblore had seen them. As they left the hut, he was on his way to the mountains, travelling with remarkable agility and speed for one of his large flabby bulk. He was carrying the rifle. Granon called on him to halt. He took no heed. Granon slung his rifle from his shoulder, raised his eyebrows at Audibert, who nodded. The *garde* sent a bullet whistling over Valdeblore's head.

Hitherto, the fugitive's course had been heading for the hills, but now he halted. Spread right across his path was the flock of sheep, a sea of wool between him and freedom, and to get in the open again and reach the refuge of the mountains, he would need to fight his way through the compact mass of animals. Such a delay would result in his certain capture. He turned to the left, ran across the pasture, and was obviously preparing to climb down the slope to the rough ground below and the cover of the forest in the valley. He looked to right and left, hesitating, his huge frame set against the skyline, his mind seeking out the best alternative to the mountains.

"I could knock him off like a sitting rabbit," said Granon.

"We must take him alive, my good Granon."

A bullet from Valdeblore's rifle hummed past Granon's ear and he and his companions took refuge behind the boulders sprinkled about on the turf.

And then the anticlimax occurred which rang down the curtain on a note of farce.

On the edge of the flock of sheep stood a large and angry billy-goat. His lyre-shaped horns flowed magnificently from his noble head. He was the boss, the champion goat of the outfit, and he was frustrated and truculent. The high altitudes had made him amorous, but he had been separated from the nannies because the shepherds had no wish to have the females heavily in kid on the long and difficult journey home. The billy-goat objected to the shots. They disturbed and challenged him and he looked around for the cause with a baleful eye. He saw Valdeblore poised on the brink of the precipitous slope to the valley and, as the fugitive looked downwards for a foothold, he lowered his head and charged.

In a circus, it would have been a great success. Valdeblore heard the sound of rushing feet and half turned to face them. There was a look of astonishment and horror in his eyes and he tried to sidestep, making a grotesque pirouette. Too late. The torpedo of angry goat caught him just above the knees and swept him off his feet into space. Man and animal shot into the air above the dreadful gorge, Valdeblore flailing as he went in a desperate effort to save himself or to fall lightly. The billy-goat vanished, but by some miracle, was found with the flock again next morning, as angry as ever. Valdeblore's body was recovered half-way down the slope among the rocks. He had broken his skull against a boulder and he was quite dead.

Thus ended the case of Samuel Cheever. Until the finish, Littlejohn had felt slight compassion for the little man who had met so horrible an end, alone, in the wilderness of a foreign land. But, as he stood before the broken body of Valdeblore and thought of his last look of hopeless terror and his absurd end, and of the way his happiness and his life had been ruined, his pity for the little twister from Francaster vanished altogether.

Toll the Bell for Murder

George Bellairs

CHAPTER I
SOMETHING WRONG IN
THE CURRAGH

In the schoolroom of the village of Mylecharaine, in the
north of the Isle of Man, the local women were holding
a 'Tay'—Manx for Tea-in preparation for a jumble sale next
day. The proceeds were to go to a fund for decorating the
church. There were around thirty there; about a third of
them occupied in laying food on long tables, and the rest
sorting out the loot which had been collected from their
own and neighbouring parishes for the morrow's big event.

It was well past tea-time. The sun had just set across the
sea behind Jurby Head, which meant it was seven o'clock, the
end of a lovely April day. All around the squat little whitewashed school stretched the flat curragh lands, marshy still
from the recent rains but green with the onset of Spring,
with wisps of mist rising from them with the coming of
night. In the background to the south, the great bastion of
the Manx hills, ending suddenly and spectacularly where
the fenlands began.

But the assembled women had no time for admiring the
evening or the view. They were busy with the spoils, assess-
ing their values with experienced eyes and hands, ticketing

them with prices, and maintaining a running commentary on the donors of the jumble.

A pile of soiled raincoats, some brass fire-irons, a wash-tub, a heap of bound religious magazines, old boots and shoes, a decrepit carpet-sweeper, a tumbledown chair with a worn horsehair seat, a musical-box, and a hand-driven sewing machine were all swiftly dealt with. Then Mrs. Lace, of Ballagot, wearing a hat which ought to have been with the jumble, opened a parcel and gingerly held aloft a pair of shabby riding-breeches, two soiled old dress-shirts, a grey morning coat and a topper to match, and a velvet smoking jacket with a red lining and the pile suffering from moths or some obscure, mangy disease.

"I can hardly persuade myself to touch them for fear they contaminate me," said Mrs. Lace, seeing nothing funny at all in the variety of the bundle or how its contents might be used.

"Who sent it?"

"You might know. Who else but a transgressor, a wicked transgressor, would wear such stuff."

"Not Sir Martin?"

"His very self."

All work ceased as the women scuffled to inspect the apparel of sin and shame, for Sir Martin Skollick, unofficial squire of Mylecharaine and tenant of Myrescogh House, had a dirty reputation. Two good-looking farm girls had already, it was said, had to go to England to bear his illicit offspring, and no woman was safe from him.

Here, in the very schoolroom itself, he seemed to have dumped the cast-offs of his sin, and some of the younger and livelier members of the party were already reconstructing Sir Martin in the sporting breeches, the flame-lined jacket, the elegant topper and the shabby Ascot coat, which once he wore in wicked haunts across the water.

All this rush of dangerous emotion was violently interrupted by a scream from one corner, occupied by Miss Caley, a maiden lady from Ballaugh, who was unwrapping parcels and surrounding herself with their contents. Barricaded by a pile of cracked plates, a black-steel kitchen fender, a pair of old Wellington boots, an ancient object like an accordion marked 'vacuum-cleaner', and two flatirons, she was now holding aloft an object which might have been, judging from her handling, red-hot. It was an old fashioned sporting-gun. In the other hand, Miss Caley balanced a cardboard box half full of cartridges.

"Whatever 'ave you got there?" said a large fat woman with a dead-pan face, called Armistead, who had arrived from England only two years ago, but who nevertheless tried to boss the show. "Give 'ere. Squealin' like that. One would think you was bein' murdered."

She took the gun savagely. "Where'd this come from?"

"Mrs. Quayle, from Balladoole."

There arose a sympathetic noise, like a dismal cheer, from the onlookers. Mrs. Quayle, following the death of her husband around Christmas, had broken-up her home, sold out, and gone to live with her son at Ballakilpheric.

"She said she'd no use for it, so we might as well have it. "It's an old-fashioned one."

It was. An ancient breech-loading pin-fire about a hundred years old. All the same, it was in good condition.

"*Two* pounds?" said one of the assessors, and the rest nodded.

"And the cartridges?"

"I'd throw that lot in. Like as not they don't make that sort anymore and they'll be needed if somebody buys the gun."

The weapon was labelled £2 and left, with its ammunition, leaning against an old chair in one corner.

"Tay's ready."

A woman arrived with a huge urn and set it at the head of the table, which was covered to capacity with plates of food. Bread and butter, jam, Manx soda cakes, scones, buns, shortbread, potato cakes and large currant slabs like solid blocks of concrete. And on top of that lot, a strapping girl entered, struggling with a huge steaming cauldron which she had to put on the floor, for there was no room on the table. It was the hot-pot.

"Where's pazon? We want him to say grace before the hot-pot gets cold."

"He's in church. Prayin', leek as not. He's in one of his bad moods to-day, poor man."

Another melancholy and sympathetic cheer from the company.

The Rev. Sullivan Lee, vicar of Mylecharaine, had arrived from London during the war, after the death of his wife in an air raid. He had been a nervous wreck and it had been thought that this scattered parish, entailing a lot of walking in good air, would do him a world of good. Now and then, Mr. Lee had relapses and behaved a bit wildly. Otherwise, he was a good priest and was well-liked.

"Somebody go get him."

Miss Caley scuttered off, chattering to herself, and the rest took their places round the table. It was almost dark outside. Lights twinkled from the scattered cottages sprinkled over the curraghs, where the menfolk were entertaining themselves whilst the women were away.

The Rev. Sullivan Lee entered. He blinked as the light of the room caught him and he looked around him as though he'd never seen the place before. A tall, well-built man, with a great dome of a head, almost bald, hollow cheeks and a Roman nose. He wore a sad, tortured look and his dark eyes might have been those of a blind man. There was no recognition or light in them. Then, suddenly, it was as if a shutter had clicked open, and he smiled at the company. It lit-up his whole face and completely changed him.

"I'm so sorry. Mustn't let the hash get cold."

"It's 'at-pot," corrected Mrs. Armistead.

Lee took his place at the top of the table. He said grace and they all fell-to. He presided like the head of some strange order. He wore a cassock with a leather belt and this, combining with the natural tonsure of his hair, gave him a monastic appearance. He enjoyed his food. They all did, and continued eating until far into the early night. Then they set to work again and he helped them. Nothing exciting happened until long after the party had dispersed.

Then, as the clock at Ballaugh was striking two musical notes which floated across the flat curraghs in the stillness, there was a terrific explosion. It seemed to hang on the air for a good half minute and then it died away.

Lights went on one after another in the upper rooms of the scattered cottages, until the curragh around Mylecharaine seemed infested by swarms of fireflies.

Mr. and Mrs. Armistead, retired from an eating-house in Oldham, awoke. He was as big as his wife and their joint bed looked like a great tent pitched in a desert of oilcloth in the low-roofed room.

"It's an atom bomb," said Armistead, pulling his trousers over the vest and long pants in which it was his habit to sleep.

He was the first abroad and the road was deserted as, shod in his carpet slippers, he gingerly made his way to the garden gate. Around stretched the dark countryside, fragrant with the scents of bog-plants, dotted with the lighted bedroom windows of the startled homesteads. Overhead swept a magnificence of stars. In the northern distance, the lighthouse at the Point of Ayre swung its great beam, like a huge besom pushing rubbish from the land into the sea. To the west, the far-off lights of the Irish coast.

Mrs. Armistead appeared at the door, her heavy features embellished by a nimbus of curl-papers. Armistead turned his head to address her.

"There's a light on in th' church. I'd better go and see what's the matter. Stay where you are, mother. Leave this to me."

By this time, others were afield. They assembled round the telephone kiosk, which shone like a beacon at the cross-roads in the middle of the village, and formed themselves in a silent group without even greeting one another. They looked in each other's faces questioningly and then some-one spoke.

"What was that explosion? Think it was a mine at sea?"

"Too loud for that. Sounded like someborry blastin'.

Like as if there was quarryin' goin' on."

"There's a light on in the church."

They went off like one man. It gave them a lead, some-thing to do. They marched to the door of the church, a motley little army, braces dangling, some of them with their raincoats over their night clothes and without collars and ties, wearing carpet slippers or unlaced boots. Two of them had hurried out without putting in their dentures. Only Mr. Jeremiah Kermode, an eccentric, was impeccably turned out. He wore his best suit and billycock, his shoes were bright with polish, and he even seemed to have had a wash and a shave. Nobody ever knew or asked how he'd done it.

The church was a little stone building, a solid-looking oblong, with a simple bell-tower rising at the west end and carrying a small bell rung by a rope which dangled outside the door. A dim light shone through the east window, illuminating the old gravestones of the churchyard and the great square vaults of the families of Mylecharaine and Myrescogh, now long departed from the neighbourhood and from human memory.

The little squad of men halted at the iron gates of the churchyard, whence a paved path, now framed in daffodils shaking in the night breeze, led to the church door. They were like visitors hesitating on the threshold of a sick-room, wondering what they would find inside. All around them' stretched the graves of the silent dead, their memorials silhouetted against the background of the night, some new and upright, others askew or fallen and forgotten altogether. Their hesitancy lasted just long enough to give dramatic pause for the final stroke of terror which was a prelude to what was yet to come.

A dark shadow emerged from the open door of the church.

It seemed, for a moment, to flutter like a great bat, and then shaped itself into the form of the vicar, his tall body leaning forward, groping for something in the darkness like a blind man. He quickly found what he sought, grasped the dangling rope, and began to ring the bell. He did it in a frenzy of despair, panting as he pulled and leaping in the air as the bell swung back and shortened the rope. Across the silent marshes, fields, roads and homesteads the silvery note floated. It wakened everybody for miles around. Those aroused from peaceful sleep to practical everyday things thought of a fire or a shipwreck. Others, less clear in their minds, fumbled about for reasons, imagined invasion tocsins or practical jokes. The superstitious-and they were thick on the ground in the curraghs-surmised the work of fairies or Things far worse. And two very old people, patiently waiting for the ebb-tide to carry them home, died, thinking they heard the bells of heaven.

The solitary ghostly note was heard for miles before the waiting men sprang to life and clawed down the frenzied parson, who seemed to be floating and flapping in mid-air in the vigour of his efforts. Silence fell, however, before the intruders gathered the Rev. Sullivan Lee in their arms and tried to calm his still jerking body, for the bell, in the fury of the attack, had finally made a complete circle over the beam, entangled the rope in its wild flight, and come to a dead stop.

The whole countryside was now sparkling with lights.

Jurby, Ballaugh, Sulby, Ballamanagh in the dark hills; some in distant Kirk Michael, and even six miles away in Ramsey heard it, too. There was a lot of quarrelling and arguing in the light of succeeding days as to who did hear it, but in the nearer places, the illuminations were proof enough that it reached them.

"Somethin's wrong in the curragh," said those who knew the unique note of the Mylecharaine bell, the like of which there was not in any other part of the isle. It was said to have been cast from the metal of an earlier one, that of the monastery of Rozelean long lost in the bogs.

Meanwhile, the men in the churchyard were trying to make head or tail of the strange behaviour of their priest. His own flock dealt more sympathetically with him than some of their nonconformist companions who, on account of his style of dress and his fondness for ritual, (mee-maw, Mr. Armistead called it) accused him of being an idolater and capable of any folly.

"What are you doin' here at this time of night, reverend?" asked Armistead, who seemed to have elected himself leader of the posse. He was wearing a cloth cap pulled down to his ears and a long woollen muffler. He sneezed, and wound the muffler tighter round his fat neck.

The vicar did not answer. Instead, he regarded his questioners with glazed eyes, holding his long hands before him as though to fend them off.

" 'ow dare you make all that row in the middle of the night, scaring the women and the little children? And what was all that bang about, too?"

Still the Rev. Sullivan Lee said nothing. He rolled his head from side to side like someone being tortured, until one of the men made for the church porch through which the light was still streaming. Then the vicar moved. He ran to get to the door before the other, turned the key, and put it in his pocket.

"You've left the lights on."

Armistead looked from one to the other of the surrounding faces under the glow from the windows. He seemed to be seeking help or inspiration as to what they should do next. "Hadn't we better put out the lights?"

But Mr. Lee was on his way home to the vicarage, standing surrounded by a circle of dark trees behind the church. The little group of men remained under the window, their bewildered faces illuminated in dim blues, yellows, purples and reds from the stained glass given in memory of a dead and gone Myrescogh and depicting Abraham about to sacrifice Isaac. He held a long knife and in the eerie glow looked alive and resentful and about to set upon the gang of interlopers who were disturbing him at his sacred task. Mr. Jeremiah Kermode sadly tried to restore his bowler to its original shape. It had been trampled on in the commotion.

Then, suddenly, one of the twinkling lamps on the curragh began to move, drew nearer and nearer, (and so did the scared men), burst into noise as well as light, and a motor-bike took shape, ridden by a shadow in a helmet.

"What's goin' on there?"

Some of the men almost cried with relief. It was as if, in a realm of hopeless shades, one living, useful, human form had intruded with help and news of another world they loved.

P.C. Killip silenced his bike, dismounted, and approached the party. They all began to talk at once, like a crowd in a theatre scene, unintelligible gibberish, with here and there an odd dear word. All except Mr. Jeremiah Kermode, who was still mournfully remodelling the hat he had bought for his wedding forty years last Easter.

"Parson's gone balmy and been firin' guns and ringin' the bell," said Armistead above all the rest.

"Where is he now?"

"Gone 'orne," said a man without his dentures and therefore unintelligible.

"Eh?"

"Gone 'ome," translated Armistead.

"And left the church lights all on?"

"He wouldn't let us go in. He locked the door."

"He did, did he? We'll soon see about that."

P.C. Killip tried the door just to be sure and then he tipped his helmet from behind and scratched the back of his head. This was like a nightmare. Cycling on patrol from Jurby to Ballaugh, he had suddenly heard a loud report which reminded him of attack fire during the war. Then a lot of lights had gone on across the curragh. And to cap the lot, bells had started to ring. He'd wondered at first if it was some sort of celebration, perhaps a royal birth. Or even God forbid! -Russian space-men invading the Island. He'd got there as quickly as he could, no easy matter among the maze of ditches, hedges, swamps and narrow roads of the curraghs. And here he was. The vicar had gone off his rocker. He hadn't thought of that one!

"I'd better go and see if things are all right and get the key at the same time. Light is too dear to waste. Some of you had better stick around. If he's gone mad, he might get a bit rough and I'll need help."

They were only too glad to find a leader. They agreed with acclamation to remain.

"Blow yer whistle if you want us," shouted Armistead, in a voice intended to convey that he wasn't afraid of anything or anybody.

P.C. Killip gingerly made his way across the parson's path between the graves to the vicarage. He was a reliable officer, solid in mind and body, red-faced, beefy, a good husband and father of four, and a good churchman, as well. He kept his mind on his job, too, otherwise he would have halted transfixed by the horror of parading among the rows of the dead he had once known, at such an unearthly hour. He protected himself from evil in the Manx fashion by holding his thumbs between his index and second fingers in the form of a cross.

The vicar lived alone and a woman from the village came daily to attend to his needs. The vicarage itself was cold and damp, a little square-built stone place in a wild garden, set in a ring of old trees, with a lot of windows, un-curtained because the rooms were empty. There was a dark pool overhung by a twisted tree with limbs like long clawing fingers in one neglected corner. Rats scuttered about the dead leaves of past summers and there was a sudden splash in the black water of the pond.

A dim glow shone through the fanlight of the house. P.C. Killip beat on the stiff rusty knocker. Nobody replied, so he tried the door, found it loose, and entered. The hall smelled of mildew and neglect and was covered in the old linoleum left by the previous tenant, a miser who had been found dead behind the door. There was a bamboo hat stand against the soiled whitewashed wall with a few coats hanging from pegs, with some walking-sticks and old umbrellas in the lower part. A staircase rose into the dark upper regions. The whole was lighted by a small smoking paraffin lamp set on a chair beside the hat stand.

P.C. Killip stood and listened. The hair rose on the back of his neck. From a dark room to the right of the hall emerged a noise like something whispering signals in Morse code. Now and then the sound changed to a wail or a great sob. The bobby's heart began to race and his feet were glued to the floorboards. Funny things happened in the curraghs. He remembered old Standish, the miser, dead behind the very door now open at his back. And ghosts and wild cries of monks brutally tortured and strangled there long ago, as their pursuers ran them to earth in their fenland hideouts. The phosphorescent wraiths of travellers, too, murdered by the Carashdhoo men. He pulled himself together, turned the beam of his lamp in the room, and met the agonized eyes of a man on his knees, praying.

"You've left the lights on in the church, sir."

It was an anti-climax and sounded out of place somehow.

The vicar seemed to think so, too, for he made no reply, but knelt there, transfixed, staring blankly at the torch without even blinking. The policeman raised him gently to his feet.

"You're not very well, Mr. Lee, are you? Better come along with me, then. We'll get somebody to make you a nice cup of tea, or maybe take you in for the night."

Mr. Lee allowed himself to be led like a child. P.C. Killip helped him on with his threadbare coat and even had to put his hat on his head for him. It was back to front and gave the priest an even wilder look.

"Give me the keys of the church and we'll switch off the lights."

No reply.

"The keys, please, sir."

"The keys? No! No!"

The parson recoiled into the blackness beyond the rays of the lamp.

"Come now, sir. Nobody's going to hurt you. You're with friends."

"No!"

This was ridiculous. Arguing with a dotty priest in the small hours. To make matters worse, Killip's lumbago was beginning to twitch. His wife had only just rubbed it away with a secret embrocation supplied by a wise woman in Smeale, and here he was.

"Give me the keys, reverend, in the name of the Law!"

"The Law! God forgive me. I'd forgotten the Law."

P.C. Killip didn't understand what the man was getting at but he took the keys obediently handed over by the parson.

"Now come along with me, sir."

Killip closed the door behind them and they set off back between the graves and joined the working-party in the churchyard. Killip left the vicar with the rest and was making for the church again.

"No! No!" shouted the parson, tore himself from the group, and leapt after Killip with large bounding jumps. "Like a bloomin' kangaroo", was how Mr. Armistead later described it to his loving wife. Killip turned and faced him.

"Take him away and keep him quiet."

Ten or a dozen hands seized the now demented man, who was babbling and praying incoherently in turn. Killip unlocked the door, sought the switches in the porch, and turned them off with hardly a glance inside. Then he paused. There was a small vestibule to keep out the draught and then a padded swing door into the main building. Killip turned again, opened the inner door, and shone his lamp round the dark church. A gust of warm air, smelling of stone and old books emerged. A few rows of plain wooden pews, with prayer and hymn-books on the racks in front of them. A large coke-stove in the middle of the aisle. Memorial tablets on the walls. *Peter Killip, who died in Burma.* His cousin Pete. And then the simple chancel, carpeted, with the altar in the background, its brass candlesticks and pewter chalice and paten reflecting the beams of the constable's lamp. A pause, a gasp, and then Killip rushed back and put on all the lights.

A body lay sprawled, face upwards, across the steps of the chancel. Killip hurried to it, gently touched it, recoiled, and then hurried out.

"Hey! Come here, two of you. I said two, not the lot." Armistead was first, hurried in, and then quickly hurried out to be sick.

He had seen quite enough of the body of Sir Martin Skollick. Half the head had been blown away by a shot-gun. The gun was there beside the body. The one which had been given to the ladies of Mylecharaine for the jumble sale.

Want another Perfect Mystery?

Get your next Classic Crime Story for FREE ...

Sign up to our Crime Classics newsletter where you can discover new Golden Age crime, receive exclusive content and never-before published short stories, all for FREE.

From the beloved greats of the golden age to the forgotten gems, best-kept-secrets, and brand new discoveries, we're devoted to classic crime.

If you sign up today, you'll get:

1. A Free Novel from our Classic Crime collection.
2. Exclusive insights into classic novels and their authors and the chance to get copies in advance of publication, and
3. The chance to win exclusive prizes in regular competitions.

Interested? It takes less than a minute to sign up. You can get your novel and your first newsletter by signing up on our website www.crimeclassics.co.uk

Made in the USA
Las Vegas, NV
18 August 2022

53504900R00152